To Wake The Dead

The Collier John Dickson Carr series includes:

THE FOUR FALSE WEAPONS

THE ARABIAN NIGHTS MURDER

THE BLIND BARBER

THE CASE OF THE CONSTANT SUICIDES

THE CORPSE IN THE WAXWORKS

THE CROOKED HINGE

DEATH WATCH

THE MAD HATTER MYSTERY

POISON IN JEST

TO WAKE THE DEAD

To Wake the Dead

JOHN DICKSON CARR

COLLIER BOOKS

Macmillan Publishing Company

New York

Macmillan Publishing Company
866 Third Avenue, New York, N.Y. 10022
Collier Macmillan Canada, Inc.

Library of Congress Cataloging in Publication Data

Carr, John Dickson, 1906–1977.
  To wake the dead.
  I. Title.
PS3505.A763T6   1984   813'.52   83–23955
ISBN 0–02–018750–5 (pbk.)

This edition is published by arrangement
with Harper & Row Publishers, Inc.

10 9 8 7 6 5 4 3 2 1

Printed in the United States of America

Contents

To Wake The Dead

Chapter 1

The Crime of Having Breakfast

AT JUST after daybreak on that raw January morning, Christopher Kent stood in Piccadilly and shivered. The air seemed painted grey as though with a brush. He was only a dozen yards from Piccadilly Circus, and the Guinness clock told him that it was twenty minutes past seven. The only thing moving in the Circus was a taxi whose motor clanked with great distinctness; it circled Ares's island and throbbed away down a quiet Regent Street. A wind had begun to blow from the east, shaking the bitter air as you might shake a carpet. Christopher Kent noticed a flake of snow, and then another, blown suddenly past him. He eyed them without animosity, but he was not amused.

At the bank round the corner, he could draw a cheque for whatever he liked. But he had not a penny in his pocket, nor was it likely that he would have one for twenty-four hours more. That was the trouble. He had not eaten since yesterday's breakfast, and he was so hungry that it was beginning to cramp him.

As though by instinct he was almost at the doors of the Royal Scarlet Hotel. It fascinated him. One day later—to

be exact at ten o'clock on the morning of February 1st—
he would walk into that hotel and meet Dan Reaper, as
had been arranged. Then the whole matter under debate
would be over. There would be satisfaction in winning
from Dan; but, at the moment, hunger and light-headed-
ness were turning his earlier amusement to a mood of
sullen anger.

As usual, the events leading to that meeting of the ways
were unreasonable. He was the son of the late Kent's
South African Ales. South African by bringing-up, he had
lived in nearly every country except his own; and he had
not seen England since they had taken him away at the
age of two. Something had always happened to prevent it.
Kent's Ales required attention, though he was nowadays
too lazy to pay much attention to them beyond the drinking. He had other views. Having been brought up on sound
principles by his father, with whose judgments he agreed
on everything except the fascination of business, he had
early acquired a liking for sensational fiction. In the middle twenties he began to write it, and at that trade he
worked like a Kaffir to make the stuff good. But Dan
Reaper was not pleased.

Standing on the more-than-hard London pavement, he
remembered a more pleasant day three months ago, with
iced drinks at hand, and the noise of the surf coming up
from Durban beach. He was arguing, as usual, with Dan.
He remembered Dan's heavy red-brown complexion, his
crisp-moving gestures, his flat positiveness. At fifty Dan
had prospered in a young man's country, and was one of
those who have made Johannesburg a new Chicago.
Though Dan was nearly twenty years older than Kent, they
had been friends for a long time, and enjoyed arguing the
worth or trash of all created things. Dan was a Member of
the Assembly, and was working his way towards becoming
an important man politically. And (again as usual) he was
laying down the law.

"I haven't got time to read novels," Dan said as usual.
"Biographies, histories: yes. That's my line. It's real. I

want something that Repays Study. About the other stuff, I feel like old Mrs. Patterson: 'What's the use? It's all a pack of lies.' But if people must turn out novels, at least they ought to write out of experience—out of a full knowledge of life—like mine, for instance. I sometimes think I could————"

"Yes," said Kent. "I know. I seem to have heard all this somewhere else. Nonsense. The job's a trade, like any other good trade; and it's got to be learned. As for your cursed experience————"

"You don't deny it's necessary?"

"I don't know," Kent had admitted honestly. He remembered studying the colours of blue water and sky through his glass. "One thing has always struck me, when I've read the brief biographical notices of writers tucked away on the back flap of the book. It's astonishing how alike they all are. In nine cases out of ten you'll read, 'Mr. Blank has been lumberman, rancher, newspaperman, miner, and barman in the course of an adventurous life; has travelled through Canada; was for a time—' and so on. The number of writers who have been ranchers in Canada must be overwhelming. One day when I'm asked for a biographical note, I am going to break this tyranny. I am going to write, 'I have *not* been lumberman, rancher, newspaperman, miner, or barman; and, in fact, I never did an honest day's work in my life until I took up writing.' "

This stung Dan on the raw.

"I know you didn't," he retorted grimly. "You've always had all the money you wanted. But you couldn't do an honest day's work. It would kill you."

From there the argument, stimulated by a John Collins or two had taken a sharper and more business-like turn, while Dan grew still more heated.

"I'll bet you a thousand pounds," cried Dan, who had a romantic imagination, "that you couldn't stand up to a test that I've been through myself. Look here, it's an idea. You couldn't start at Johannesburg without a penny in your pocket, say; you couldn't work or beat your way to the coast—Durban, Capetown, Port Elizabeth, anywhere you like—you couldn't work your way to England aboard ship, and turn up to meet me there at a given rendezvous on a date, say, ten weeks from now. I mean, you couldn't do it without cashing a cheque or using your own name to be helped along. Bah!"

Kent did not tell him that the idea, in fiction, was not original. But it interested him.

"I might take you up on that," he said.

Dan regarded him suspiciously; Dan looked for a catch in everything.

"Are you serious? Mind, if you did a thing like that—or tried to do it—it would do you all the good in the world. Teach you what Life is like. And you'd get material for some real books instead of these footling stories about master-spies and murders. But you don't mean it. You'll think better of it to-morrow morning."

"Damn your hide, I believe I do mean it."

"Ho ho!" said Dan, and gurgled into his glass. "All right!" He pointed a heavy finger. "At the beginning of January I've got to go to England on business. Melitta's going with me, and your cousin Rod, and Jenny; and probably Francine and Harvey as well." Dan always travelled like an emperor, with a suite of friends. "I've got to go down to Gay's place in Sussex when we first get there. But on the morning of February 1st, sharp, we're to be in London. Do you think you could make that trip and meet me in my suite at the Royal Scarlet Hotel at ten o'clock on the morning of the first? Think it over, my lad. A thousand pounds you can't—no cheating, mind."

Two more snowflakes curled over in the air and were blown wide by that bitter wind. Kent looked up Piccadilly, figuratively tightening his belt. Well, he had done it. Here he was; or, at least, he would have done it in twenty-four hours more if he could hold out until then. And his chief impression now was that nearly everything Dan had so confidently predicted was wrong.

Experience? Material for books? At the moment he did not know whether to laugh or swear. None of these things had come on adventurous wings. To Dan himself, going out to South Africa in a cattle-boat after the War, there might have come some vision of high adventure or mystic twilights: though Kent doubted this. Exhilaration be hanged. It had been nothing but monotony and work; bone-cracking work, which—if he had not been solidly put together—would have broken him in the first two weeks. His own stubbornness had carried him through. He could have learned as much about human nature from a boarding-house in Johannesburg, and nearly as much about adventure.

But here he was. Nearly a week ago he had landed from the *Volpar* at Tilbury, with a trimmer's pay in his pocket; and had spent most of it in one glorious bust with a couple of messmates. Possibly, with time to lend joke and point, a sense of adventure on the high seas would come in retrospect. At the moment he knew only that he was devilish hungry.

He moved a little closer to the great revolving doors of the Royal Scarlet Hotel, which towered up in white stone over Piccadilly. Inside he could see charwomen finishing their work on the marble floors; carpets were being put down again, silently; and the hush of early morning was disturbed only by the echo of footsteps.

The Royal Scarlet was an imposing but not expensive place. Dan Reaper always preferred to go there, though as a rule he hired half a floor and in the end paid nearly as much as he might have paid at the Savoy. It was the principle of the thing, Dan said, never to let high-priced hotels make you pay for a name. Besides, the manager was a fellow South-African and a friend of his. For Coronation year they were building a top-floor annex which was predicted to be something new in the way of luxury rooms, and which had also attracted Dan.

Christopher Kent moved closer. It was warm inside those glass doors; warm and drowsy; and you might rest even hungry innards in a comfortable chair. Looking through into the lobby, he was conscious of an irrational resentment against Dan—Dan, expansive *père de famille*

without any family, Dan, who exulted in going to all kinds
of trouble if he could get a ten-shilling article for nine and
elevenpence three farthings. At this moment Dan would
still be at Gay's house in Sussex, snugly tucked into bed.
But he would be here presently, with his suite of friends
and employees. Kent ran them over in his mind. Melitta,
Dan's wife. Francine Forbes, his niece. Rodney Kent,
Christopher's cousin, and Rodney's wife Jenny: Rodney
was Dan's political secretary. Harvey Wrayburn, a great
friend of the family, would probably have made the trip
too. And in another day they would be descending on
London. . . .

That was a real cramp in the stomach this time. He
would not have thought it possible to be so hungry.

Something white, something that was too large to be a
snowflake, caught the corner of his eye. It was drifting
down from the sky; it slipped past his shoulder; and automatically he put out his hand for it. It was a little folded
card, of the sort they gave you when you were assigned to
a room. It said in red letters:

THE
ROYAL SCARLET
HOTEL

Date: 30/1/37.
Room: 707.
Charge: 21/6 (Double).

The charge includes room, bath, and
breakfast. No responsibility can be accepted for valuables unless they are
placed in the manager's safe.

"Room, bath, *and* breakfast—" Kent stared at the card;
first the idea occurred to him as a good thing for a story,
and then with a rush of hesitant surprise he realised that it
might be practical.

He remembered how these things were done. You walked into the dining-room and gave your room-number either to the waiter or to someone sitting at the entrance with a book. Then you were served with breakfast. If he walked in boldly and gave the number of a room certain to be occupied, he could breakfast well—and then walk out again into the void. Why not? How were they to know he wasn't the occupier of the room? It was now barely seven-thirty. The chances were slight that the real occupant of the room would be down so early; and, in any case, it was something that would have to be risked.

The idea appealed to him enormously. Though he had pawned most of his possessions, and needed a haircut, still his suit was presentable; and he had shaved the night before. He pushed through the revolving doors into the foyer, removing his hat and overcoat.

It was a mild enough form of swindle; but Kent suddenly realised that he had never felt so guilty in his life. An empty stomach gives very little assurance; still, he wondered whether they were all looking at him hard or peering at the thoughts in his head. He had to get a grip on himself to prevent himself from hurrying across the foyer as though he were pursued. Only a hall-porter—in the neat dark-blue uniform naturally adopted by any hotel calling itself the Royal Scarlet—seemed to be looking at him. He strolled casually through the foyer, then through a palm-lounge, and into a big dining-room which seemed to be just waking up from sleep.

There were, he was relieved to see, already several people at the tables. If he had been the first there, and a swindler at that, he might have bolted. He almost did bolt at the sight of so many waiters. But he tried to walk with cool assurance, like a man carrying a morning paper. Then a head waiter bowed to him; and the thing was done.

He has afterwards admitted that his heart was in his mouth when the waiter drew out a chair for him at an isolated table.

"Yes, sir?"

"Bacon and eggs, toast, and coffee. Lots of bacon and eggs."

"Yes, sir," said the waiter briskly, and whipped out a pad. "And the number of your room?"

"Seven-o-seven."

It seemed to excite no surprise. The waiter noted it down, tore out a duplicate slip made on carbon-paper underneath, and hurried away. Kent sat back. It was pleasantly warm; the scent of coffee in the air made him a little more light-headed; but he felt like a man unsteadily getting his grip at last. Before he had time to wonder whether it might be snatched away from him, there was put before him a plate of what seemed the finest eggs and the most succulent bacon he had ever seen. A rack of toast and a coffee-service of polished pewter added silver to the already bright colours of the table; the yellow and red-brown of bacon and eggs, against shining white china and cloth, might make a painting of rare quality.

"Banners," he thought, looking at the eggs, " 'banners yellow, glorious, golden, From its roof did float and flow ———————.' "

"Sir?" said the waiter.

" 'We fight to the finish, we drink to the dregs,' " quoted Kent recklessly, " 'And dare to be Daniels on bacon and eggs.' That's all, thanks."

Then he dug in. It was difficult at first, for his insides appeared to be opening and shutting like a concertina; but presently a soothing sense of well-being began to creep into him. He sat back drowsily, feeling at peace with the world, and wished for something to smoke. But that would not do. He had had his meal; now he must get out of here before———

Then he noticed the two waiters. One had just come into the dining-room; they were looking towards his table and conferring.

"That's done it," he thought. But he felt almost cheerful.

Getting to his feet with as much dignity as he could, he

started to walk out of the room. Behind the waiters, he noticed, was a hotel-attendant of some sort, wearing the dark-blue uniform. He could guess what that meant even before the attendant stepped out and spoke to him.

"Will you come this way, sir, please?" asked the man, with what seemed a very sinister inflection.

Kent drew a deep breath. That was that, then. He wondered if they put you in jail for this sort of thing. He could imagine Dan Reaper's roars of laughter (and the laughter of everyone else) if they arrived next day and found him in clink for cadging a breakfast; or washing dishes to pay it off. It made him furious, but there was no way out unless he ran for it; and he was not going to do that. He walked as sedately as he could beside the attendant, who led him through the palm-lounge, and then to the lodge of the hall-porter. That dignitary, a burly man with a sergeant-major's moustache and bearing, did not look sinister; he looked polite and disturbed. After glancing round as though he suspected the presence of enemy spies, he addressed Kent with confidential heartiness.

"I'm very sorry to trouble you, sir," he said; "but I wonder if you'd be good enough to help us out of a difficulty? You're the gentleman in 707?"

"Yes, that's right."

"Ah! Well, sir, it's like this. The room you're in—707— was occupied up to yesterday afternoon," again the sergeant-major looked around, "by an American lady who's sailing home in the *Directoire* late to-day. She rang us up late last night; but of course we didn't like to disturb you until you were up and about. The fact is, sir, that when she left here she forgot a very valuable bracelet; pushed it down in the drawer of the bureau, it seems, inside the paper lining, and clean forgot about it. The lady prizes it very highly, she tells us, and doesn't want to go home without it. It's too bad the chambermaid didn't spot it when the room was made up yesterday before you came in; but you know how these things happen. Now, sir, I know it's an imposition on you; but if we found that bracelet right now, we could get it to Southampton in time to catch her boat. I wonder if you'd mind just stepping upstairs with me, and looking in that drawer?"

Kent had begun to feel a trifle ill.

"I'm afraid I have to go out," he said slowly. "But there's no reason why *you* shouldn't go upstairs and look —or the maid, or whoever wants to. You have my full permission, and you could get in with a pass-key."

The hall-porter assumed an even more heavily reluctant air.

"Ah, but that's just the trouble, sir," he pointed out, shaking his head. "Under the circumstances————"

"What circumstances?"

"Your good lady being asleep up there, and having hung a 'quiet' sign on the door," said the porter, with an air of handsome frankness, "you can see we hardly liked————"

"My good lady?"

"Your wife. It would hardly do for us to wake anyone up with a request like that. But I thought if you wouldn't mind going in and explaining to your wife————"

Even as his mind registered the word "sunk," Kent found himself being urged by some hypnotic power in the direction of the nearer of the two lifts.

Chapter 2

The Crime of Murder

THERE were, he afterwards realised, very few courses open to him. No course, in fact, except that of walking sternly and quickly out of the hotel: an action into which his inflamed conscience put an interpretation of guilt bringing about immediate pursuit. Also, with a stomach now lined with good food, he began to take a pleasant interest in the situation. It was like a situation in one of his own books; and it stirred in him the quality of devilment. Apparently he would have to break into the room of a blameless husband and wife, now asleep upstairs—and get away with it somehow. Adventures (he could have told Dan Reaper) are to be found within walls, not on the plain.

Going up in the lift, the hall-porter was affable.

"Have a good night, sir? Sleep well?"

"Pretty well."

"I hope you weren't disturbed by the men in the hall getting ready that second lift. That top floor where you are, you know, is very new; we're quite proud of it; and it isn't quite finished. They haven't finished installing the second lift. They're working double-time to get all that floor ready in time for Coronation. Ah, here we are."

The seventh floor of the Royal Scarlet was constructed on the principle of fewer and larger rooms. It had four wings, of which wing A (immediately to your right as you stepped out of the working lift) was the only one with which Kent ever had any concern. A broad descending staircase faced the two lifts, set side by side, and on the second lift workmen were now tinkering with the mechanism under a powerful light.

Wing A was spacious and luxurious enough, although Kent could have wished for a little of the less frantically modern note in chromium, glass, and murals. To the right of the lifts, a broad corridor ran some distance down before turning again at right angles. Underfoot was a very thick grey carpet; and the walls were decorated in a way which suggested the smoking-room or lounge of a liner. On one side ran a full-length representation of a scene round a prize-ring, and the other side appeared to be composed of a coloured alphabet gone mad. Dim lights illuminated it with a chrysalis effect. It was very new, and not quite out of its smooth rawness; you could almost smell the streamlining as you could smell the paint.

Kent was growing even more uneasy as he came to face it. Number 707 was in the corner at the turning of the corridor, its door being round the corner and out of sight from the direction of the lifts. Kent, a little ahead of the hallporter, was the first to see that door. Outside it stood a pair of woman's brown shoes: of what material he could not tell or did not notice. And hanging from the knob was one of those cardboard notices reading, "Quiet is requested for the benefit of those who have retired." But that was not what made him stop dead, instinctively shielding the card with his body. Across the notice had been scrawled, half-writing, half-printing, in red ink:

DEAD WOMAN

In Kent's mind it took on a weird clearness. At the end of this bend in the corridor there was a window, and outside the window a fire-escape; he seemed to notice a dozen things at once. He noted also the linen-closet at the end of the corridor: there was a bright light inside it, and a chambermaid in a blue-and-white uniform. Yet it all concentrated on those words, "Dead Woman," hanging helpfully outside the door.

Surely if the chambermaid had already passed the door, those words would have been noticed? His own voice sounded very queer when he said:

"I'm afraid I haven't got my key."

(Well, should he own up now, or bolt for it?)

"Oh, that's all right, sir," the hall-porter assured him, in a surprisingly natural tone. "We'll have the maid here in half a tick. S-sss-t!"

He was already hurrying down the hall to get the maid. Christopher Kent remained where he stood: he did nothing because he could think of absolutely nothing to do. But one thing he did not like. He put out his hand quickly and reversed the card, so that its inner side (printed in the same way except for that curious note in red ink) was now outwards.

"Here we are, sir," said the hall-porter. The key clicked in the lock and the door opened an inch. Even if the porter had not tactfully stood aside, Kent was instantly in front of him.

"If you'll just wait here a moment—?" he said.

"Of course, sir. No hurry."

Gritting his teeth, Kent slipped in and let the door swing shut after him; it was one of those which automatically lock on closing.

The room inside was almost dark. Heavy cream-coloured blinds had been drawn full down on its two windows, and made opaque blurs against the gloom. Neither window could have been up, for the place smelt heavily stuffy. In the wall to his left he could dimly make out the line of twin beds; and he momentarily expected someone to sit up in one of them and ask him what the devil he was doing there. But nothing stirred, not even the quilted counterpane on either, and he saw that both beds were empty. Nothing stirred, that is, except his own scalp; for he began to realise that the notice on the door was probably true.

A little way out in the big room he could discern a wardrobe trunk, of the sort that stands on end and opens out like a book. It now stood part way open towards him, and something was projecting along the floor from between its leaves. First it was a dark mass; then it had a leg in a grey silk stocking; then a hand. It was a woman's body lying on its side with the head between the leaves of the trunk. Something white was partly draped over the shoulder.

Those interested in such matters have argued what an ordinary man in the street would do if he were thrown into a bad position with a dead person before him; Kent had argued it himself. He did nothing. The time he actually spent in that room he afterwards computed as about three minutes.

First he must bring himself to go and look. His hand was moving uncertainly in the air, and to the right of the door his fingers brushed something which made him draw back. A little table stood there: on the table was a huge pile of neatly-folded bath-towels.

He did not think of turning on a light or raising a blind. In his pocket he had a box of matches, with two or three left. He went over to the woman as quietly as he could, bent down, and hurriedly struck a match. That this was murder he had not doubted from the first. And, after a quick look, he blew out the match with equal haste: swallowing to keep down that feeling of revulsion which creeps on you before you are aware of it.

To the best of his knowledge, he had never seen the woman before. She seemed to be young, and had brown bobbed hair: which was one of the few details of which he could be sure. She was fully dressed, in a dark grey tailored suit and white silk blouse, except that instead of shoes she wore soft black slippers trimmed with fur. Evidently she had been strangled: the murderer having wrapped on his hands, to avoid leaving any marks, the ordinary crumpled face-towel which now lay across her shoulder. But this was not all that had been done. Her face had been heavily beaten or stamped on—undoubtedly after death, for there was not a great deal of blood despite the damage of that vicious afterthought. She was quite cold.

Kent crept across the room. There was a chair near the window and he sat down on the edge of it, though he automatically refrained from touching anything. He said to himself, coolly and half aloud, "My lad, you're in one terrible mess."

He had claimed he had spent that night in the room, with a woman he did not know from Eve. Logically, one thing ought to sustain him: he was in no danger of eventual arrest or hanging. The woman had been dead many hours. He had spent the night at a coffee-stall on the Embankment, and he could prove it by much congenial company; fortunately, his alibi was secure.

But that was only eventually. If he did not wish to spend the next day or so in a cell—to say nothing of being obliged to reveal his real name, losing a thousand-pound wager to Dan, and making himself a laughing-stock—he would have to get out of there somehow. All his stubbornness butted against this mess. Flight? Certainly; why not, if it could be managed? But in decency he could not leave that woman lying there———

There was a discreet knock at the door.

Kent got up quickly, searching for the bureau. One name and address now stood out in his mind as clearly as the lettering on the card. It was the name and address of a man whom he had never met, but with whom he frequently corresponded: Dr. Gideon Fell, number 1 Adelphi Terrace. He must call Dr. Fell. In the meantime, if he could find that infernal bracelet which someone had left behind in the bureau, he might get rid of the hall-porter.

He found the bureau, which was between the two windows; he had to touch things now. Through the sides of the blinds, pale light illuminated it. But he did not find the bracelet, because it was not there. A sense of something even more crooked and dangerous stirred in Kent's brain: he did not exactly suspect the waxed moustaches of the hall-porter, now waiting patiently outside the door, but he thought there must be something wrong besides murder. There was nothing at all in the bureau, whose drawers had each a clean paper lining.

Gingerly lifting a corner of the window-blind, Kent peered out. The windows of the room opened out on a high enclosed air-well faced with white tiles. Something else was wrong as well. A little while ago, the folded card bearing the number 707—the card that had brought him here—had floated down from some high window into his hand. But he had been standing in front of the hotel. Ergo, it had come from someone else's room. . . .

The discreet knock at the door was repeated. This time he thought he could hear the hall-porter cough.

Kent turned round and studied the room. In the wall now on his right there was another door; but this side of the room formed the angle with the two corridors outside. He made a quick and correct calculation. Unless it were a cupboard, that door must open directly into the corridor on the side out of sight of the hall-porter. It did: he drew back the bolt and opened it, now in sight of the men working on the lift. Accept what the gods give; in other words, here goes! Slipping out, he closed the door behind him and made off towards the stairs. Fifteen minutes later, in the midst of a thickening snowstorm, he was ringing the doorbell at number 1 Adelphi Terrace.

"Aha!" said Dr. Fell.

The door was opened by the doctor himself. He stood as vast as the door itself, projecting thence like a figurehead on a ship, and beaming out into the snow. His red face shone, as though by the reflection of firelight through the library windows; his small eyes twinkled behind eye-glasses on a broad black ribbon; and he seemed to peer down, with massive and wheezy geniality, over the ridges of his stomach. Kent restrained an impulse to cheer. It was like meeting Old King Cole on his own doorstep. Even before the visitor had mentioned his name or his errand, Dr. Fell cocked his head affably and waited.

His visitor arrived at a decision.

"I'm Christopher Kent," he said, breaking the rule and losing his bet. "And I'm afraid I've come six thousand miles to tell you I've walked into trouble."

Dr. Fell blinked at him. Though his geniality did not lessen, his face had become grave. He seemed to hover in the doorway (if such a manoeuvre were possible), like a great balloon with an ivory-headed stick. Then he glanced round at his own uncurtained library windows. Through them Kent could see a table laid for breakfast in the embrasure of the bay, and a tall, middle-aged man pacing round as though with impatience.

"Look here," said Dr. Fell seriously, "I think I can guess why and who. But I've got to warn you—you see that chap in there? That's Superintendent Hadley of the Criminal Investigation Department; I've written to you about him. Knowing that, will you come in and smoke a cigar?"

"I'd like to."

"Aha!" said Dr. Fell, with a pleased chuckle.

He lumbered into a big room lined to the ceiling with books; and the watchful, cautious, explosive Hadley, whose mental picture Kent had been able to build up already, stared when he heard the visitor's name. Then Hadley sat down quietly, smoothing out his noncommittal face. Kent found himself in a comfortable easy-chair by the breakfast-table, a cup of coffee in his hand, and he told his story with directness. Now that he had decided to lose his bet and let Dan's triumph go hang, there was satisfaction in feeling like a human being again.

"—and that's the whole story," he concluded. "Probably I was a fool to run out of there; but, if I'm going to jail, I'd rather be sent to jail by the head-man than explain to the hotel-staff how I cadged a breakfast. I didn't kill the woman. I never saw her before in my life. And, fortunately, I'm pretty sure I can prove where I was last night. That's the full list of my crimes."

Throughout this Hadley had been regarding him steadily. He seemed friendly enough, if very worried.

"No, it wasn't the thing to do," Hadley said. "But I don't suppose there's any great harm done, if you can prove what you say. And in a way I'm glad you did. (Eh, Fell?) The point is—" He drummed his fingers on his brief-case, and moved forward in the chair. "Never mind about last night. Where were you last Thursday fortnight: the 14th of January, to be exact?"

"On the *Volpar*, from Capetown to Tilbury."

"That ought to be easy enough to prove?"

"Yes. But why?"

Hadley glanced at Dr. Fell. Dr. Fell was sitting back in an enormous chair, several of his chins showing over his collar, and looking in an uneasy fashion down his nose. Over Kent's account of the wager he had made rumbling noises of approval; but now his noises were of a different sort.

"It would not be either striking or original," he observed, clearing his throat, "if I observed that I did not like this. H'mf. Ha. No. The business itself is neither striking nor original. It is not very bizarre. It is not very unusual. It is merely completely brutal and completely unreasonable. Dammit, Hadley————!"

"Look here, what's up?" demanded Kent. He had felt a tension brush that snug and firelit room.

"I know you found a woman in that room," Hadley said. "The news was phoned to me here not five minutes before you arrived. She had been strangled. Then, presumably after death, her face had been so battered as to be almost unrecognisable. You saw her by the light of a match with her head against the floor. Now, Mr. Kent, I assume you're telling the truth." His eyelids moved briefly. "And therefore I'm afraid I've got some bad news for you. If you had got a better look at her, you might have recognised her. The lady was Mrs. Josephine Kent—the wife of your cousin, Mr. Rodney Kent."

He looked from Hadley to Dr. Fell, and saw that neither of them was in the mood for joking.

"Jenny!" he said. "But that's————"

He stopped, because he did not know what he meant himself. It was simply that the two ideas, Jenny Kent and death, would not coincide; one was a stencil that would not go over the other. He tried to build up a picture of her. Small, plump, neat woman; yes. Brown hair; yes. But the description would fit a thousand women. It seemed impossible that it should have been his cousin's wife over whom he had struck a match not half an hour ago; yet why not? That piece of clay beside the trunk would not carry Jenny's extraordinary attractiveness.

Hadley looked hard at him. "There's no doubt it is Mrs. Kent if that's what you're thinking," the superintendent said. "You see, Mr. Reaper's party arrived at the Royal Scarlet last night, and they're occupying that wing on the seventh floor."

"The whole party? Then they were already there when I walked in?"

"Yes. Did you know Mrs. Kent well?"

"I suppose I should have expected that;" muttered Kent, reflecting that much trouble could have been saved had he known it. He tried to arrange his thoughts. "Jenny? I don't know," he answered, honestly doubtful. "She wasn't the sort you did know well, and yet everybody in the world liked her. It's difficult to explain. I suppose you could call her 'nice.' Not unpleasantly nice; but you couldn't imagine her on a party or doing anything that wasn't strictly according to Hansard. And she was amazingly attractive without being beautiful: bright complexion, very quiet. Rod worshipped her; they've been married only a year or two, and——" He stopped. "Good God, that's the worst of it! This will just about kill Rod."

The figure of his cousin Rodney was very distinct in his mind then. He sympathised more with Rod than with the woman who was dead, for he had grown up with Rod and liked him very well. To Christopher Kent things had always come easily. To Rodney they came by plodding. Rodney was in simple earnest about everything. He was admirably suited to be Dan Reaper's political secretary; to answer letters with interest and thoroughness; to assemble the facts for Dan's speeches (Rodney Kent's facts could never be questioned); and even to write the sincere prose into which Dan stuck a tail-feather of rhetoric.

"The double room at the hotel, of course." Kent remembered it suddenly. "Rod would have been with her. But where was he? Where was he while she was being murdered? He wasn't there this morning. I tell you, it'll just about kill him————"

"No," said Dr. Fell. "He has been spared that, anyhow."

Again he became aware that both Dr. Fell and Hadley were looking at him.

"We may as well get this over with," the superintendent went on. "You may have wondered how I come to know so much about you and your affairs. I knew about this wager of yours; Mr. Reaper told me. We have been trying to get in touch with you, but nobody knew what ship you would be on or even what name you would use. . . . This isn't the first time I've been in touch with that party. Your cousin, Mr. Rodney Kent, was murdered on the 14th of January in exactly the same way that his wife was murdered last night."

Chapter 3

The Statement of Ritchie Bellowes

CONSEQUENTLY," pursued the superintendent, "I think you can help us." For the first time a human look appeared on his face, the shadow of an exasperated smile. "I've come to *this* duffer for help," he nodded towards Dr. Fell, who scowled, "because it seems to be another of those meaningless cases which delight his heart so much. Here are two young people, a happily married couple. It is universally agreed (at least, it's agreed by everyone I've spoken to) that neither of them had an enemy in the world. They certainly hadn't an enemy in England, for neither of them has ever been out of South Africa up until now. There seems no doubt that they were as harmless a pair as you'd find anywhere. Yet somebody patiently stalks and kills them—one at Sir Gyles Gay's place in Sussex, the other here at the Royal Scarlet Hotel. After killing them, the murderer stands over them and batters their faces with a vindictiveness I've not often seen equalled. Well?"

There was a pause.

"Naturally I'll help all I can," said Kent with bitterness. "But I still can't believe it. It's—hang it, it's indecent! As you say, neither of them had an enemy in— By the way,

29

how is Jenny fixed? I mean, does she need money or anything, for—no, I forgot; she's dead. But haven't you got any idea who did it?"

Hadley hesitated. Then, pushing his finished breakfast-plate to one side, he opened his brief-case on the table.

"There's a fellow we've got in jail: not on a charge of murder, of course, though that's actually why he's there. Fellow named Bellowes. A good deal of the evidence points to him as the murderer of Rodney Kent———"

"Bellowes," said Dr. Fell blankly, "has now become the most important figure in the case, if I understand you properly."

"I don't think you do understand. Whether or not Bellowes killed Rodney Kent, I'm ruddy sure he didn't kill Mrs. Kent, because he's in jail."

A long sniff rumbled in Dr. Fell's nose. The light of battle, never very far away between these two, made them momentarily forget their visitor. Dr. Fell's face was fiery with controversy.

"What I am patiently attempting to point out," he returned, "is that Bellowes's statement, which seemed so ridiculous to you at the time———"

"Bellowes's statement can't be true. In the first place, his finger-prints were in the room. In the second place, when any man, drunk or sober, seriously maintains that he saw a man in the resplendent uniform of a hotel attendant walking about a Sussex country house at two o'clock in the morning———"

"Here!" protested Kent.

"I think," said Dr. Fell mildly, "that we had better enlighten our friend about a few things. H'mf. Suppose you go over the evidence again, Hadley, and ask for any information you want. Speaking for myself, I cannot hear too much of it. It's like one of Lear's nonsense rhymes: it flows so smoothly that for a second you are almost tricked into thinking you know what it means. The hotel attendant in a country house is a difficulty, I admit; but I can't see it's a difficulty that tells against Bellowes."

Hadley turned to Kent. "To begin with," he asked, "do you know Sir Gyles Gay?"

"No. I've heard Dan talk a lot about him, but I've never met him. He's something in the government, isn't he?"

"He used to be. He was under-secretary for the Union of South Africa: that means, I gather, a sort of buffer or liaison-officer between Whitehall and Pretoria. But he retired about a year ago, and it's been less than a year since he took a house at Northfield, in Sussex, just over the border of Kent." Hadley reflected. "Reaper's chief reason for coming to England was to see him, it seems. It was a business-deal: some property in Middelburg that Reaper was either buying or selling for Sir Gyles, and a friendly visit as well. Gay is a bachelor, and seems to have welcomed a lot of company in his new country house."

Again Hadley reflected. Then, as though frankly getting something off his chest, he got up and began to pace about the room, measuring the spots in the carpet while he talked. His voice was as indeterminate as his clipped moustache. But Kent had an impression that his watchfulness never relaxed.

"On Tuesday, January 12th, Reaper and his party went down from London to Northfield; they had arrived in England the day before. They intended to stay there for a little over a fortnight, and return to London on the evening of January 31st—that's actually to-day—in time for Reaper to meet you at the Royal Scarlet *if* you won the wager and appeared to-morrow. Everybody in the party seems to have been speculating about it.

"In the party at Northfield there were six persons. Sir Gyles Gay himself, the host. Mr. and Mrs. Reaper. Miss Francine Forbes, their niece. Mr. Harvey Wrayburn. And your cousin, Mr. Rodney Kent," continued Hadley. He was as formal as though he were giving evidence. "Mrs. Kent was not there. She has two aunts in Dorset—we checked up on them—and she decided to pay them a visit; she had never seen them before, although she had heard about them for years. So she went down there before coming on to Northfield. I suppose you know all the persons in Reaper's party?"

"Oh, yes," said Kent, thinking of Francine.

"And you'll be willing to supply any information I need about them?"

Kent faced him frankly.

"Look here, it's no good saying I don't see your implication. But you'll never find a murderer in that group. It's a funny thing, too: I know most of them better than I knew my own cousin."

"Oh, a murderer—!" said Hadley, with a slow and dry smile, as though he brushed the matter aside as being unimportant. "At the moment we're not finding a murderer; we're merely finding facts.

"Now the facts about the business are simple enough. Nobody was running about the place at the wrong times. No group of people cross each other's trails or contradict each other's stories. But the background is the unusual part of the business, which seems to appeal to Fell.

"The village, Northfield, is an attractive sort of place such as you find frequently in Kent and Sussex. It consists of a village green with a church, a pub, and a dozen or so houses round it. It's rather secluded, set in the middle of all those thousand little lanes designed exactly like a maze for motorcars; it runs to half-timbering and an 'old-world' atmosphere."

Dr. Fell grunted.

"This back-handed lyricism," he said, "is inspired by the fact that Hadley, in spite of being a Scot, is a good Cockney who hates the country, and profoundly resents the circumstance that roads antedated motor-cars."

"That may be," admitted Hadley quite seriously. "But all the same I was looking for a hint in it. Say what you like, it can't be—it wasn't—a very exciting place in the dead of winter. I was just wondering why *all* Reaper's party wanted to go down there for a fortnight and dig in. You'd think they'd prefer to stay in town and see some shows.

"Well, for the past forty years one of the great local characters thereabouts was old Ritchie Bellowes: the father of our chief suspect. He's dead now, but they thought a lot of him. Old Bellowes was both an architect and a practical builder, with a taste for doing a lot of the work with his own hands. He built half the modern houses in the district. He seems to have had a fondness for wood-carving and all sorts of gadgets; but his particular hobby was building replicas of Tudor or Stuart houses so cleverly faked, with beams and floor-boards out of other houses, that the most expert architect would be deceived about the age of the house. It was a sort of village joke, and the old man seems to have had rather a queer sense of humour himself. He loved putting in trick doors and secret passages—stop! I hasten to assure you, from absolute knowledge, that there's no secret passage or the like in the house I'm telling you about.

"This house, the one he built for his own use, was bought by Sir Gyles Gay some months ago. It's a fairly large place—eight bedrooms—and stands at the foot of a lane going down past the church. It's an imitation Queen Anne place, and a really beautiful job if you don't mind something on the heavy and grim style. Some of the windows look straight out across the churchyard, which is hardly my idea of rural grandeur.

"What we have to consider is the position of young Ritchie Bellowes, the old man's son. I tell you quite frankly I'm damned if I see how he fits into this, and I should feel happier if I could. He's a character also. He was born and brought up in that house. From what I've been able to learn, he's had the best of educations, and he's certainly a clever chap. What seems to impress everyone is his phenomenal power of quick observation, drunk or sober: the sort of person before whom you can riffle a pack of cards and he can afterwards name you consecutively every card he saw. As a matter of fact, he gave a little entertainment of this kind, mental tests, before Sir Gyles's guests during the first few days they were at the house.

"He was left very well off when the old man died. Then the dry rot set in. He doesn't seem to have had any actual vices: he was simply plain lazy, added to a slight paralysis in the left arm, and he liked the drink. The slide down the incline was first gradual, and then abrupt. First his business dropped to pieces; the slump hit him and he didn't improve it by the way he squandered money. Then his wife died of typhoid at the seaside, and he caught it too. He kept on quietly drinking. By this time he's become something like the village drunk. He gives no trouble and makes no fuss. Every night of his life he leaves the bar-parlour of the Stag and Glove under his own steam, with great politeness. Finally, he had to sell his favourite fake Queen Anne house —Four Doors, it's called—for whatever it would bring. He's been living in lodgings with a pious widow; and almost haunting the old place since Sir Gyles Gay bought it. That may have been the root of the trouble.

"Now we come to the bare facts about the night of the murder. Exclusive of servants there were six persons in the house. Sir Gyles and his five guests all slept on the same floor. They all occupied separate rooms (Mr. and Mrs. Reaper were in connecting ones); and all the rooms opened on a central passage running the breadth of the house. Like a hotel, you'll say. The household retired together about midnight. So far as I can find out, there had been absolutely nothing unusual, abnormal, or even suspicious about anyone or any event that night; on the contrary, it seems to have been a fairly dull evening. After midnight only one person—according to the testimony—left his room at any time. At about five minutes past two o'clock Mr. Reaper woke up, put on his dressing-gown, turned on the light, and went out in the hall to go to the bathroom. Up to this time it is agreed that no noise or disturbance of any kind had been heard.

"Next, compare this with our knowledge of Bellowes's movements for that night. Bellowes left the Stag and Glove, which is off the village green about two hundred yards from the lane leading to Four Doors, at just ten o'clock: closing time. He had drunk no more than usual that night; six pints of ale, the landlord says. But on the last round he called for whisky, and, when he left, he bought a half-bottle of whisky to take with him. He then seemed to be his usual self. He was seen to walk off along the road towards Porting, the next village, and to branch from there into a lane leading to a wood called Grinning Copse: another favourite haunt of his, where he often sat and drank alone. The 14th was a cold night, with a very bright moon. There we lose sight of him.

"At five minutes past two, then, Reaper at the house opened his bedroom door and walked out into the main passage. Along one wall of this passage—not far outside the door of the room occupied by Rodney Kent—there is a leather-covered sofa. By the moonlight through the window at the end of the passage, Reaper could see a man stretched out on this sofa, asleep and snoring. In that light he didn't recognise the man; but it was Bellowes, unquestionably dead drunk.

"Reaper turned on the lights and knocked at Sir Gyles's door. Sir Gyles knew Bellowes, of course, and seems to have sympathised with him. They both assumed that Bellowes, drunk, had simply come here by instinct, as he had been doing all his life: a key to the house was found in his pocket. Then they noticed that the door to Rodney Kent's room was wide open."

Outside the windows the snow was falling with silent insistence, shadowing this book-lined room. In a sort of hypnosis induced by reaction or firelight, Christopher Kent was trying to fit the person he had always known under warmer skies—ginger-haired, serious-minded Rodney—into this bleak atmosphere of a sham Queen Anne house by a churchyard. During the recital Dr. Fell had not moved, except to ruffle his big mop of grey-streaked hair.

"Well," Hadley went on abruptly, "they found your cousin dead there, Mr. Kent. He was lying at the foot of the bed. He wore his pyjamas and dressing-gown, but he had not yet gone to bed when the murderer caught him.

He had been strangled by hands wrapped in a face-towel; the towel itself, which came from the wash-hand-stand, was lying across his shoulder. (That particular room is furnished in heavy eighteen-sixties style, with marble-topped bureaux and the old massive stuff.) After being strangled, his face had been bashed in by about a dozen blows—our old friend the blunt instrument, of course—but the blunt instrument wasn't found.

"It was a nasty bit of work, because the blows must have been delivered some minutes after his actual death, out of deliberate hatred or mania. But it was not enough to prevent positive identification, so there's no doubt as to the victim. Finally the murderer must have caught him almost as soon as he'd retired to his room, because the medical evidence showed he had been dead nearly two hours. Is all that clear?"

"No," said Dr. Fell. "But go on."

"Stop a bit," interposed Kent. "There's something even more queer here. Rod was thin, but he was as tough as wire. The murderer must have been very quick and very powerful to catch him like that without any noise; or was there a struggle?"

"Not necessarily. No, there was no sign of a struggle. But on the back of his head there was a bad bruise which did not quite break the skin. It might have come from the scrollwork and curves on the footboard of the bed—you know the sort of thing—when he fell. Or the murderer might have stunned him with the instrument that was later used to batter him."

"So you arrested this fellow Bellowes?"

Hadley was irritable. His measurement of the spots in the carpet had now become a matter of painful preciseness.

"Not on a charge of murder. Technically, of housebreaking," he retorted. "Naturally he was the suspect. First of all, his finger-prints were found in the room, round the light-switch: though he says he has no recollection of being in the room and is willing to swear he didn't go in. Second, he is the only person likely to have committed the crime.

He was drunk; he may have suffered from a sense of grievance about the house; he may have come back there and gone berserk——

"Wait!" Hadley interrupted himself, forestalling objection. "I can see all the holes in it, and I'll give you them. If he killed his victim at midnight and then went out and fell asleep on the sofa in the hall, what happened to our blunt instrument? Also, there was no trace whatever of blood on him or on his clothes. Finally, it so happens that his left arm is partially paralysed (one of the reasons why he never took to work), and the doctor is of the opinion that he couldn't have strangled anybody. The drunken motive is also weak. If he had a grievance against anybody, it would have been against Sir Gyles Gay. He would hardly have walked in and—(with malice aforethought, since there was a weapon)—assaulted a complete stranger at random, especially as he didn't make the least noise in doing it. I also admit that nobody in a village where he's been drinking for a good many years has ever found him savage or vindictive, no matter how much he had aboard. But there you are.

"Then there's his statement, which seems a mass of nonsense. He wasn't coherent until the next day, and even in jail he didn't seem to realise what was happening. When he told his story for the first time, Inspector Tanner thought he was still drunk and didn't even bother to write it down; but he repeated it when he was cold sober, and he's stuck to it since.

"According to him—well, here you are."

Opening his brief-case, Hadley took a typewritten sheet from among a sheaf of others and ran his finger down it.

I remember being in Grinning Copse, going there after the pub closed, and I remember drinking most of the bottle I had. I have no idea how long I was there. At one time I thought there was someone talking to me; but I may have imagined this. The last thing I remember distinctly is sitting in the copse on one of the iron seats.

The next thing I knew I was back at Four Doors, sitting on the sofa in the upstairs hall.

I cannot tell you how I got there; but it did not seem strange to find myself there. I thought, "Hullo, I'm home," that's all. Since I was already on the sofa and did not feel like moving, I thought I would just stretch out and take a nap.

At this time I do not think I went to sleep immediately. While I was lying there I saw something; I think I looked round and saw it. It was bright moonlight in the hall; there is a window at the end of the hall, on the south side, and the moon was high then. I do not know how it caught the corner of my eye, but I saw him in the corner there, by the Blue Room door.

I should describe him as a medium-sized man wearing a uniform such as you see in the big hotels like the Royal Scarlet or the Royal Purple. It was a dark blue uniform, with a long coat, and silver or brass buttons; I could not be sure about colours in the moonlight. I think there was a stripe round the cuffs, a dark red stripe. He was carrying a kind of tray, and at first he stood in the corner and did not move.

Question: What about his face?

A.: I could not make out his face, because there seemed to be a lot of shadow, or a hole or something, where his eyes ought to be.

Then he moved out of the corner, and moved or walked down where I could not see him, past my head. His walk also made me think of a hotel attendant.

Q.: Where did he go?

A.: I do not know.

Q.: Did it not surprise you to see a hotel-attendant walking along the hall with a tray in the middle of the night?

A.: No, I did not even think much about it that I remember. I rolled over and went to sleep; or at least I do not remember anything more. Besides, it was not a tray he had; it was more like a salver to carry visiting-cards.

"Which," commented Hadley, slapping the typewritten sheet down on the table, "makes it all the more nonsensical. A salver, mind you! Blast it, Fell, this is either delirium tremens or prophecy or truth. A salver for what? For carrying the weapon? I don't say this fellow Bellowes is guilty; just among the three of us, I don't think he is. But if he's quite sincere in telling this, and if the hotel-attendant isn't the same kind of vision as a brass-buttoned snake, where are we?"

"Well, I'll tell you," said Dr. Fell modestly. He pointed his ivory-headed stick at Hadley, and sighted along it as though it were a rifle. "That toper of yours, you recall, is the same man who can describe a shop-window full of articles after one glance at 'em. A little *causerie* with Ritchie Bellowes, now languishing in clink, is indicated. Dig into that statement; find out what he really saw, or thinks he saw; and we shall probably have a glimmer of the truth."

Hadley considered.

"Of course," he said, "there's the theory that Bellowes committed the first murder while drunk; and that some other person merely used it, used the way of the crime and Bellowes's story about a phantom hotel-attendant, to kill Mrs. Kent later at the Royal Scarlet Hotel————"

"Do you believe that?"

"Frankly, no."

"Thank'e," said Dr. Fell. He wheezed for a moment, regarding Hadley with what can only be called ruddy dignity. "These two murders are the work of one person: anything else, my boy, would be artistically wrong: and I have an unpleasant feeling that someone behind the scenes is managing matters with great artistry." For a time he remained blinking, in a vacant and somewhat cross-eyed fashion, at the hands folded over his stick. " 'Mf. Take this business at the Royal Scarlet last night. All of Reaper's party were present again, I take it?"

"All I know," said Hadley, "is what Betts told me over the phone a few minutes ago. Yes. And Gay himself was with them again—making six persons, just as there were at Four Doors."

"Gay went with 'em to the hotel? Why?"

"Instinct to stick together, I suppose. Gay and Reaper are as thick as thieves."

Dr. Fell looked at him curiously, as though interested by the choice of phrase. But he turned to Kent. "This," rumbled the doctor apologetically, "is hardly what you would be inclined to call fine old English hospitality. I've been looking forward to meeting you, because there are one or two points concerning sensational fiction which I should like to debate with some vehemence. But, frankly, I should like to ask some questions now. These friends of yours—I haven't met any of them, and I want you to describe them for me. Not (heaven forbid) any complicated backgrounds. Just give me one word or phrase about them, the first word or phrase that jumps into your head. Eh?"

"Right," said Kent, "though I still think————"

"Well: Daniel Reaper?"

"Talk and action," replied the other promptly.

"Melitta Reaper?"

"Talk."

"Francine Forbes?"

"Femininity," said Kent, after a pause.

Hadley spoke in a colourless voice. "I understand from talking to Mr. Reaper that you were a good deal interested in the young lady."

"I am," the other admitted frankly. "But we don't get on very well. She is vitally concerned with the importance of new political movements, new theories of all kinds; she *is* The Intelligent Woman's Guide to Socialism, Capitalism, Sovietism, and so on. I'm not. In politics, like Andrew Lang, I never got any farther than being a Jacobite; and I think that, if a man's got the gumption to go out and make himself a fortune, more power to him. Consequently, she regards me as a pig-headed Tory and reactionary. But one of the main reasons why I took up this fool bet was to show her————"

"Heh," said Dr. Fell. "Heh-heh-heh. I see. Next name on our list: Harvey Wrayburn."

"Acrobat."

"Is he?" inquired Dr. Fell, opening his eyes. "I say, Hadley, this is interesting. Do you remember O'Rourke in the Hollow Man case?"

"He's not an acrobat literally," interposed Hadley. "But I think I see what you mean." His eyes narrowed as he regarded Kent. "Very versatile fellow, Fell. He seems to know a good deal about, or to have had some personal experience with, every subject you could mention. He buttonholed me on the subject of crime, and was spouting encyclopaedia after your own heart. He seems a decent sort and," added Hadley, with innate caution about saying this of anyone, "straightforward enough."

"He is," agreed Kent.

"And that's the lot. Now," argued the superintendent, "I don't want to say too much before we've got all our facts. But, by George! a more sterile, harmless lot, as far as suspicion is concerned, I never came across. We've looked up the pasts of all these people. I've talked to them until I'm blue in the face. No one hated or disliked anyone else. No one is financially crooked or even financially crippled. There is not even a hint of a last stand-by in someone's having a love-affair with someone else's wife. There seems to be absolutely no reason why two ordinary young people, whose death would not benefit or even please anyone, should be carefully stalked and murdered. But again —there you are. They were not only murdered: they were battered with patient fury after death. Unless some member of that group is homicidally mad (which I refuse to believe, because I never met a case of it in which signs didn't crop out plainly even when the person was not in a seizure), it makes no sense. What do you make of it?"

"There's just one thing, Hadley. After the man was murdered, you at least had his wife to question. Couldn't she tell you anything to throw any light on it?"

"No. Or she said she couldn't, and I'll swear she was telling the truth; so why should anyone kill her? As I told you, she was with the aunts in Dorset when it happened.

She went half out of her mind, and took to her bed under the soothing hysterics of the aunts. She only got out of the doctor's care long enough to rejoin the rest of the party in London: and on her first night here *she's* murdered. I still ask, what do you make of it?"

"Well, I'll tell you," said Dr. Fell. He puffed out his cheeks, seeming to loom even vaster as he leaned back in the chair. "I can give no assistance at the moment, I regret to say. I can only indicate the things which seem intriguing. I'm interested in towels. I'm interested in buttons. And I'm interested in names."

"Names?"

"Or their permutations," said Dr. Fell. "Shall we get on to the hotel?"

Chapter 4

Hotel-service for Murder

WHEN they were introduced to the manager of the Royal Scarlet Hotel, Kent had expected to meet a suave autocrat in a morning coat, a sort of super head-waiter, of foreign and possibly Semitic extraction. Quite to the contrary, Mr. Kenneth Hardwick was a homely, comfortable, and friendly island product, who wore an ordinary grey suit. Kenneth Hardwick was a grizzled man of middle age, with a strong face, a hooked nose, and a twinkling eye; the keynote of himself, as of his hotel, seemed to be an untroubled efficiency which was shaken by a murder but prepared to deal with it without fuss.

Superintendent Hadley, Dr. Fell, and Kent sat in the manager's private rooms on the seventh floor. The ordinary business office was downstairs; but two rooms on the new floor, in Wing D, had been set apart for him. His living-room, a severe but comfortable place in dark oak, had two windows looking out on the white-tiled air-well. Hardwick sat behind a big desk, where a desk-lamp was burning in the gloom of the day, and tapped a plan of Wing A spread out before him. He constantly put on and took off a pair of eyeglasses, his only sign of perturbation in a business-like recital.

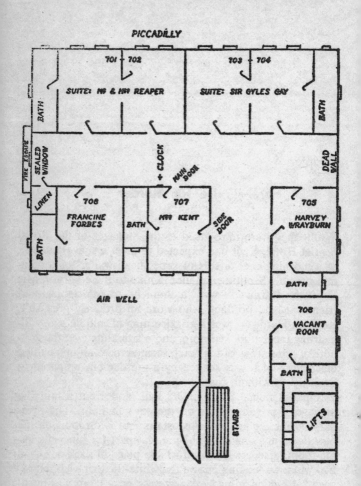

PLAN OF WING A
SEVENTH FLOOR, ROYAL SCARLET HOTEL

"—so," he concluded, "before the other Mr. Kent came here this morning, that was the position. Mr. Reaper booked the rooms for his party six weeks ago, and asked particularly to have the accommodations on this floor. Of course I knew about Mr. Rodney Kent's death two weeks ago, and a bad business it was." He seemed to draw himself together, setting his glasses on more firmly. "Although there was practically nothing about it in the Press, and certainly no hint of anything except—um—a drunken attack. . . ."

"No," said Hadley. "The Home Office have instructed us to keep it out of the public eye. The inquest has been adjourned."

"I see." Hardwick leaned a little farther forward. "Now the position is this, superintendent. Ordinarily I should be a fool if I asked whether this affair could be kept quiet. I had and have no intention of asking that. But what's the situation? If there has been a certain amount of secrecy about Mr. Kent's death, does the same thing apply to Mrs. Kent? Right up to this minute nobody, except those immediately concerned, knows anything about it. Business as usual, you see. This has been easy, because Mr. Reaper's party are the only persons in Wing A; they're more or less cut off————"

"Cut off," repeated Hadley. "Until I get my instructions, it will certainly be kept quiet. Now for details. Just which rooms are these various persons occupying?"

Hardwick pushed the plan across the desk. "I've marked them here," he explained. "You'll see that number 707 says, 'Mr. and Mrs. Rodney Kent.' It was down like that in our books; and it was not changed. That was why, this morning, the staff saw nothing odd in there being a second occupant of the room when someone asked for breakfast."

There was a knock at the door. Sergeant Betts, Hadley's aide-de-camp, came in with a note-book significantly displayed.

"Doctor's just finished, sir," he announced. "He'd like to see you. I've checked up on the other points you asked about."

"Right. Where are the—guests?"

"All in their own rooms. I had a bit of difficulty with Mr. Reaper, but Preston is standing guard in the hall."

Hadley grunted, hitching his chair closer to study the plan. There was a long silence. The light of the desk-lamp shone on Hardwick's face, moulded with attention, a half-smile fixed there. Dr. Fell, a great bandit figure in the black cape, with his shovel-hat in his lap, stared down over Hadley's shoulder. Faintly they were aware of the music of the orchestra from the lounge below, coming up the airwell; but it was a background, a vibration, rather than something actually heard.

"I see," the superintendent began abruptly, "that all the rooms have private bathrooms. And only one of them is unoccupied."

"Yes; number 706 is unoccupied. Nearest the lifts. The workmen are still there, and I was afraid it might disturb anybody who was too close."

"Do you take charge of these arrangements personally?"

"Not ordinarily, no. But in this case, yes; I know Mr. Reaper, and I used to live in South Africa myself."

"Were these rooms assigned some time ago?"

"Oh, yes. The only difference was that the party arrived here a day earlier than they had intended."

"How was that? Do you know?"

"Well, Mr. Reaper rang me up from Northfield yesterday afternoon. He said—their nerves were all on edge, you see—" Hardwick made a slight deprecating gesture; "he felt they had better not stay in the country any longer, and the police had no objection to their coming to London. It was easy enough to fit them in; this is a slack season. As a matter of fact, only one of the rooms had been occupied —707—by a lady who was vacating it yesterday afternoon."

Hadley glanced at Kent. "That's the American lady who said she left a valuable bracelet behind in the bureau of the room?"

"Said?" repeated the manager. "I don't know what you

mean by that exactly. She *did* leave a bracelet in the bureau. Myers, the day hall-porter, found it there at the same time he found—Mrs. Kent."

Christopher Kent stared at him. He had too vivid a recollection of that maplewood bureau, with its sleek-moving drawers and their paper linings, to let this pass.

"Wait. There's a mistake here somewhere," he interposed. "During my little adventure this morning I looked all through that bureau; and I'll swear by anything you like that there was no bracelet in it then."

Hardwick spoke after a pause. The small lines had returned to his forehead; it was as though they were poised there. He looked quickly from one to the other of his guests.

"I don't know what to say. All I know is that I have the bracelet now; a fairly clinching argument. Myers brought it to me when he came to report the other business. Here, have a look at it."

He pulled out a drawer at the left-hand side of his desk. Tearing open a sealed envelope, he put down the bracelet under the light. It was of white gold, set in broad links, and in the centre was one stone of curious design. Square, black, polished and dully gleaming, it had engraved on it two lines in Roman script just large enough to read. *Claudite jam rivos, pueri,* said the inscription, *sat prata biberunt.* Behind Hadley's shoulder Dr. Fell was making vast and seething noises of excitement.

"Yes, it's unusual," Hardwick commented. "That stone —obsidian, black opal, what is it?—looks as though it had been taken out of a ring and set into the bracelet. But the inscription is still more unusual. The remains of a once-passable stock of Latin don't help me. I should render it irreverently as, 'Shut up the liquor, boys; the meadows have had enough to drink'—which seems to be nonsense."

He regarded Dr. Fell with a dry and inquiring grin, which had a sudden keenness in it.

"Oh, Baachus!" growled Dr. Fell, not informatively. "I say, no wonder she wants to get this back! The stone is not intrinsically valuable; but there are several museum-curators who would cut your throat to get it. If it's what I think it is, there must be very few of them extant. As for the inscription, you're not far off. It's a string of metaphors in Virgil's coyest style; his injunction to the shepherds; and a schoolbook softener would render it, 'Cease to sing, lads; recreation enough has been taken.' H'mf. Ha. Yes, I should say this had certainly been taken out of a ring and set into the bracelet. White gold; broad links—nothing there. Only the stone is old. Of course the scheme originated in Greece, and was only copied by the Romans. It's unique! Wow! Dammit, Hadley, you are looking at one of the most ingenious devices of the ancient world."

"Ingenious devices?" demanded Hadley. "Ingenious device for what? You mean it's a poison-stone or bracelet or something?"

"The professional touch," said Dr. Fell with austerity. He stared at it. "No, nothing of that sort; and yet it is as severely practical as one. The Romans were a practical race. Who is the owner of this, Mr. Hardwick?"

The manager looked puzzled. "A Mrs. Jopley-Dunne. I have her address here."

"You don't happen to know her, do you?"

"Yes, quite well. She always stays with us when she is in England."

Wheezing, Dr. Fell sat down again and shook his head. An exasperated Hadley waited for him to speak; but, when the doctor's eye wandered off towards vacancy, Hadley gave it up in favour of more practical matters.

"The bracelet can wait; one thing at a time. Just at the moment, we're following Mr. Reaper's party. At what time did they arrive here?"

"About six o'clock last evening."

"What were they like then? I mean, what was the mood of the party?"

"Definitely glum," said Hardwick, with a gravity which Kent felt was hiding a bleak smile. It did not pass un-noticed by Hadley.

"Go on," said the superintendent. "What happened then?"

"I met them, and took them upstairs. As I told you, I know Mr. Reaper personally. Well, under the circumstances, I advised him to take his friends out and see a show, preferably something funny. You know."

"And did he?"

"Yes; he took six tickets for *She Will When She Won't.*"

"Did they all go?"

"Yes. I don't think Mrs. Kent wanted to go, but she was persuaded. I happened to be leaving my office—downstairs that is—about a quarter past eleven, and I met the party returning from the theatre. They certainly seemed in much better spirits. Mr. Reaper stopped to buy a cigar, and told me that they had all enjoyed the show."

"And then?"

"They went upstairs. At least," said Hardwick, cocking his head on one side and choosing terms carefully, "they got into the lift. I did not see any of them again. The next thing I knew of the business was next morning, when Myers came in to report the discovery of the body." He removed his eyeglasses, put them into their case, and shut it with a snap. For a time he remained looking meditatively at the blotter. "I am not," he added, "going to make any more comments on the ugly nature of this business. You know it; I know it; and it's bad enough to speak for itself." He looked up. "Have you seen that woman's face?"

"Not yet," said Hadley. "Now one question in particular. You say that there were men working on one of the lifts. Were they working all night?"

"Yes."

"Do you know what time they came on and went off duty?"

"Yes."

"Yes. That shift—three men—began at ten last night and worked until eight this morning. They were still there when the body was discovered."

"Suppose some other person—some outsider, someone

not connected with Mr. Reaper's party—had gone into Wing A or come out of it at any time during the night. Those men would have seen him, wouldn't they?"

"I should certainly think so. The wing is lighted all night. A person could have come up or down only by the lift or by the staircase; and the workmen were standing between both."

Hadley gave an interrogative glance at Sergeant Betts, who nodded.

"Yes, sir," agreed the sergeant. "I've got a statement from all three men. They seem straightforward enough and they all tell the same story. They remember Mr. Reaper's party coming upstairs about a quarter past eleven. As a matter of fact, Mr. Reaper stopped and asked them some questions about how the lift worked, and how they were getting on with it. They saw the party separate at the turning of the corridor. Afterwards, they're willing to swear no other person came in or went out of the wing all night."

"So. But is there any other way an outsider could have got in?"

Hadley's question was directed midway between Betts and the hotel-manager. After a pause the latter shook his head.

"Unlikely," he said.

"Why?"

"Look at your plan. I don't say it's impossible, but you're the judge of that." Hardwick twisted the plan round on the table. "There are two other ways, theoretically. An outsider—I suppose you mean a burglar?—might have climbed up the fire-escape to the window at the end of the wing. But, as it happens, that particular window is not only solidly locked on the inside: it was reported to me yesterday as being so stuck in its frame that it couldn't be opened at all. A man was to have seen to it this morning. The only other way in would have been for your burglar to have climbed up the face of the building—either on the outer side towards Piccadilly, or else inside by way of the air-well—barged through someone else's room without being seen, and got out the same way. Knowing what I do of this hotel, I should say it's so unlikely as to be nearly impossible."

"You see where these questions are leading?"

"Oh, yes. I see it."

Hadley turned to Betts. "Well, excluding outsiders, did *anybody* go in or out of that wing during the night? What about employees of the hotel?"

"Nobody except the chambermaid, sir. She went off duty at half-past eleven."

"Yes, but—" Hadley scowled at his note-book. "What about the Boots? Wouldn't there be a Boots, or whatever you call him? You put your shoes outside the door at night, and they take them away to be polished————"

Betts nodded. "Yes, sir. But the Boots—he's actually an under-porter—wasn't in the wing until early this morning, a good many hours after the murder. It seems they don't pick up your shoes and take them away during the night, in case someone comes in very late. They wait until five o'clock in the morning; then they gather up the lot, polish them, and put them back. The Boots went through at five o'clock, and spoke to the men working on the lifts. But only one person in the wing had put out a pair of shoes— Mrs. Kent. And the Boots knew there was some mistake."

"Mistake?" said Hadley sharply.

"In the first place, they were a pair of brown suède shoes; and you can't polish suède. In the second place, they weren't a pair, though they looked alike at first glance. One was a lighter brown than the other, and had a small flat buckle on it. The Boots knew there had been a mistake somewhere, so he left the shoes there and came away."

Dr. Fell interposed, with an expression of painful interest on his face. "Just one moment. I'm interested in the mechanics of this citadel. Just how is a hotel run? Who would be in and out of the place at that time of night?"

"There are some three hundred people employed here," said Hardwick, "and it would take some time to explain how everything is run. But I can tell you this: after eleven-thirty at night, nobody would have any business upstairs at all—nobody—except one of the four under-porters.

"It's like this. The maids, who are on duty to answer bells and the rest of it during the day, go off for the night at eleven-thirty. That's for moral reasons," he explained blandly; "you don't want a crowd of girls about when you're turning in. At that time, also, any employees who would have had occasion to go upstairs during the day (like waiters or page-boys) are also off duty. The upstairs is left to the four under-porters on the staff of the night hall-porter."

"There are two shifts, I suppose?" asked Hadley.

"Oh, yes. The night men come on at eight o'clock, and go on until eight the next morning. Each man takes care of one or two floors, according to how full we are. If a bell rings from his floor, he answers it. If luggage has to be carried up, or a guest forgets his key or comes home tight —all the odd jobs, you see. They also collect the shoes at five in the morning, as the sergeant says."

"The point is," insisted Hadley, "*did* anyone go upstairs last night except the maid?"

"No, sir," said Betts. "That seems to be pretty certain."

With a very brief preliminary knock, the door opened and Dan Reaper walked in. After him came Francine Forbes, as though for a rear-guard.

Kent got up automatically. She saw him, although Dan did not notice anything. More than ever, in London, Kent realised that Dan was built on a large scale like a relief map of Africa, and he required room in which to breathe. Yet, despite Dan's buoyant energy, he looked ill; there was a part of his brain which for ever worried and worried and worried. His hair, turning dry and greyish at the temples, was cut short in the Teutonic style; his very light eyes, in a face whose brick-dust tan had not faded, were surrounded with little wrinkles which made the heavy face seem to have been gone over with a nutmeg-grater. His mouth, which expressed at once generosity and suspicion, had been pulled in so that the lower lip was drawn over the lower teeth.

In appearance Francine offered a contrast, though in a few mental features she might have been his daughter. She was calmer than Dan, possibly even more determined: it was that determination which brought her and Christopher Kent into conflict whenever they met. She was slender, with that very fair skin which does not tan or burn, but seems to keep a kind of glow in its whiteness: emphasised by fair hair curtly bobbed, and dark brown eyes with long lids. She looked—there is no other word for it—overbred, though the overbreeding seemed to have run to vitality rather than anaemia. You knew that her brown dress was an extreme in fashion less because it was so plain than because it was so completely right for her.

"Look here, Hardwick," said Dan, with restraint. He put the palms of his hands flat on the desk, and then he saw Kent.

Dan whistled.

"How in the world—?" he added, with a subdued roar.

"I think," said Hadley, "that you know Mr. Kent?"

"Lord, yes. One of my best—" said Dan. He stopped again, and looked up quickly. "Did you tell him who you were, Chris? Because, if you did————"

"I know: I lose. Never mind the bet, Dan. Forget the bet. We're in the middle of too serious a mess for that. Hello, Francine."

Dan flushed, rubbing the side of his jaw. He looked at a loss, the other thought, because his innate tact was struggling with his innate desire to explain himself.

"Rotten," he said. "Rottenest nightmare I ever stumbled into. We tried to find you, Chris, but of course— Don't worry, though; don't worry a bit. I took care of everything. He was buried in Hampshire: you know his people came from there; everything of the best: cost me over five hundred, but worth it." After these jerky utterances, even Dan's strong nerve seemed to falter. He spoke querulously. "But I wish I were back having a nice comfortable drink at the SAPC. Now it's Jenny. Have you got any idea what's been happening to us?"

"No."

"But you can tell them, can't you, that nobody would want to kill Rod or Jenny?"

"I can and have."

Hadley let them talk, watching both of them. After barely acknowledging Kent's greeting, Francine Forbes waited with that same air of just having emerged from a cold bath; it was a glow of the skin, he thought, as well as a mental atmosphere. But she was not at ease. Although the long eyes did not move, her hands did: nervously brushing the sides of her dress.

"If we are through discussing Chris's gallant gesture," she said in her brittle voice—it made him hot and angry in a fraction of a second—"perhaps we'd better tell you, Mr. Hadley, why we are here. We form a deputation of two to tell you that we're jolly well not going to stay caged up in separate compartments, like isolated cases, until we know what has happened. We know Jenny is dead. And that's all we do know."

Hadley was at his suavest. He pushed out a chair for her, although she declined it with a turn of the wrist which indicated that she saw nothing except the matter in hand.

"I'm afraid it's all we know ourselves, Miss Forbes," the superintendent told her. "We were coming round to see each of you as soon as we had gone over the room where the murder was committed. Yes, murder: the same as the other one, I'm afraid. By the way, let me introduce Dr. Gideon Fell, of whom you may have heard."

She nodded curtly: a salutation which the doctor, who had got up with vast wheezings, acknowledged by sweeping his shovel-hat across his breast. He also surveyed her through his eyeglasses with an expression of vast and benevolent interest which she seemed to find irritating. But she kept her eyes fixed on Hadley.

"Was she—strangled?"

"Yes."

"When?" asked Dan. He seemed to wish to assert himself.

"We don't know that yet; as I say, we haven't been to the room or seen the doctor. I know," pursued Hadley smoothly, "that it's difficult to remain in your various rooms just now. But, believe me, it would help to keep matters quiet and prevent attracting attention to what's happened—and to yourselves as well—if you would just follow my advice and go back there now. Unless, of course, you have anything important to tell us about last night?"

"N-no," said Dan, clearing his throat. "Not that, God knows!"

"I understand your party came back here from the theatre about a quarter past eleven last night?"

"Yes, that's right."

Hadley paid no attention to his suspicious glance. "When you came back, Mr. Reaper, did you visit one another's rooms or did you all go directly to your own rooms?"

"Straight to our own rooms. We were tired."

By this time Francine had assumed so bored an expression that Kent longed to administer a whacking in the proper place. What he could never determine was whether these moods of hers were quite genuine or an elaborate shell of affectation.

"Well, then: did you see or hear anything suspicious during the night?"

"No," said Dan rigorously.

"You, Miss Forbes?"

"Nothing, thank you," said Francine, as though she were refusing something to eat or drink.

"Did either of you leave your room at any time?"

"No," answered Dan, and hesitated. "No; that still goes. I didn't leave the room. I put my head out and looked into the hall, that's all."

"Looked out into the hall? Why?"

"To see the clock. There's a clock on the wall in the hall there, near Francine's door. My watch had stopped. I called out to my wife to ask her if she knew what time it was; but she was in the bathroom with the bath running, and couldn't hear me. So I opened the door," said Dan, making a heavy gesture of lucidity, "and looked out at the clock. That's all."

"At what time was this?"

"At two minutes past midnight," replied the other promptly. "I set my watch then."

Sergeant Betts moved unobstrusively round behind Hadley's chair. He wrote a few words on the margin of his note-book and held it out. Kent, who was sitting nearest, could read it before Hadley noncommittally passed the note-book to Dr. Fell. It read: *Doctor says she died about midnight.*

"Did you see or hear anyone then, Mr. Reaper? Anyone in the hall, for instance?"

"No," said Dan. "Nobody," he added, "except one of the hotel-attendants, outside Jenny's door, carrying a big pile of towels."

Chapter 5

The New Iron-maiden

WHAT Kent could not understand was whether or not Dan realised what he had said—even whether he threw it off deliberately, and had come here to do so. It was difficult to think that a man of Dan's practical intelligence would not think of it. But he spoke with his own casual air of flat positiveness, as though the matter were of no importance. Something brushed the atmosphere of that room, and they all felt it.

"But—" protested Hardwick suddenly; then he adjusted his expression and remained polite.

"Sit down for just one moment, Mr. Reaper," Hadley said. "At two minutes past midnight you saw a hotel-attendant in the hall carrying towels? A man?"

"Yes."

This time the atmosphere in the room brushed Dan like a touch on the shoulder. His look responded to it.

"A man in uniform?"

"Yes, naturally. I think so."

"What kind of uniform?"

"What kind have they all got? Dark blue; red stripe on the cuff; brass or silver buttons; something like that."

Abruptly Dan's heavy eyes grew fixed, and then opened slightly like those of a man making out something from a great distance away. "Oho!" he said.

"You realise it, then. At the time Mr. Kent was murdered, a man in the dress of a hotel-attendant was seen at Sir Gyles Gay's house————"

Dan summed it up. "Ah, *vootzach!*" he said. After a pause he went on: "I see what you're getting at, of course. But do you think it surprised me to see a hotel-attendant *in* a hotel? Do you think I'd regard it as suspicious? What the blazes should I expect to see? I didn't even notice the fellow, particularly. I simply looked out—saw it out of the tail of my eye—and shut the door again. Like that."

Dan used many gestures when he argued. He was arguing now, with some heat. And there was reason in his position.

"That's not the point, Mr. Reaper. We have evidence, or seem to have evidence, that no employee of the hotel was in that wing between half-past eleven last night and five o'clock this morning."

"Oh," said the other. He assumed his buttoned-up "business" expression, and he had assumed it suddenly. "I didn't know that, superintendent. All I can tell you is what I saw. What evidence?"

"The men working on the lifts say that nobody went upstairs or came down during that time."

"Staircase?"

"Nor by the staircase."

"I see," said Dan abruptly. "Well, what does that make me?"

"An important witness, possibly," Hadley answered without heat. "This man in the hall: did you see his face?"

"No. He was carrying a big pile of—bath-towels! That's it! Bath-towels. Must have been a dozen of 'em. They hid his face."

"He was facing towards you, then?"

"Yes, he was walking along. . . . Just a minute—I've got it now! I was standing in the door of the bedroom of our suite, looking towards the left—towards the clock on the wall, naturally. He was coming towards me. As I was saying, he was just about outside Jenny's door."

"What was he doing?"

"I've told you," replied the other, in a tone as expressionless as Hadley's own, "that I hardly noticed him. I don't suppose I had the door open more than a couple of seconds, just long enough to see the clock. I'd say he was either walking towards me or standing still."

"Which? All I want is your impression, Mr. Reaper."

"Standing still, then."

It was no very terrifying ghost to be found in the halls of an ordinary hotel; but it was a patient kind of ghost which strangled its victims and then battered their faces in. Kent found himself thinking that it was all the more unpleasant because it had been described as "standing still" near Josephine's door.

"Bath-towels," said Hadley. "A number of bath-towels, we've heard, were found in the room where the murder was committed. It looks as though your mysterious man had at least gone into that room. . . ."

"Was her face—?" Francine cried suddenly.

"Yes. And a face-towel was used to strangle her, as in another case we know about," said Hadley. The girl did not falter, or anything of a dramatic nature; but her eyes suddenly grew so bright they thought she was going to cry. Hadley was not uncomfortable. He turned to Dan. "About this man: didn't it strike you as odd to see an attendant carrying bath-towels? Wouldn't it have been a job for the maid?"

"I don't know whose job it was," retorted Dan. "It certainly didn't strike me as odd, and wouldn't have done even if I had noticed all the subtleties you're putting into it. At home, in the hotels, you hardly ever find a maid at all. All the work is done by boys—Indians, mostly. I can see now that it's queer enough; but why should it strike me then?"

"Can you give us any description of this man? Tall, short? Fat, thin?"

"Just ordinary."

Hardwick interposed. He had been standing unobstrusively on the fringe of the group as on the fringe of thought; but he looked so solid and so dependable that Dan turned to him as though he were going to shake hands.

"You have been speaking about a uniform," he said slowly. "What sort of uniform was it? We've got several, you know."

Hadley swung round. "I was coming to that. What uniforms have you got, to begin with?"

"For that time of night, not many: as I told you a moment ago. If this had happened during the day, there would be a pretty broad range. But when you get to a time as late as midnight, there are only three kinds of employees who wear a uniform at all; everybody else, from car-starter to page-boy, is off duty. First, there's the night hall-porter, Billings, and his four under-porters. Second, there are the two liftmen. Third, there are the two attendants in the lounge—you know, serving late drinks. That's all."

"Well?"

"The hall-porter," replied Hardwick, half shutting his eyes, "wears a long blue tunic, frock-coat effect: double-breasted, silver buttons, opening high at the neck: wing collar and black bow tie: red stripe on cuff and collar. The four under-porters wear a double-breasted coat with wing collar and black four-in-hand tie; red insignia. The liftmen wear a short single-breasted coat high at the neck; silver buttons, shoulder epaulets. The lounge attendants have a uniform like blue evening clothes, with silver buttons and red insignia. But as for the last two being upstairs———"

"I had no idea there were so many of 'em," growled Dan. "It's no good. If I try to keep on thinking, I'll only put ideas into my own head and probably lead you wrong. I remember the coat and the buttons; that's all I can swear to. You could see the buttons under the pile of towels. He was holding up the towels in front of his face."

Hadley frowned at his note-book.

"But can you tell us, for instance, whether it was a long or a short coat? Or an open or a closed collar?"

"I couldn't see his collar. I've got a fairly strong impression that it was a short coat; but I wouldn't swear to that either."

Hardwick interrupted with abrupt explosiveness.

"This is a worse business than you think. There's something you'd better know, superintendent, though it won't help you much. Some years ago we had a night under-porter who turned out to be a thief—and as neat and ingenious a thief as I've come across. His method of robbing the guests was very nearly fool-proof. He would have his two floors to attend, as usual. In the middle of the night he would go upstairs to answer a bell, or to 'look round' as they often do. Up there he had hidden a pair of pyjamas and slippers, and sometimes a dressing-gown as well. The pyjamas would go on over his uniform. He had, naturally, a master-key to the rooms in his circuit. So he would simply slip in and steal what he liked. If the occupant of the room woke up, or was disturbed in any way, he had a magnificent excuse which never failed, 'Sorry; wrong room; I've barged in.' In any case he would be taken for a guest. If he were seen coming out of a room, or walking in the halls, he would excite absolutely no suspicion; he was a guest going to the lavatory, or wherever you like. When the robbery was discovered a guest would naturally be suspected. Well, he did that for some time, until one victim refused to accept the 'wrong room' excuse, and grabbed him."[1]

[1] It is unwise, I know, to thrust out an editorial head from behind the scenes; but, in case it should be thought that I am plagiarising from fiction, I should like to say that this really happened. For obvious reasons I cannot give the name of the hotel, but it is a large one in Bloomsbury.—J. D. C.

Hardwick paused.

"Don't," he added, with dour amusement, "run away with the idea, please, that you're in a wayside den of thieves. But I thought I had better mention it. It's what made me put up those signs in every room, 'Please bolt your door.' "

Francine took up the challenge—if it was a challenge. "It seems to me that there is a moral there," she said without inflection. "If an employee can dress up as a guest, a guest can also dress up as an employee."

There was a heavy silence, while the room seemed very warm.

"I beg your pardon, Miss Forbes," said Hardwick, not too quickly. "I honestly did not mean that at all. I—um—merely mentioned it. In any case, I can check up on the movements of all those people last night."

"You might do that immediately," Hadley suggested, and got up with decision. "In the meantime, we'll have a look at the body. Just one more question. You were speaking about 'master-keys.' Are the locks on the doors the same in every room?"

"Hardly. The locks are something of a fine art in gradation. As a rule, each maid has assigned to her a certain number of rooms to do: usually twelve, though it may be less. She carries only one key, which opens any door in her group. And each group of rooms has a different lock. Lock-patterns may be repeated in different parts of the hotel, of course, but there are nearly twenty different combinations. The under-porters carry a master-key which will open any lock on their two floors; and so on up in gradations, until I have a key which will open any door in the building. *But* that general rule does not apply to our top floor, the new addition. We're trying out an experiment, probably not successful, of having Yale locks on all the doors, and no two locks the same. It will be a hundred times more trouble, and cause a lot of confusion; but it's absolutely impossible for any unauthorised person to open even so much as a linen-closet."

"Thank you. We'll go round to 707, then. You had better come along, Mr. Kent." Hadley turned to Francine and Dan. "Will you wait here for us, or would you rather go back to your own rooms?"

For answer Francine went to the chair he had previously drawn out for her, and sat down in it with the air of one who folds her arms. Dan—rather deprecatingly—said that they would stay.

It was very warm in the corridors outside, crossed in zebra-fashion with cold where someone had left open a window or raised a skylight in this hive. The raising of windows gave brief glimpses deep into the life of the hotel, and brought together the noises that make up the hollow hum which is its background. Ghostly voices talked in the air-well. You heard a plate rattle, and the buzzing of a vacuum-cleaner. Indistinct figures crossed the line of vision at windows; Kent felt certain that there would be roast chicken for lunch. All this was built up layer upon layer below them, leading to the sedate modernness of Wing A. The three of them, with Sergeant Betts following, looked down that wide corridor, with its bright mural decorations and each of its lights enclosed in a chrysalis of frosted glass.

"Well?" prompted Hadley.

"I have found the essential clue," said Dr. Fell earnestly. "Hadley, I'll let you into the secret. It's the wrong sort of bogey-man."

"All right," said the other with some bitterness. "I was wondering when it would commence. Fire away, then."

"No, I'm quite serious. For a murderer deliberately to dress up as a hotel-attendant is wrong; and therefore—I say, therefore—it means something."

"I suppose you wouldn't consider the startling theory that the murderer was dressed like a hotel-attendant because he really *is* a hotel-attendant?"

"Perhaps. But that's what I want to emphasise," urged the doctor, plucking at Hadley's sleeve. "In that case the business becomes much worse. We have here a menace which is undoubtedly peering round corners and dogging this party. Now, a menace may or may not be frightening; but it's usually appropriate. Unless it is appropriate there's no point to it. For the first murder we have as a setting an isolated house by a churchyard in Sussex: a setting appropriate to nearly every kind of lurking menace except a hotel-attendant in full canonicals stalking through the passage with a salver. Considering what has happened here in the hotel, I don't think we can dismiss that business at Northfield as a coincidence or the mere hallucination of a drunken man.

"You see, these two murders were committed either by a real hotel-attendant, or by a member of Reaper's party dressed up to look like one. But if it is the first, why should the murderer deliberately put on his workaday uniform to wander through a Sussex country house in the middle of the night? And, if it is the second, why should a member of Reaper's party put on the infernal costume at all?"

Hadley was troubled.

"Here, stop a bit!" he protested. "Aren't you jumping to conclusions all over the place? It seems to me you're being hag-ridden by the idea of a double-murderer in fancy dress. Suppose what Bellowes saw at Northfield was a hallucination: suppose the attendant carrying the towels, here, was an innocent member of the staff who somehow escaped being noticed as he came upstairs—" He stopped, because he could not convince himself of this. But about the principle of the thing he was dogged. "I mean, there's not a shred of actual evidence to show that either Mr. or Mrs. Kent was killed by someone dressed up like that. It seems probable, but where's the evidence?"

"Well," said Dr. Fell mildly, "our friend Hardwick should be able to check up on the movements of his staff last night at midnight. Eh?"

"I should think so."

"H'mf, yes. And suppose they can all account for their whereabouts? That would mean, I think (let's face it) that it was somebody in masquerade? Ergo, what becomes of your innocent figure who is first a hallucination and then an accident?" The doctor was lighting his pipe, and his vast puffs sent the smoke skew-wiff round his face. "I say, Hadley, why are you so opposed to the idea?"

"I'm not opposed to the idea. Only, it seems ruddy nonsense to me. Why should anyone dress up like that? Unless, of course————"

Dr. Fell grunted. "Oh, yes. We can always say (soothingly) that the murderer is a lunatic with a complex for doing his work in that particular kind of fancy costume. I can't quite believe that, because to my simple mind the dress of a hotel-porter is hardly one I should associate with an avenging angel or any form of secret violence. But look at your cursed evidence! The crimes appear to be completely without motive; they are wantonly brutal; and there seems to be no reason why the murderer should insist on strangling his victims with his hands wrapped up in a towel, which I submit would be a clumsy and uncertain process. Finally, there's that."

They had come round the turn in the corridor, where Sergeant Preston was on guard. Dr. Fell indicated the "quiet-is-requested" sign still hanging from the knob of the closed door, with its announcement in red ink of the presence of a dead woman inside. Then he reached out with his stick and touched the brown suède shoes a little to the left of the door.

"Shoes that don't match," he said gruffly. "Mind, I must caution you against too many deductions. But kindly note —shoes that don't match."

Hadley turned to Sergeant Preston. "Anything new?"

"Two sets of finger-prints, sir. They're developing the pictures now; the manager lent us their regular dark-room here. The doctor's waiting for you."

"Good. Go downstairs and get that hall-porter; also the chambermaid who was on duty here last night. Bring them up here, but keep them outside until I call."

Then Hadley opened the door. The cream-coloured blinds were now drawn up on the windows, so that Kent had a good view of the room he had first seen in dimness. For a second or two he was not sure whether he could force himself to go in. He knew what was lying on the floor; he knew now that it was Jenny; and he felt a certain nausea choking him. For several hours he had been telling himself that it was not as though he had lost someone very close to him, either in Jenny or even in Rod. He bore their name in law; but other friends, and particularly Francine, were much closer to his feelings than this amiable young couple who had dodged about on the fringes of his life. But it was the meaningless nature of the crimes which took his nerves; suddenly it disgusted him with his own crime-fiction.

Then Hadley touched his elbow and he went in. Two broad windows opening on the air-well, their grey velvet curtains drawn fully back, showed the white tiling outside like the wall of a cold-storage vault; and snow patched the window-ledges. It was a room about twenty feet square, with a ceiling somewhat low in proportion. Its tint was uniformly grey and blue, with light outlines in the panelling, and sleek maplewood furniture after the prevailing fashion. It showed little sign of disturbance. Towards his left were the twin beds, their blue silk counterpanes undisturbed. In the wall on the left was the other door leading to the corridor; and, farther on, a dressing-table. The bureau—as he had good reason to know from his first visit—stood between the windows. In the wall on the right he now noticed a door open on a bathroom, and a large wardrobe. Completing the circuit of the room, the pile of bath-towels still lay on the little table to the right of the door.

Evidently Jenny had been unpacking her trunk when the murderer entered. The wardrobe door stood ajar, and he could see just one frock hanging up inside from the many still hanging in the trunk; there were also several pairs of shoes in the wardrobe. But he saw one great difference from this morning. The trunk stood in its former position, facing the door and some eight feet out from the right-hand window, its leaves well open. Yet the body, which

formerly had lain on its right side with the head just inside
the trunk, now sprawled face upwards some three or four
feet closer to the door. He was relieved to see that the
towel had now been draped over her face. Then Kent
caught sight of his own face reflected in the mirror over
the bureau, and dodged back instinctively.

"I see," he said, clearing his throat, "you've moved her."

A middle-aged man in glasses, who had been sitting
across the room with a medical bag on the floor beside
him, got up quickly.

"Moved her?" repeated Hadley. "She certainly hasn't
been and wouldn't have been moved. That's how she was
found—that right, Betts?"

"Yes, sir," agreed the sergeant. "Aside from the con-
stable, I was the first person here; and that's how *I* found
her."

"Well, it isn't how I found her," said Kent. He described
the position. "I've got good reason to know that. Somebody must have pulled her out this distance after I had
gone."

Hadley put his brief-case on the bed. "We want that
hall-porter. Where the devil's that hall-por— Ah, I've sent
for him. Look round, Mr. Kent; take your time. Does anything else look different?"

"No, not so far as I can see. I didn't get a good look at
the room; the blinds were down; but everything seems
about the same. I didn't notice that wardrobe, though it's
unlikely that *it* wasn't here a couple of hours ago. But
there's another point besides the position of the body: that
missing bracelet which the woman who vacated the room
last was supposed to have left behind in the bureau. If
that's the bureau you mean,"—he pointed—"I'll swear
again there was no bracelet in it at eight o'clock this morning. Yet according to the manager, it was found by the
hall-porter after I had gone. I'd like to know how long it
was between the time I left the room and the time he
opened the door."

"We'll attend to that," said Hadley. "In the meantime —well, doctor?"

Hadley knelt beside the body, twitched the towel off Jenny's face, and grunted noncommittally; Kent was glad that his back hid the sight. The police-surgeon approached with interest.

"So she's been moved," the latter commented, with a quick look at Kent and a beam of satisfaction. "I'm not surprised. That would account for it. If I'm right, this is a new way of committing murder."

"New way of committing murder? She was strangled, wasn't she?"

"Yes, yes, strangled, asphyxiated, what you like; but with a difference. She was probably stunned first, though there are eight blows on her face and head, and I can't tell which of them might have done the stunning. I should say, roughly, that she died about midnight—allow a margin one way or the other." The doctor peered over his spectacles, and then knelt beside Hadley. "But look here! Look at the front and back of the neck."

"Creases. As though," muttered Hadley, "there'd been a cord or wire tied round. But———"

"But there's no cord or wire, and the creases don't extend round as far as the sides of the neck," the other pointed out. "It explains everything, including the towel, though I should have imagined the fellow would have used a thick bath-towel rather than this. Now take a look at that wardrobe trunk. It's a big trunk—plenty of space at one side where the dresses hung—and she's a small woman. You also notice that the dresses inside look a bit rumpled and tossed about. It's a job for you, of course: but I should say her neck was put between the sharp jaws of the trunk as it stood upright, with the towel round her neck so that the edges wouldn't cut. . . ."

Hadley got to his feet, snapping his fingers.

"Oh, yes. Nasty business, of course," agreed the other. "As I say: the towel muffled her neck, and her body was in the part of the trunk where the dresses are hanging. Then the murderer slowly pressed together the edges of the trunk until she was very effectually strangled. Afterwards she was allowed to drop, and the blows were administered for good measure. Neat idea, though. There's death in everything nowadays, isn't there?"

Chapter 6

Fifteen Bath-towels

THERE was a silence, after which Hadley dropped the towel back on the face and drew a deep breath. The big trunk, very suggestive despite the pink frock that hung uppermost in the space to the left, drew all their eyes.

"This is one murderer," said Hadley, closing his hands deliberately, "that I'm going to see hanged if it's the last thing I ever do. Look here, doctor: you examined the other one—her husband—didn't you? *He* wasn't killed with any such hocus-pocus as that, was he?"

"No, that seemed to be a straight case of strangling with the hands wrapped in a towel. Pretty powerful hands, too; or else—" He put his finger to his temple and made a circling motion with it. "Dementia praecox, superintendent. The whole case smells of it; or has so far. The trouble is that this looks like too reasoned and deliberate a plan of campaign. However, that's your job. Unless you want me for anything more, I'll be pushing off. They'll bring the body along whenever you say."

"Thanks, doctor. Nothing else," said Hadley. For a time he moved slowly in a circle, studying the body and the trunk, and making careful notes. "Betts!"

"Yes, sir?"

"That 'quiet' sign on the door: could you find out where it came from?"

"It came from here," said the sergeant. "There's one of them supplied to every room; it's put in the bureau drawer, in case the guest wants it. New-fangled notion, apparently. And as for the writing in red ink on it—here you are, sir."

He walked across the room to a small writing-desk, placed cater-cornered in the far right-hand corner near one window. The dark-blue carpet was so thick that no football sounded here when either Hadley or the sergeant moved. Kent also suspected that these new walls were sound-proof. Drawing away the chair before the desk, Betts indicated the blotter. In addition to the hotel pen and inkwell, with stationery in the rack above, there was a small agate-coloured fountain-pen.

"Probably hers," the sergeant suggested. "It's got her initials on the band, and it's filled with red ink."

"It is hers," said Kent, who recognised it even at a distance. The stuffy warmth of the room was growing heavy on his forehead. "She had two of them, one filled with blue and the other with red ink. They were something like—mascots."

Hadley frowned at the pen. "But why red ink?"

"Capable business-woman. She had a part interest in a dress-making shop in Pritchard Street, although she never let it appear. Apparently she thought it wasn't dignified." Suddenly Kent felt tempted to laugh. Many images rose in his mind. The term "capable business-woman" seemed the last to describe Jenny, for it did not convey the extraordinary attractiveness which (in a purely spiritual way) turned so many people's heads. Harvey Wrayburn had once remarked that she appealed to the adolescent mentality. Through those memories he heard Hadley's voice:

"Finger-prints on this?"

"No, sir."

"But if she had two pens, where's the other one?"

"Must be in her trunk," said Betts. "It's not in her handbag, over on the dressing-table."

Disturbed, Hadley examined the trunk. Though solid, it was an old, worn one; and her maiden name, "Josephine Parkes," had almost faded out in white lettering on one side, the surname now being replaced with a bright white, "Kent." The top compartment on the right-hand side of the trunk formed a kind of tray, filled with handkerchiefs and stockings neatly arranged. In the middle of a pile of handkerchiefs Hadley found the second pen, together with a little gold box, the key in its lock, containing costume jewellery. He juggled the two pens in his hand, muttering.

"This won't do. Look here, Fell, what do you make of it? She was undoubtedly beginning to unpack the trunk when the murderer got her. She'd begin with the dresses— my wife always does, anyway, to see that they don't crumple. But she had taken out only one dress and some shoes; the shoes apparently to change them, for she's wearing bedroom slippers. The only other thing she removed was this red-ink fountain-pen, which was buried under a pile of handkerchiefs. Unless, of course . . ."

During this whole examination Dr. Fell had been leaning back against the wall, his shovel-hat over his eyes. Now he roused himself, putting away his pipe.

"Unless the murderer took it out himself. And in that case he knew where to look for it. H'mf, yes," said Dr. Fell, wheezing in slow laborious breaths. "But I say, Hadley, I should be very much obliged if you would just recapitulate what you think happened here. It's rather important. Again we have one blessed gift from heaven. The guests seemed to have remained quietly in their rooms— except the murderer. We are not obliged to remember a complicated time-table of people treading on each other's heels through the halls, or who met whom in going to post a letter at 9:46. What we have got to do is merely to read the indications of the physical evidence. But, oh, Bacchus, I've got an idea it's going to be difficult! Begin, will you?"

"Where?"

"With the entrance of the murderer."

"Assuming that the murderer is the 'attendant' Reaper saw outside the door at midnight?"

"Assuming anything you like."

Hadley studied his note-book. "I know that tone of yours," he said suspiciously. "Just let me tell you this: I'm not going to stand here and get a whole analysis worked out while you merely wave your hand and say you knew it all the time, but that it's not the important point. By the Lord Harry, I'm going to have one case where you play fair. Agree or disagree, I don't give a damn which; but no misleading. Is it a go?"

"You flatter me," said Dr. Fell with dignity. "All right; fire away."

"Well, as I see it, there's one main difficulty. There are eight blows on the face and on the front of the skull, and no blow or bruise on the back of the head. But she certainly couldn't have been conscious when she was put into that Iron-maiden trunk over there; she had to be fitted into the machine; and she'd have cut up a row that would have been heard. I know the walls look fairly solid, but sound-proof walls are like noiseless typewriters: you can still hear through them. This seems to mean that the murderer must have attacked her face to face with our blunt instrument, and that one of the blows from the front stunned her."

"Undoubedly. Whereas, you remember," Dr. Fell pointed out, screwing up his face, "Rodney Kent was hit on the back of the head."

"If the murderer, then, used a weapon large enough to do what's been done to that face afterwards, how was it that she didn't sing out, or run, or put up some kind of struggle, when she saw him coming? And—in a brightly lighted hotel—how was he able to carry the weapon about without being observed?"

Dr. Fell pushed himself away from the wall. Lumbering over to the tall pile of bath-towels on the table, he began picking them up quickly one after the other, shaking them out, and letting them fall. At the sixth towel, when the floor was littered with them, something dropped with a soft thud and rolled to Hadley's feet. It was an iron poker some two feet long; its head was covered with lint where stains had made it stick to the towel.

"Look here, my boy," said Dr. Fell, turning to Kent apologetically; "why not go downstairs and get a drink? It can't be very pleasant for you to see her like that, and ————"

"I'm all right," said Kent. "It was the way the thing jumped, that's all. So that's how it was done?"

Drawing on his gloves, Hadley picked up the poker and turned it over.

"It's what we want, right enough," he said. "I see. It was not only a good concealment; but, with your hand on the grip of this thing, and the towels hiding the sight of it from the other person, you could whip it out and hit before the other person knew what you were doing."

"Yes. But that's not the only consideration. It is also reasonable to ask: why are there *so many* towels? There are fifteen of the blighters; I counted. If your purpose is merely to hide the poker, why do you stack them up like that and badly encumber your movements when you have to strike? But fifteen towels would not only serve to hide the poker: they would also hide————"

"The face," said Hadley.

Again Dr. Fell got the pipe out of his pocket and stared at it blankly. "The face. Quite. Which leads us to the question: if the murderer is a real hotel-attendant, why should he bother to hide his face either in the halls or before Mrs. Kent? In the halls he is in his proper sphere; open to no suspicion so long as he is not seen entering this room; and carrying such a great pile of towels will actually serve to call attention to him. Before Mrs. Kent, when he knocks at the door, he is a hotel employee with an obvious errand. But if he is some member of her own party—some person she knows very well—he *must* hide his face. He cannot run the danger of being seen walking about in that elaborate uniform with his well-known face bared. Mrs. Kent will certainly be surprised and probably alarmed if she opens the door and sees a friend in fancy-dress: particularly the same sort of fancy-dress that appeared in the house when her husband was murdered. And he must get inside that room before she is suspicious. Add to all this the fact that the liftmen swear no real attendant came up here last night between eleven-thirty at night and five in the morning: you begin to perceive, my boy, that the Royal Scarlet Hotel houses an unco' dangerous guest with an odd taste in clothes."

There was a pause. Hadley tapped on his note-book.

"I've never suggested," he returned, "that she was killed by a complete stranger. But in that case—unless he pinched a real attendant's uniform, the clothes he wore must still be in one of these rooms?"

"So it would appear."

"But why? Why carry about an outfit, and wear it only for murders?"

Dr. Fell clucked his tongue. "Tut, tut, now! Ne'er pull your hat upon your brows. There are other things to claim our attention. Since you won't recapitulate, I will.

"Several things were done in this room besides murder. First, someone picked up a pair of mis-mated brown shoes and put them outside the door. It seems unlikely, to say the least, that Mrs. Kent would have done it. They were not only shoes that did not match; they were suède shoes that could not be cleaned. So the murderer did it. Why?"

"At first glance," replied Hadley cautiously, "you'd say it was because the murderer didn't wish to be interrupted by anybody, as he might have been. He was in the midst of a clutter of shoes. So he picked up a pair, which looked alike to a man in a hurry, and put them outside the door so that it would be assumed Mrs. Kent had gone to bed. That was why he also—hold on!"

"Exactly," agreed Dr. Fell. "That was why, you were going to say, he also hung a 'quiet' sign on the door. But there we take a dismal header. The murderer takes a (hidden) 'quiet' sign out of the bureau drawer; he takes a (hidden) fountain-pen out of Mrs. Kent's trunk; on this card he writes 'Dead Woman' in large letters, and hangs it on the door-knob. It seems rather a curious way of making sure you avoid interruption. Why does he appear to need so much time, and to take so many precautions?"

"Any suggestions?"

"Only to conclude this account by indicating what happened this morning. We assume,"—he pointed his stick towards Kent, who had been swept aside in the backwash of this argument—"we assume that our friend here is telling the truth. H'mf. At about eight o'clock he comes up here with the hall-porter. At this time the bureau does *not* contain a bracelet left behind by an American lady who departed yesterday, the body is lying with head almost inside the leaves of the trunk. While the hall-porter waits, our friend gets out. Presently the porter has the door opened again. The missing bracelet is then found in the bureau, and the body has been moved some feet out from the trunk. The conjuring entertainment is over: ladies and gentlemen, I thank you."

Kent thought that the glance Hadley turned towards him was speculative enough to be ominous.

"If I were judging the matter from outside," Kent admitted, "I should say I was lying. But I'm not lying. Besides, what about that bracelet? I certainly didn't come here last night, pinch a bracelet I'd never seen from a woman I'd never heard of; and then come back here this morning and return it. Where does the bracelet fit in?"

"The alternative being," said Hadley, ignoring this, "that the hall-porter is lying?"

"Not necessarily," said Dr. Fell. "If you will look _____"

There was a knock at the door. Preston brought in the hall-porter and the chambermaid.

The girl was an earnest blonde in a starched blue-and-white uniform which made her look stout; she seemed to jingle like the bunch of keys (all Yale keys) at her waist; but she appeared excited rather than frightened, and a nerve twitched beside one eyelid. Myers, the hall-porter, stood in massive contrast. Though Kent again noted his pointed moustaches and slightly pitted face, the most conspicuous thing in all their eyes was the porter's costume: notably the long double-breasted frock-coat with the silver buttons. Myers, after one glance, affected not to notice Kent's presence. That glance was not belligerent; it was one of dignified but hideous reproachfulness.

Hadley turned to the maid first. "Now there's nothing to worry about," he assured her. "Just look here, please, and answer a few questions. What's your name?"

"Eleanor Peters," said the girl, hardly lifting her eyes from studying the figure on the floor. She seemed to carry an atmosphere of strong soap.

"You were on duty here last night, weren't you, until half-past eleven?"

"Yes."

"Look up at me, please; never mind that!—Now. You see these towels? Do you know where they come from?"

A pause. "From the linen-closet down the hall," she answered, reluctantly following instructions. "Or at least I suppose they do. There was fifteen of them gone from there this morning, and the place was pulled all about, sir."

"Do you have charge of that linen-closet?"

"Yes, I do. And I locked it up last night, too, but somebody got in and pulled it all about."

"Was anything else gone?"

"Nothing but one face-towel. That one, I'll bet." She nodded in a fascinated way towards Jenny Kent's body; and Hadley moved over to obscure her sight of it.

"Who else has a key to the linen-closet?"

"Nobody, far as I know."

"What time did you come on duty this morning?"

"Quarter-past seven."

Hadley went over to the door, opened it, and detached the "quiet" sign from outside. Standing well back in the room, Kent could now see out diagonally across the corridor towards the door which, on the plan, had been marked as that of Sir Gyles Gay's sitting-room. This door stood part-way open, and a face was looking out with an air of alert and refreshed interest. If this were Sir Gyles Gay, Kent was conscious of surprise. He remembered Dr. Fell's mention of interest in names, whatever might have been the significance of it. The name itself had a spacious Cavalier ring, as of one who would down tankards on the table and join a businessmen's chorus in full Cavalier style. Actually, he was a little wizened, philosophical-looking man with an air of interest in everything and a complete lack of embarrassment. After giving Hadley an amiable, somewhat marble-toothed smile reminiscent of the portraits of Woodrow Wilson, he withdrew his head and shut the door. The mural design on that wall was a representation of a cocktail party. Hadley closed the door of 707.

"You came on duty at a quarter-past seven," he said to the maid. "I suppose you passed this door?"

"Oh, yes, sir. Naturally."

"Did you notice this card on the door?"

"I noticed the card, but I didn't notice what's written on it. No, I did *not*," said the excited Eleanor, who evidently wished she had.

"Between the time you came on duty and the time this gentleman came upstairs with the porter," he nodded towards Kent, "did you see anyone else in this wing?"

"No. That is, nobody except a page. He came up about half-past seven and looked at the door of number 707 here, and turned round and went away again."

Myers, the porter, was about to come into action. He had been waiting with several slight clearings of the throat, like a nervous orator who has several speakers before him. Now he began, with massive respectfulness, to explain; but Hadley cut him short.

"Just a moment. . . . About last night. Were you in this part of the wing when Mr. Reaper's party got back from the theatre?"

"That's the handsome one in 701," said the maid; and stopped, covered with a pouring confusion. She added rapidly: "Yes, I was."

"Did you see—?" Hadley stood aside and indicated Jenny.

"Yes, I did. I saw them all except the one with the moustache, in 705."

"What was Mrs. Kent wearing then? Do you remember?"

"Same as she's wearing now, but with a mink coat over it. Except that she'd got on shoes instead of slippers," added Eleanor, after another careful inspection. "The other, the fat one"—Melitta Reaper, undoubtedly—"was in evening dress, gold lawn, with a white fur wrap. But this lady, and the hoity-toity one in 708 were both in ordinary clothes."

Myers, evidently furious, was about to quell this style of talk with cold authority; but Hadley's glance at him was even colder.

"Did you hear them saying anything?"

"Only good night, that I remember."

"Did they go directly to their rooms?"

"Yes, sir. They all stood with their hands on the knobs of the doors, looking round, as though they were waiting for a signal or something; and then all of a sudden they all turned round together and went into their own rooms."

Hadley studied his note-book; then he turned to Myers.

"First, about this bracelet: when did you hear it had been left behind in this room?"

"Eight o'clock this morning, sir, when I came on duty," replied the other instantly. He had a good parade-ground manner of giving evidence, and he was on his mettle. His answers bristled up as though you had given him a shake by the shoulders. "I'm the day-porter, you see, and I come on duty at eight. But Billings, the night man, told me about it when he went off duty. Mrs. Jopley-Dunne, who occupied this room last, had telephoned last night about the bracelet. Mrs. Jopley-Dunne was then staying overnight with friends in Winchester, intending to go on to Southampton next day to catch the *Directoire*. But she telephoned so late that Billings would not disturb Mrs. Kent at that hour."

"What hour? Do you know when the call came through?"

"Yes, sir, there's always a record. At 11:50."

"At 11:50?" the superintendent repeated quickly. "Was anyone sent up here to inquire?"

"No, sir, nor even telephone. As I say, he would not disturb Mrs. Kent at that hour."

"Where were you at that time, by the way?"

"Me sir? I was at my home, in bed." A new, somewhat hoarser tone, had come into Myers's voice; he showed a kind of Gibraltaresque surprise.

"Go on: about next morning."

Myers retold the familiar story. "—so you see, sir, Billings had already sent up a page-boy at seven-thirty, and the page said there was a 'quiet' sign on the door. When I came on duty, and Billings passed the word along to me, Hubbard (that's one of the under-porters) said he thought the gentleman in 707 was just finishing his breakfast in the dining-room. I took the liberty of asking this gentleman, thinking naturally—you understand.

"We went upstairs. I got the chambermaid to open the door, and he went in. He asked me to wait outside, of course. When he had been gone about two or three minutes, and there was no sound out of the room, I tapped on the door: meaning to tell him, you see, sir, that the matter could wait if he could not find the bracelet. There was no answer to that. A minute or so later I tapped again; I was beginning to think it was queer. Then my coat or something brushed that sign on the door. It had been turned round so that the dead-woman part was facing the wall, and I hadn't seen it until then." Myers drew a quick whistling breath. "Well, sir, I knew I was taking a responsibility, but I asked the maid to open the door. And I went in. This gentleman—wasn't there."

"Where was the body lying then?"

"Just where it is now."

"What did you do first when you went in?"

"I went to look for the bracelet."

"For the bracelet?"

"Sir," replied Myers, in a sudden lofty passion, "I had been told to go and get that there bracelet. I did it; and I don't see why everyone should think it was so out of the way. I walked across, like this"——he illustrated——"I opened the right-hand bureau drawer, like this; and there it was, stuck down by the paper lining. I put it in my pocket. Then I went and told the manager I had got it, and that the lady in here was dead. I know there's been mistakes; and I don't *say* this gentleman here killed her; but I've heard nothing about nothing; that's all *I* say."

Hadley turned to Kent.

"How long should you say you were in here before you slipped out that side door into the other angle of the corridor?"

"It's hard to tell. About three minutes, I should think."

"And you?" the superintendent asked Myers. "How long between the time Mr. Kent came in here and the time you followed him?"

"Well, sir, say five minutes."

"While you were waiting outside what we'll call the main door, the one with the sign on it, I suppose nobody went in or out past you?"

"Not by that door they didn't! No, sir!"

"Then here is the order of events, if we say both of you are telling the truth. Mr. Kent comes into this room. After three minutes he goes out by the side door. At the end of five minutes you come in. During the space of two minutes, then, someone has entered by the side door——must have been, because you were planted in front of the only other entrance——someone has put the bracelet in the drawer, moved the body, and gone out the same way. This, I repeat, happened in the two minutes between the time Mr. Kent left the room and the time you entered it. Is that right?"

Myers was aggrieved. "I can't speak for him, sir, that's all I say. But I can speak for myself, and what I say's the truth."

"Just one last thing. While you were outside the main door, you could see the doors of all the rooms in this angle of the corridor?"

"Yes, sir," replied the other—and stopped, evidently taken backwards by a rush of thought.

"During that time, did any of the guests come out of their rooms? Would you have noticed?"

"I should have noticed. And, sir," said Myers, with massive simplicity, "none of 'em did. That I'll swear to."

"What about you?" inquired Hadley, and turned to the maid.

"Stop a bit!" urged that young lady, examining the past. "Yes, I'll agree to that. *I* should have noticed, I'm sure. But there's one door I couldn't see from there; I mean it was round the corner. That's the side door to 705, facing the side door of this one across the hall."

Hadley shut up his note-book. "That's all, thanks. You can go; but don't talk about this, either of you." When they had been dismissed, he looked for Dr. Fell with some satisfaction. "This looks dangerously like a bit of luck. It's what you would call a logical certainty. Either this one is lying—" he put his hand on Kent's shoulder—"which I don't believe. Or *both* the porter and the maid are lying, which I don't believe either. Or—we come to it—the person in this room must have been Harvey Wrayburn, from 705."

Chapter 7

A Square Black Stone

DR. FELL had again played his disconcerting trick of never being in the place you expected him, which was a physical as well as a mental trait. When Hadley looked round, the doctor was bending over the dressing-table at the other side of the room, so that they could see only a vast expanse of back and black cape. A red face now turned round and rose to the surface like Leviathan, while he blinked over his eyeglasses.

"Oh, it's possible," admitted the doctor, with a petulant wheeze. "It's still more possible since—" He flourished a snake-skin handbag.

"Since what?"

"Since I can't find her key. The key to this room. I've been looking all over the place for it. You remember, we heard a very interesting account of the spring-locks with which all the doors on this floor are supplied; no two locks alike. Except, I dare say, when one room has two doors, like this one: then the same key would open both. But where is the key? If someone used that side door to sneak in here and return the bracelet in two minutes—well, he had to get in. On the other hand, there are certain curious

85

suggestions which occur to me, especially after a closer examination of that trunk, and they do not fit in with your friend Wrayburn."

There was the sound of an argument outside the partly-open main door to the hall, cut short by a faint "Pah!" Into the room, with the utmost composure, came the wizened and calm-faced man whom Kent had seen peering out of the doorway across the hall. Though he was of middle height, he seemed much shorter by reason of his bony leanness; he was carefully dressed, to the point of the dapper, in a blue double-breasted suit and (very) hard collar. That collar, like the set if pleasant expression which suggested false teeth, seemed to give him a high glaze like the polish on a tombstone. While preserving the most careful decorum, he nevertheless contrived to suggest the same air of refreshed interest. His thin hair, carefully parted, was whitish at the top and dull grey over the ears; its smoothness contrasted with his wizened face. He stopped by the body, as though performing a conventional rite; he shook his head, cast down his eyes, and then looked at Hadley.

"Good morning, superintendent."

"Morning, Sir Gyles."

"And this, I think," the other went on gravely, "will be the celebrated Dr. Fell. And the other—?" Introductions were performed, while Gay's shrewd eye appraised them. "Gentlemen, I have come for you, and I will not be denied. You must come over to my rooms and————

"—and take a cup of China tea," he added, when by some mysterious power of eye he had got them out of the room. "I could not say it in there. I don't know why."

Despite his poise he was a trifle white. Dr. Fell beamed down on him as though on some interesting phenomenon.

"Heh," said the doctor. "Heh-heh-heh. Yes. I particularly wished to speak to you. I want a fresh viewpoint on character, so to speak; the others are able judges, I don't doubt, but they have lived too close to each other to be free from bias."

"You flatter me," said Gay, showing the edge of a marble-toothed smile. "I am entirely at your service."

While Hadley remained behind to give brief instructions to Betts and Preston, Gay took the others into his sitting-room. It was a pleasant place, furnished (surprisingly) in eighteenth-century fashion, though the noise of traffic from Piccadilly boiled up below the windows. From this height you could see far down the slope of grey barrack-like roofs, past the curt solidity of St. James's, to the bare trees of St. James's Park. The dapper old man fitted into this. On a table by the window there was a steaming tea-service; and, when the others refused tea, their host poured a cup for himself with a steady hand.

"You will find cigars in the box beside you," he told Dr. Fell. "And now, gentlemen, to business: though the business will be mostly theory. One thing, though, I can tell you at the start," he said vigorously. "I know no more of this—this bloody business than when that young man was murdered in my house. I did not leave my room last night, and I don't know who did. All I *know* is that we seem to be pursued by an exacting and business-like murderer."

"H'm," said Dr. Fell, who was endangering a frail-looking chair. "Well, look here: what do you think of Mr. Reaper's party in general?"

Gay drew a deep breath. There was an expression of pleasure on his bony face, which faded as he seemed to reflect.

"Up to the time young Kent was murdered," he answered gravely, "I had never had so much fun in my life."

He paused to let this sink in.

"I must explain. In business I have been known as a terror, a spolier of the Egyptians and everyone else; and I confess that my conduct in the City, as the Wodehouse story puts it, would have caused raised eyebrows in the fo'c'sle of a pirate sloop. Also, I have been a successful government official: hence my surprising knighthood. Also, there is no arguing with the mirror—and the mirror displays a stern and shrivelled look. Therefore it is taken for granted. Therefore people, coming in contact with my bleak atmosphere, talk about the weather. I think it has been years since anyone invited me to have a second drink.

. . . Well, Reaper's party paid no attention to that, or never thought of it. They came into my house, and after a decorous interval they cut loose. They banged the piano. They got up games in which I found myself blindfolded, inadvertently pinning a paper donkey's tail to the posterior of Mrs. Reaper. Young Wrayburn, and even the Grim Reaper himself, when he forgot he was an M.A. and a business man, introduced the novel note of 'Ride 'em, cowboy!' In short, they made the damn place resound!—and I loved it."

He ended with a surprising and deep-throated crow of mirth, lifting his neck to do so, and showing an extraordinary animation which twinkled up to his eyes.

"And murder came next," said Dr. Fell.

The other grew sober. "Yes. I knew I was enjoying myself too much for it to last."

"You're an intelligent man," Dr. Fell went on, in the same sleepy and abstracted fashion. "What do you think happened?"

"Oh, I don't know. If this hadn't happened to me, I should have said, Read your psychology: but those books don't apply—to personal cases. They never do."

"Was Rodney Kent one of the persons who promoted the hilarity?"

Gay hesitated. "No, he was not, though he tried to be. It was not in his nature, I think. He was too conscientious. I think you have met the type. He is one of the persons who stand, smiling but uncertain, on the edge of a group who are enjoying themselves; and you think over and over, 'What in blazes can I do to amuse so-and-so?' till it amounts to a point of desperation. But you never succeed."

It was, Christopher Kent reflected, a perfect description of Rod, who was really in his element only when he had facts to dig out.

"But he was murdered," said Gay.

"What about Miss Forbes?"

"Ah, Miss Forbes," said Gay dryly, and again showed the edge of the marble-toothed smile. "I think you misunderstand her, Dr. Fell. You should have seen her, when *she* forgot herself, standing by the piano and singing a ballad whose drift I need not repeat." He turned to Kent, and added: "She is in love with you, you know."

As startled as though he had got two successive blows in the wind, Kent sat up.

"She's— What makes you think that?"

"Secrets," said Gay reflectively. "You would be surprised at the number of secrets that have been confided to me in the past fortnight. Nothing damaging, nothing helpful, I am afraid; but I was surprised and pleased and a little touched. It is flattering. In the old days nobody would have thought of confiding a secret to me. That person would have been afraid I should use it to extract his back teeth or collar-stud. And I fear he would have been right. But I mention this particular secret in the hope that it may be helpful." He considered. "Now listen, and I'll sum up. In South Africa to-day there is a minority political group called the Dominion Party. They are excellent fellows, although they haven't a dog's chance; the government is eighty per cent *Afrikaans*. But they try to keep up English traditions—including the wholly mythical one of English reserve. Nearly all the members of Reaper's crowd are touched with that brush. Reaper himself is, though he professes to be a United man." He looked at Kent. "*You* are, I suspect. But I don't think Miss Forbes realises that it is not really necessary nowadays to stand on her dignity. The spectacle of me lapping up sherry out of a saucer as a forfeit for failing to do something else equally dignified—I forget what—should have corrected that. You understand, Dr. Fell?"

The doctor chuckled, though he kept a speculative eye on their host.

"I'm not sure I do understand," he rumbled. "Are you trying to tell us something? Do I detect, as a sinister undertone to these games, a suggestion that there is a repression or neurosis which takes the form of murder?"

Gay's face did not change, though it was a second or two before he answered. "I'll be quite candid," he said with a broad air. "I don't know what I bloody well do mean."

"H'mf. Still, there's one person, you know, whose character you haven't described. I mean Mrs. Josephine Kent."

Gay got up, with his dapper walk, and passed round a humidor of good cigars. Each accepted one; and, in a perplexity of thought, Kent looked out across the grey roofs patched in snow. The scratching of a match, and the ritual of cigar-lighting, roused him. Their host was again sitting quietly on the edge of his chair; but his face had hardened.

"You forget," he continued, "that I met the lady for the first time last night, and that I knew her only a few hours before this happened. She was with her aunts during the other business; she met us in London. Nevertheless, I'll tell you what she was. She was a dangerous girl."

"Nonsense!" exploded Kent. "Rod's wife?"

Sir Gyles Gay's face was alight with a great pleasure, so that it seemed to shine as at the discovery of a toy.

"Hadn't you discovered that?"

"Yes," said Dr. Fell. "But go on."

"I don't mean," said Gay, with a quick and sharp look at the doctor, "I don't mean a crooked girl, or an evil one. (By the way, she must be rather older than she looks, you know.) I don't suppose there was ever a consciously crooked thought in her head; I doubt whether she would have recognised one of her worst and most radiant thoughts as being crooked, even if such a thought had been there. Since you object to the term 'dangerous,' though, I'll describe her in another way. She would have made an ideal wife for me. And she knew it."

Kent grinned in spite of himself. "Was that why she was dangerous?"

"You still don't understand. The sort of character she had is common enough, but it's elusive and difficult to describe. So I'll merely tell you something. I met her last evening for the first time. Within fifteen minutes she was making up to me. Object, matrimony. For my money."

There was a pause. "Sir Gyles," Kent said, "you're a very intelligent man, as Dr. Fell has said; but don't you think that's rather an asinine statement?"

The other did not seem offended, though there was a gleam in his eye. On the contrary, he appeared pleased as at more confirmation of a theory. After taking several deep pulls at his cigar, and savouring the smoke, he leaned forward.

"And," he insisted, "I should have fallen. Oh, yes. Was I attracted? Damme, yes! Even though I knew—well, I have now got the phrase that describes her. She was the ideal Old Man's Darling. Hadn't you realised all this?" His calm certainty on the point sent through Kent a sudden discomfort that was like a touch of belief. "Tell me if I've read her character correctly on other points. I judge that she was an excellent business woman: probably with a business of her own: very likely something to do with clothes or millinery. I also judge that nobody ever saw her disturbed or out of countenance: that nobody ever really knew her. She slid through things. That little—er—*half pint* (a word I've picked up) could not actually be touched by anything. That, gentlemen, is the quality which would drive our sex crazy; and she had the particular kind of attractiveness, blessed-Damozel and kiss-me-lightly style, which turns a lot of heads to begin with. Of course she would marry a well-meaning chap like Rodney Kent. Of course she would sweetly expect all the favours; and get 'em. But when she saw the possibility of a better match, or was merely tired, she would say he was too gross, or something; that she had been entrapped or sold into the marriage; that her soul had been snatched; and she would pass on to what she wanted amid general murmurs of sympathy. Dignity she had, I've no doubt—and for some curious reason there persists among our countrymen a belief that if you have dignity you're probably right."

It was a thrust so straight and deep that Kent stirred again. Jenny, instead of lying over there with her face covered by a towel, now seemed to walk in the room. Dr. Fell seemed to be half asleep; but you could see the steady shining of intentness in his eyes.

"Forgive the long oration," Gay concluded abruptly.

Dr. Fell examined the end of his cigar. "Not at all," he said with offhand affability. "Do you think that quality had anything to do with her murder?"

"I didn't say anything about the murder. You asked about her character."

"Oh, here! Do you mean that a person's character has nothing to do with his or her murder?"

"Undoubtedly. But I haven't had a chance to deduce anything about the murder yet. I haven't even heard about the circumstances. So I must stick to what I know."

At this invitation Dr. Fell merely opened one eye. "Yes, but—" he said with an air of stubbornness. "Tell me: is there anything you know, or can deduce, which would lead you to suspect that Mrs. Kent wasn't what she seemed?"

"Wasn't what she seemed? I don't understand."

"Then I won't ask it. It is another of those subtleties which grieve Hadley. 'For *nutu signisque loquuntur* is good consistorial law.' It also has some reference to a blind horse, which I may be. I take it you regarded Mrs. Kent, then, as a kind of painted Roman statue, hollow inside?"

"That's it exactly. If you knocked on it, you'd get the same kind of sound. Knock, knock—" Gay paused with another interested expression, as his agile brain seemed to go after a new line of thought. "Ahem! By the way, doctor, I have been introduced in my old age to a game which offers considerable possibilities. It consists in taking various good English words and twisting them out of the shapes God gave them. For example! I say to you, 'Knock, knock.' You are now to reply, 'Who's there?' "

"All right. Who's there?" inquired Dr. Fell, with interest.

"Beelzebub. You now say, 'Beelzebub who?' "

"Beelzebub who?" said Dr. Fell obediently.

What particular gem of this genus was about to be perpetrated Kent never learned, although he was interested by the spectacle of the two grave philosophers playing it. At this point there was, in actual fact, a knock at the door, and Hadley came in. The theories were dispelled. Kent wondered whether the superintendent had been listening at the door, for his face wore a curiously exasperated look.

"Wrayburn," he said to Dr. Fell, "will see us in a minute. He's just getting up, it seems." Then Hadley looked at Gay. "In the meantime, Sir Gyles, would you mind answering a few questions? Also, would you have any objection to this suite being searched?"

"Searched? Not at all; go right ahead. But may I ask what you're looking for?"

"For a hotel-attendant's uniform." Hadley waited, and Gay put down his cigar on the edge of the saucer; he tried to flash his marble-toothed smile, sardonically, but he displayed the first sign of uneasiness he had yet shown.

"Ah, I thought so. I knew it. The ghost has been walking again. I tried, by applying the spur of silence, to extract some information from Dr. Fell. But it doesn't seem to work as well with schoolmasters as with business men or lesser breeds without the law."

Hadley gestured to Sergeant Betts, who went towards the bedroom. "—and also, if possible, we hope to find a key."

"Key? What sort of key?"

On the polished round centre table a key was lying now: a Yale key through whose thumb-hole was threaded a little chromium tag bearing the number 703. Hadley picked it up.

"A key like this. This is yours, naturally?"

"Yes, it's the key to the suite. Why?"

Hadley was at his most offhand. "Someone, presumably the murderer, stole the key to Mrs. Kent's room. It must be somewhere in this wing now, unless it was—thrown out of the window, for instance." The tone of the last few words was curious, though he looked amused. "*You* haven't see it, have you?"

Their host was thoughtful. "Sit down, superintendent; make yourself comfortable. No, I have not seen it. Not since last night, that is."

"Last night?"

"Yes. I noticed Mrs. Kent opening the door of her room with it."

"How was that?"

"It is customary," explained Gay, with icy testiness, "to open doors with a key." He had adopted a harder guard with Hadley than he had attempted with Dr. Fell. "No, see here—it was like this. I don't know whether you've heard it; I suppose you have; but we all went to the theatre last night, and when we came back we turned in immediately. We made a kind of military drill of saying good night, each standing in the door of his own room. Well, Mrs. Kent's room is directly across the hall. She opened the door with her key. She turned on the light just inside. Then, just after she went inside, I remember that she dropped the key in her handbag."

Dr. Fell woke up. "I say, you're sure of that?" he demanded with some excitement. "You're certain she put the key in her handbag?"

"Yes, I'm quite certain of that." Gay's interest was aroused again. "Why do you ask? She was standing with her back to me (naturally); but turned round a little towards the left, so that I could see her left arm. I think she was holding the door open with her right knee. She wore a fur coat, and her handbag was snake-skin. She turned round to say good night over her left shoulder; she went in—I am following this carefully—and at this time the bag was in her left hand. She dropped in the key and closed the bag. I remember that left hand because on the wrist she was wearing a white-gold bracelet, with a square black stone in it, and I noticed it when the sleeve of the coat fell back."

He stopped abruptly, aware of the expression on his companions' faces.

Chapter 8

The Card from the Window

I SEEM to have startled you," Gay observed, picking up his cigar. "Is anything wrong?"

Though Hadley remained impassive, he wore a heavier look. "A white-gold bracelet with— Are you telling us that Mrs. Kent was wearing Mrs. Jopley-Dunne's bracelet?"

"No indeed, superintendent. I never heard of Mrs. Jopley-Dunne, and I can't say I like the name. I merely said she had on *a* bracelet of that kind. It had a Latin inscription on the stone, I believe; though I didn't get close enough to examine it. I'm fairly sure she had it on at the theatre. One of her friends ought to be able to identify it."

Dr. Fell, after spilling cigar-ash down the ridges of his waistcoat, spoke in a hollow voice. He said:

"That has torn it, Hadley. That has most definitely torn it. Oh, my sacred hat. We grope through a spiritual abyss; and all because, by the innate mental workings of guests at hotels, Mrs. Jopley-Dunne drops a brick. It's a curious fact, worthy of consideration by psychologists, that whenever someone away from home mislays anything, he or she is always firmly convinced that it was Left At The Hotel.

Don't you see the sinister significance of it now? The elusive Mrs. Jopley-Dunne didn't leave her bracelet. It wasn't her bracelet at all. It was Mrs. Kent's. . . . There ought to be a house-telephone here somewhere. I strongly advise you to get hold of Hardwick, bring him up here with the bracelet and Reaper and Miss Forbes, round up Mrs. Reaper as well: and if one of them can't identify that thing as belonging to Mrs. Kent, I'm a son of Boetia."

"But, according to everybody, Mrs. Jopley-D. seemed pretty positive she had left it," Hadley muttered. "And why are you so excited? Even if this is true, how does it help us?"

"Help us?" roared Dr. Fell, who was stirring with spark and cigar-ash like the Spirit of the Volcano. "Help us? It is the most enlightening and stimulating thing I have heard this morning. It solves a good many of our difficulties. Grant me the fact that the bracelet belonged to Mrs. Kent," he argued, "and I'll take you a little farther along an exceedingly murky road."

"How?"

"Just tell me this, Hadley: what happened in that room last night?"

"How the hell should I know? That's what———"

"No, no, no," said Dr. Fell testily. "I've had occasion to tell you about this before. You're concentrating so exclusively on the murder that you don't stop to ask yourself what *else* happened there. Why, we were asking a while ago, did the murderer need so much time in that room? Why did he need to be free from interruption for a fairly long time? What was he doing in there?"

"All right. What was he doing?"

"He was making a very careful and intensive search of the room," replied Dr. Fell, making a hideous pantomime face by way of emphasis. "Without, apparently, finding what he wanted or pinching anything. Consider the following points. He found a fountain-pen which had been hidden under a pile of handkerchiefs in the tray of the trunk: therefore he had been through at least that part of the trunk. He found a 'quiet' sign hidden in the bureau drawer:

therefore he had been into the bureau. He got the key of the room out of Mrs. Kent's handbag: therefore he had been through the handbag. So much it requires very little cerebral activity to determine, and we are pretty safe in postulating a search. The trouble was that, so far as I could see, nothing appeared to be missing. If we prove that the bracelet belonged to Mrs. Kent, and that for some reason the murderer pinched it last night————"

Hadley was staring at him. "After which the murderer came back and returned it this morning? You call that making things clearer? And, anyway, what's the point of the bracelet? You were making a great fuss about its being one of the most ingenious devices of the ancient world, or some such nonsense; but you haven't said a definite word about it yet."

"Oh, I know," said Dr. Fell despondently. "And yet—and yet—well, I still think you'd better get on to that telephone."

"There it is, on the table," suggested Gay.

Hadley roused himself to the fact that he was indiscreetly talking before witnesses. After asking to be put through to the manager's office, he showed the newspaperman's trick of speaking to the telephone in such a way as to be inaudible four feet off. The others shifted uncomfortably until he put back the receiver again.

"Hardwick will phone through to Mrs. Jopley-Dunne," he said. "Then he'll come round here with Reaper and Miss Forbes. We may as well have them all here. Mr. Kent, you know Mrs. Reaper. Will you go down to their suite and ask her to come here?" (Kent suddenly realised that the superintendent found Melitta a difficult proposition.) "In the meantime, Sir Gyles, those questions . . ."

"I am at your service," assented Gay, with a sort of ancient vivacity. "Though, as I told Dr. Fell, I am afraid I can't help you. Nothing suspicious happened last night so far as I know. I turned in immediately, and read in bed until half-past twelve; but nothing disturbed me in any way. . . ."

That smooth, hard voice was the last thing Kent heard

as he went out into the hall. But he did not go immediately to Dan's suite. He stood for a time in that muffled corridor, the stump of the hot cigar almost burning his hand, and tried to rearrange his thoughts.

Two things were becoming apparent now. In spite of himself he was beginning to credit Gay's deadly sharp analysis of Jenny. He had always been credited with being unobservant about people; and certain vague scenes, gestures, inflections, returned to trouble him now. It was like trying to remember a passage or a quotation in a book, in which you can remember the appearance of the book, the page on which the passage occurred, and even the part of the page on which the passage occurred; but you cannot remember the quotation itself. But, even granting all Gay had said, this did nothing to explain her murder—and certainly gave no ghost of a reason why Rod should be killed.

Next, Harvey Wrayburn was in a bad position. You had only to look at this corridor in order to see that. The maid and the hall-porter had been outside one door; they were in a position to testify that nobody else could have stirred out of a room, and Wrayburn's side door was the *only* one they could not see. But why? Why? Why? He thought of Wrayburn, with his brushed-up moustache, his bouncing energy, and his vast mine of information on all the most useless subjects: in appearance a little like that Laughing Cavalier who does not (you recall) really laugh. Then there was this odd business of Wrayburn being still asleep at eleven o'clock in the morning; so far as Kent could remember, he had never done that before.

From hotel-attendant to bracelet to Iron-maiden trunk, it was all a bogging mass of whys. Kent walked slowly down the hall; and, about to knock at the door of Dan's suite, he stopped to inspect the linen-closet. Its door was now ajar; through a frosted-glass window, partly raised, the dull light showed that it served another purpose besides housing the neat shelves of sheets and towels. Other shelves contained tea-services, evidently for those guests who wished early-morning tea before breakfast. He inspected it gloomily, without much enlightenment. Then he knocked at the sitting-room door of Dan's suite, and Melitta's voice told him to come in.

Well, you would not unduly upset Melitta even by the presence of murder, for Melitta lived in a perpetual state of being mildly and stoically upset. It was as though she had taken a tonic which kept her always in the same state of disturbance, and her voice at the same monotone. Twenty years ago she had been a very beautiful woman. She would still have been a beautiful woman if it were not for her soft stoutness, or a certain expression by which the angles of her face seemed to have drooped plaintively out of line: as though the whole woman had been pushed down squatly from above.

But her eyelids were reddish this morning. She sat in a deep chair by a table on which were the remains of a large breakfast, and a box of chocolates. She seldom touched the chocolates, however; she remained bolt upright as a Sphinx, her hands flat along the arms of the chair. The large body was exceedingly well if a little hastily dressed. Her voice struck him like a familiar tune; she showed no surprise at seeing him, but simply picked up the conversation as though it had been broken off five minutes ago, while the handsome blue eyes never left his face.

"—and it is all very dreadful, I know, and of course I know how dreadful it must be for you, and I quite sympathise; but what I say is that it seems so *inconsiderate*, when we had been looking forward to such a nice holiday; but it just does seem as though there would always be something wherever I go. Did you have a nice trip out?"

"Melitta," said Kent, "do you know what's happened? The superintendent wants to see you."

Her monotone never noticed a change of subject; she accepted it, and slid into it as easily as though they had been discussing it all the time. But, even while seeming to regard him vacantly, she showed her frequent disconcerting shrewdness.

"My dear Christopher, I got it all out of the maid a little while ago, and gave her a shilling for it too. Not that I begrudge the shilling, heaven knows; though I do think that things in England are *too much*, and when I see the prices on things in the shops I simply gasp, and I cannot understand how they can pay so much when at home I could get that same hat for twenty-seven and six. Poor Jenny; her shop was much nicer, and Parisian models too. Poor Jenny: my heart does bleed for her, it does really," —and undoubtedly it did—"but I wish Dan would not let them talk such nonsense as they do. But you know how men are, and Dan especially, wanting to get on well with everybody————"

In conversation with Melitta, Kent had discovered, the best policy was to find some train of thought you could understand, and trace it back to its devious beginning: at which time you usually found something worth hearing.

"Nonsense? Nonsense about what?"

"Christopher, you know perfectly well what I mean. Why should any of us do anything like that to Rod or Jenny? We never did at home, did we? I have said before, and I say again, though you needn't repeat it, I do *not* trust that Sir Gyles Gay, even if he has got a title. I have heard about him at home, though of course Dan wouldn't listen, and in business he has the reputation of being nothing better than an absolute Twister. But of course Dan is easy and soft-headed"—it was hardly a description Kent himself would have applied to Dan—"when he finds someone he thinks is a good fellow. Yes, I know what you're going to say, but all men are like that; and I admit he made me laugh, but, as my grandfather used to say, beware of people who make you laugh, because they're usually up to no good."

"That," said Kent, a trifle stunned, "is just about the most cynical remark I've ever heard. But what has it all got to do with Jenny or Rod?"

"I'm sure I don't know," she told him placidly. "But what Rod knew, Jenny knew; you can be sure of that."

"Meaning? It doesn't seem to make any sense."

"Oh, fiddle-de-dee!" cried Melitta, losing a little of her injured air and showing some of that sparkle which could still make Dan Reaper beam with pride. "Who wants to make sense? *I* don't pretend to, thank heaven, though I've always been more sensible than most, and a good deal more sensible than any of you. If you want to know what happened, you just think of everything that could have happened; and one of them is the right explanation; and there you are."

Kent looked at her with a certain reverence. If she had taken just two glasses of champagne at that moment, the hump would have lifted from her face as well as from her feelings, and she would have been a genuinely beautiful woman.

"I suppose it's a sound principle in detective-work," he admitted. "But, since you have a suspicious mind and secrets are coming out all over the place, how did Jenny strike you?"

"Strike me?" she asked quickly.

"I mean what's your version of her character?"

"Version fiddlesticks. People do not have versions of character in families: they take what they can get, and thank heaven it isn't worse, as Uncle Lionel used to say. I do think you ought not to talk in such a silly way, Christopher, though I dare say it's all very well in novels. Jenny was a sweet girl, or as much as could be expected."

"Well, you'd better make up your mind before you see Superintendent Hadley and Dr. Fell." This was the sort of talk from Melitta which always stung him. "There seem to be more niggers in the woodpile than you'd think. As old friend to old friend, Melitta, you're only fifty; don't try to talk like a grandmother before your time."

He was sorry a moment later, that he had said it. It pierced something that was not a fancied complaint. But there was nothing now that could be done. When he took her down to Gay's room, he asked only one more question.

"Did you ever notice in Jenny's possession a white-gold bracelet with one black stone, like an obsidian?"

"No," said Melitta, her first monosyllable.

Yet she was complacent, amiable, even cheerful in Gay's room, where Hadley was concluding his questioning. Gay preserved towards her an attitude of great gallantry, and, when he presented her to Dr. Fell, she was almost effusive. Hadley, his note-book on his knee, forged ahead as steadily as an army lorry.

"—and you did not wake up, Sir Gyles, until half-past nine this morning?"

"That is correct," agreed the other with great gravity.

"How did you first learn of the murder?"

"From one of your men. Sergeant Somebody. I rang for the maid to get hot water for my tea," he nodded towards the table. "The maid answered the bell, but the sergeant came with her. He told me Mrs. Kent had been killed, and asked if I would stay in my suite. I obeyed orders."

"One last question. I believe it is the usual thing, when you take a room at this hotel, for them to issue a little folded card with the number of the room, the price, and so on?"

Gay frowned. "I don't know. It certainly is so at a number of hotels. This is the first time I have ever been here."

"But didn't you get such a card?"

"No."

Hadley's pencil stopped. "I'll tell you why I ask. Mr. Kent here was standing in front of this hotel between seven-twenty and seven-thirty this morning. One of those cards—let me have it, will you?—dropped down out of a window; from up here somewhere, anyhow." He took the card Kent handed him. "This, you see, is for room 707, Mrs. Kent's room. But her room looks out on the air-well. This card, apparently, could only have come from your suite or Mr. Reaper's. What we want to know is how the card for 707 came to be in here, and why it was dropped out of a window at seven-thirty in the morning."

There was a pause. Gay returned the look unwinkingly.

"I don't know, superintendent. So far as I know, it was not dropped out of here."

"Can you tell us anything, Mrs. Reaper?"

"My husband attends to all that," Melitta said vaguely. The lines of dissatisfaction pressed down her face again, so as to make its expression unreadable; Kent guessed that she and Hadley were not favourites of each other. "I remember quite well that there were a number of those little cards. And naturally they gave them to my husband in a batch, because of course he was the host and paid for all the rooms. I am quite *sure* he put them all down on the bureau in our bedroom. And, though I cannot and do not expect to be consulted about it, I should think it was easy. It blew out."

"Blew out?"

"The card blew out," she told him with an air of patience. "Out of the window. And since my husband will insist on sleeping with both of the windows wide open, and they always put the bureau between the windows, I cannot say I am surprised. There must have been a high wind this morning,"—this was true, Kent remembered, for he had been standing out in it when the card whirled down,—"because I know he got up at some time to close the windows, and things were blown all about on the bureau."

Hadley wore a look of unspoken profanity. If this attractive clue turned into a mere gust of wind, it would be a final bedevilment.

"Are you certain the card for 707 was among them?"

"I am not certain; I don't know anything about it. All I know is that I simply glanced at them, to make sure my husband had told me the truth about what the rooms cost. I never noticed the numbers at all. I am afraid, as usual, you will have to ask my husband."

There was an opportunity to ask him. Dan, shouldering in at that juncture, stopped short and seemed disturbed to find her there. Francine was behind him, with a worried-looking Hardwick, the latter carrying a sheet of notes.

"That bracelet—" exploded Dan. "No. You tell 'em, Hardwick. Fire away."

The manager gave a careful and courteous greeting to

everyone before he took up a task he did not seem to relish. He resembled a grizzled clerk studying a ledger, and had a pencil poised.

"About the bracelet, as Mr. Reaper says. It belonged to Mrs. Kent; Miss Forbes has just identified it. But we're not through with the other one yet. I've talked to Mrs. Jopley-Dunne on the telephone. Her bracelet is a silver linked one set with small diamonds; it's worth three thousand dollars, and she says that beyond any doubt she left it in that bureau." He looked up. "I think she means it, Mr. Hadley. She—er—she can't claim any liability; but, all the same, we don't want this unpleasantness and I have got to find the bracelet somehow."

Dr. Fell sat up. "Steady!" rumbled the doctor. "Let me understand this. You say there were *two* bracelets in that bureau?"

"It looks like that," admitted Hardwick.

"Two bracelets. Both were stolen, and then one was returned. But the one that was returned was Mrs. Kent's bracelet, which very probably has some meaning in this case. And the one that was taken and *not* returned was a bracelet belonging to Mrs. Jopley-Dunne, a woman whose belongings have absolutely nothing to do with the case at all. If it had been the other way round, we should have had sense. But it isn't and we haven't. Oh, my eye, Hadley! This won't do."

Hadley gave a sharp glance round.

"Not so fast," he snapped. "Anything else, Mr. Hardwick?"

"Yes. I've checked up on the night-staff. I take it," inquired Hardwick, "Mr. Reaper saw this 'hotel-attendant' in the hall at two minutes past twelve?"

"That's right. Well?"

The manager peered up over his eyeglasses. "Then every solitary soul employed on the night-staff has what you'd call a complete alibi. It's a long story, but it's all here for your convenience in checking. I've had them routed individually out of their beds as quickly as I could. Shall I read this out?"

"Fine," said Dan without enthusiasm. "I hope that clears the air. But, since I'm chiefly interested in my own tight little circle— You haven't got any mechanism, have you, to prove an alibi for all of us?"

"As a mater of fact, in one case I can." Hardwick forgot himself and put his pencil behind his ear. "It goes along with the alibi of Billings, the night-porter, who was in his lodge downstairs. A telephone-call from up here came through at just midnight. Billings answered it. The guest wanted information, and they talked until three minutes past. Billings is willing to swear to the voice of the guest who spoke to him; and an under-porter heard Billings's side of it. So—er—well, it's your affair; but that seems to let both of them out of it."

"Who was the guest?" demanded Hadley.

"Mr. Wrayburn, in 705."

Chapter 9

Men in the Case

HADLEY did not comment; for a short time it was as though he had not heard. But he avoided Dr. Fell's eye and studied the ring of faces which, blank or interested, now included all of the *dramatis personae* except one. A very clever person (had he known it) was then within sound of his voice.

"We'll go into that later," he observed. "Thanks for the information, though. At the moment, have you got that bracelet? Good! Miss Forbes: you identify this as belonging to Mrs. Kent?"

Kent had been looking at her ever since she had come in, wondering about Gay's maunderings, wondering about the nature of the mess in which they had been landed. Francine's expression baffled him as she regarded the bracelet; it was not an expression he knew.

"Yes. She was wearing it last night."

"Will someone else identify it? Mrs. Reaper? Mr. Reaper?"

"I'm sure *I* never saw it before," said Melitta.

"Neither have I," Dan asserted, wheeling round as though surprised. "Funny, too. You'd notice a thing like that, with the inscription and the rest of it. Do you suppose she bought it since she landed over here?"

Hadley gave a quick look at Dr. Fell, who did not respond. "It doesn't look the sort of thing you could buy in Dorset; or possibly even in London, according to the doctor. However! She was wearing this at the theatre last night?"

"Yes, she was," Francine said in a cool tone which gave the impression that her truthfulness might be doubted. "Perhaps the others didn't notice it because she wore her fur coat all last night. But I saw it beforehand. I————"

"We don't doubt you, Miss Forbes," Hadley said at that curious tone, as though to prod her. "When did you see it?"

"Before we went to the theatre, and just before we went out to dinner. I went to her room to ask her whether she was going to dress for the theatre last night."

"Time?"

"About seven o'clock."

"Go on, please."

"She said she was much too tired and queer inside to dress. She said she wouldn't even go to the theatre if it weren't for sticking to the party; she said she thought it wasn't decent." Francine stopped. Under the long eyelids her dark brown eyes, which gave vitality to the too-fair complexion, flashed towards Hadley as though pondering. "She said————"

"Just a moment. She talked about 'sticking to the party.' Do you mean she was alarmed or frightened?"

"No, I don't think so. It would have taken a great deal to frighten her." Another pause. The emotional temperature was so low that Kent wondered about it. "When I went in her trunk was open but not unpacked; she said she would unpack after the theatre. She was standing in front of the dressing-table, with her wrist out, looking at that bracelet. I admired it, and asked whether it was new. She said yes. She also said, 'If anything ever happens to me, which I don't anticipate, you shall have it.'"

Hadley looked up quickly.

"She was a great friend of yours?"

"No. I'm not sure whether she liked me. But I think she trusted me."

This was a curious remark from Francine; both Dan and Melitta Reaper seemed to find it so, for there was a shifting and muttering in the group.

"Anything else, Miss Forbes?"

"Well, she looked very hard at me, I thought, and asked if I had ever seen anything like the bracelet before. I said I hadn't, and looked at it closer. I asked her whether the inscription had any meaning; any personal meaning, that is. She said, 'Only if you're able to read it; that's the whole secret.'"

Again Hadley glanced at Dr. Fell, who seemed intrigued and sardonically amused. "'Only if you're able to read it; that's the whole secret.' Wait!" muttered the superintendent. "You mean that Latin inscription is, or contains a cryptogram or cipher of some sort? Oh, Lord, haven't we had enough———"

"Be careful, Hadley," warned Dr. Fell. "I rather doubt that. Anything else, Miss Forbes?"

"No, that was all. I don't know what she meant. I certainly never suspected her of subtlety. So I went back to my room, and she didn't refer to the matter afterwards. May I have it now?"

"Have what?"

"That bracelet. She promised———"

This was so frankly and blatantly out of character that even her voice sounded wrong. Francine corrected herself, with a little husky cough, and tried to assume her earlier impersonal air. Hadley, with a smile that was not pleasant, closed up his note-book; he sat back with a look of luxurious patience.

"Now let's have it, Miss Forbes. What is it you're hiding?"

"I don't think I understand."

"But I do think you understand," said Hadley patiently. "You ought to know the consequences. I'm not going to sit here and howl at you; I simply warn you that I'll act on the assumption you're keeping something back. Some exceedingly dirty work has been done in this hotel and I mean to find out what. I'm going to ask your friends some questions; and then I'm going to ask you again. See that you have something to tell me."

"Oh, really?" said Francine in a high voice. "You don't know how you frighten me. Well, I still have nothing to tell."

Hadley ignored this. "Some general questions, please. I got you all together because, if anyone can add anything to the pool, we want to know it. You all swore to me two weeks ago that there was no reason why Mr. Kent—Mr. Rodney Kent—should have been murdered. Now his wife is killed. You all must know quite well that there is a reason somewhere. Mr. Reaper!"

Dan had sat down in a chair opposite Melitta, with Sir Gyles Gay between them like a referee. When Dan got out his pipe, unrolled an oilskin tobacco-pouch, and began to press in tobacco with a steady thumb, it was as though he were loading a gun: say a twelve-bore shotgun.

"Fire away," he invited, shaking himself.

"I think you told me that Mr. and Mrs. Rodney Kent lived in your house in Johannesburg?"

"Right. They had the top floor."

"So you and Mrs. Reaper must have known Mrs. Kent as well as anybody?"

"Yes, certainly."

"Do you share this general belief that nobody knew her very well?"

"I don't know," said Dan, and stopped. "I never thought of it. What do you mean by 'knowing' her, anyway? Term makes no sense. I didn't watch her go to bed at night and get up in the morning."

Sir Gyles Gay interposed, with Cheshire-cat effect. "I think the superintendent is wondering, though, whether anybody else did. The seeds are taking root."

"*You* put them there," said Hadley. "What I mean, Mr. Reaper, is this. Do you know of any love affair Mrs. Kent may have had before her marriage—or afterwards?"

"Good God, no!" said Dan, who seemed to be genuinely shocked as he dug back into his memory. "That's the last thing I should have thought of Jenny. Afterwards, I mean. I know you hinted at something like that after Rod's death; but I knew you didn't mean it seriously. She wasn't like that. She was a—a kind of sister. Wasn't she, Mel?"

Melitta nodded with such earnestness that she seemed to be waggling her head like a China figure.

"What was her attitude towards divorce, Mr. Reaper?"

"Divorce?" repeated Dan with a blank look.

"She was absolutely and unalterably opposed to it," interposed Melitta suddenly. "She told me so any number of times; she said it was shocking and disgusting the way they go on in Hollywood because someone drops a shoe on the floor or something.

"But what are you getting at?" asked Dan.

"The devilish respectability of many murderers," Sir Gyles Gay put in with the effect of a pounce. "Now that I have got a policeman in a corner, I should like to get his practical opinion on the matter. It's the only thing that's puzzled me about murderers. I don't care what causes crime in general, whether it's the thickness of a gland or the thinness of a lobe or anything that the doctors wrangle about. To my forthright mind the explanation of most crime is simple: somebody wants something and so he simply goes and grabs it———"

Dan grunted approvingly. Hadley did not stop this oration; he was watching the group while Gay, with the pleased expression of a wizened small boy, continued:

"—but one kind of crime is plain nonsense. It's this: A. falls in love with Mrs. B. So, instead of separating from Mr. B., instead of doing anything rational about it, Mrs. B. gets together with A. and they murder Mr. B. This seems to me to be carrying respectability too far. I know it isn't an original thesis. But I'll make an extra point: it's the only kind of murder case which is certain to cause a big splash of noteriety in the Press, to be eagerly followed and read by everyone, and to be remembered for many years in the public mind. Millionaires are shot, chorus-girls are gassed, matrons are dismembered in trunks; that kind of case may or may not attract great notice. But the case of A. and Mrs. B. always does. Think of the criminal cases which most readily jump to your mind, and you'll see what seven out of ten of them are. Now, that seems to indicate that it strikes home. It's close to the great British household. It affects us—a disturbing thought. Maybe A. and Mrs. B. are prowling closer round our own doors than we think. Mrs. B. doesn't get a separation, or a divorce, or go and live with A.; she simply has her husband murdered. Why?"

Francine could not keep out of this. "Because," she said curtly, "most people aren't well off and can't afford emotional luxuries. Get a decent social state, and you'll change all that. Under our present state the only emotional luxury the poor can afford is murder."

"They don't really intend to do any dreadful thing like that," said Melitta with the same air of suddenness, "though I suppose most women have thought about it at one time or another, like that terrible woman who wrote all the letters that are shocking, but you wish more of them had been printed in the book. But all of a sudden they get drunk or lose their heads or something, and before they know it it's all over: like adultery, you know."

"What do *you* know about adultery?" said Dan with restraint. He blinked at her, after which a grin crept over his face. "Here! If the parade of epigrams has finished, I'd like to know just what all this has to do with Jenny. She wouldn't—er—lose her head."

Francine, folding her arms, looked straight at Hadley though she addressed Dan.

"Don't you see what they're hinting at? The background of the idea is that someone has fallen in love with Jenny, but *she* knows Rod will never give her up under any circumstances; and above all things she mustn't be touched by any scandal. That would horrify her. So she encourages this man to kill Rod. But for that reason she won't go down to Sussex and stay in the house while the killing is done; so she remains with her aunts. It may be delicacy or caution. Then she discovers that she can't stick the man—possibly she says her soul is revolted, or possibly she wanted Rod killed for some other reason, and now that it's done she needn't encourage the murderer any longer—so she tries to send him about his business. But he kills her."

"Could you believe that about *Jenny*?" demanded Dan. "Didn't she make Rod a good wife?"

"Oh, uncle, my darling," said Francine, "I didn't say it was my theory. But, as for the last part of it, yes. I've watched her making him a good wife, and, frankly, it made me sick. She cared no more for Rod than I do for that lamp-shade."

"I am glad to have my judgment," observed Gay, tilting up his chin with shining pleasure, "confirmed by outside witnesses. I warned Dr. Fell, and later Mr. Hadley, that she was that very dangerous and insidious thing, a sweet and dignified woman."

"Well, I'll be—" said Dan. "What kind of a woman do you want, then? Sour and undignified?"

"Hey!" roared Dr. Fell.

There was an abrupt silence after that thunderous blast. Dr. Fell pounded on the floor with his stick, but his eye twinkled over eyeglasses coming askew on his nose. Then he cleared his throat for pontifical pronouncement.

"Much as I dislike to interrupt," he said, "this discussion appears to have turned into an argument about matrimony. I am always willing to argue about matrimony; or, in fact, anything else; and at any other time I shall be happy to oblige. Both murder and matrimony are stimulating and exciting things: in fact, an analogy could be drawn between them as regards the interest they excite. Harrumph! Ha! But Miss Forbes has made at least one point—point of fact—which is so good that we can't let it drop. Eh, Hadley?"

"Thank you," said Francine. Her chilly manner was in contrast to the fervor with which she had spoken last; but in spite of herself she smiled under the beam of Dr. Fell's presence. "I didn't say it was my theory."

"H'mf, no. That odious burden shall rest elsewhere. But in this theory, how did that bracelet fit into it?" He pointed his stick towards the table where the bracelet lay. "Was it a kind of pledge or token given by this X, this unidentified man, to Mrs. Kent?"

"Well—yes."

"Do you believe that to be actually the case?"

"Yes. I—oh, I don't know! That's just it: I don't know anything! I've already said a dozen times more than I intended. . . ."

"Yes," agreed Hadley placidly, "I thought you would." He seemed to gain his point by ignoring her. "Mr. Reaper: let's get back to the subject we started on, before we continue about this. What do you know *about* Mrs. Kent? I met her only once, and she was ill then, or said she was; so it's little enough I got out of her. For instance, where was she from? Johannesburg?"

"No, she was born up country, Rhodesia. I knew her parents well, when she was a kid in curls. Good old stock; gentlemen-farmers; not very go-ahead."

"Are her parents living?"

"No. I lost touch with them some years ago. They left her very well provided for, though I shouldn't have suspected that. She came to Johannesburg about three years ago; she and Rod have been married for two."

Dr. Fell interposed a sleepy question. "I say, was she fond of travelling? Did she do much of it?"

"No," said Dan, sighting behind his pipe. "Funny you should ask that. She detested it; never did any. Trains and ships made her sick, or something; even coming from Salisbury to Johannesburg was something to set her teeth about. Didn't want to make this trip, either. As it happens," he added, staring down at the packed tobacco with a heavy and lowering embarrassment, "I wish she hadn't. I wish nobody had. And then—" He spoke quietly. "Right down to brass tacks: did you mean all that about A. and Mrs. B.?"

"That was Sir Gyles's suggestion." Hadley was still

prodding, and he saw Dan look sideways with abrupt suspicion. "I'm merely trying to get at the truth. But do you think someone in your party is a homicidal lunatic?"

"My God, no!"

"Then we've got to look for a motive, if you'll help. Think. Was there *any* reason why someone should have killed both Mr. and Mrs. Kent? By this time you've all got to face it: it wasn't an outsider or a member of the hotel staff. So was there any reason? Money? Revenge? You shake your head—you all do. Then, Mrs. Kent being the sort of person some of you think she was, the only indication we've got is a possible affair in which Rodney Kent is killed by X in collusion with Mrs. Kent, and X later kills Mrs. Kent herself. If," Hadley's tone grew sharper, "Miss Forbes will now tell us what she knows. . . ."

"Which is still nothing," said Francine. "The sum and substance of it is this. I wasn't actually told a word. I inferred, from the way she talked, that some man she was very much interested in had given her the bracelet; someone she either loved or————"

"Or————?"

"Feared, I was going to say. There you are. I couldn't tell you because I didn't want to sound silly," she drew in her breath with hard effect, "like one of Chris's melodramatic novels. Maybe I was imagining it all, because it seems a little too melodramatic to be true. But I did understand that if I looked hard enough at that bracelet I might learn something."

"About what? About the person who gave it to her?"

"Yes."

"And that is why you wanted me to give it to you a while ago?"

"Well, yes."

Hadley picked up the bracelet and turned it over in his hand. "You can see for yourself that there's not a scrap of writing, or place for writing, or any secret hanky-panky, except that Latin inscription. Do you mean there's a secret hidden in that, like an acrostic or some such thing? *Clau-*

dite jam rivos, pueri, sat prata biberunt. This is more in your line, Fell."

"I still think," Gay urged, "that you're making too much of a small thing. If I may suggest it, the inquiries should be broader. If there has been a man in the case, there ought to be traces of him. Find that man, and you'll be a good deal closer to finding the murderer."

"No, you won't," said a new voice.

The door to the hall had opened and Harvey Wrayburn came in. He did not come with his usual bounce or bustle. In appearance he was stoutish and undistinguished, except when some enthusiasm animated him—as it often did. Then his gingery hair and moustache, his alert eyes under a bump of a forehead, would all take on a vividness of self-assurance in which few could disbelieve. He had a fondness for wearing old grey worsted suits, and a habit of jamming his fists into the coat-pockets so that the coat always looked bulging and long. At this time he was self-assured enough, except for a look of strain round his eyes. He seemed poised on the edge of speech, as though he had just been put in front of a microphone and told that the red light would flash on in half a second.

"For the last five minutes," he said, "I've been listening outside that door. Who wouldn't?" he added, raising his neck up a little. "The question was whether I should get our friend Hadley in a corner and explain, or else get it all off my chest in front of all of you—and have done with it. I've decided to get it off my chest. All right: I'm the man you want."

Hadley jumped to his feet. "Mr. Wrayburn, you may make a statement if you like, but I must caution you ———"

"Oh, I didn't kill her," said the other rather irritably, as if he had been robbed of an effect. "I was going to marry her; or she was going to marry me. Your grand reconstruction also misfires on one other point: that bracelet. I didn't give the bracelet to her. She gave it to me."

Chapter 10

Shipboard Idyll

WRAYBURN'S next statement was in a slightly different key. "I feel better," he said in a surprised tone. "No balloon or aneurism seems to have burst. You don't look any different. Oh, hell."

After a violence of expelled breath, he perched himself on the edge of the table as though he were addressing a class, and went on:

"I know about the penalty for suppressing evidence. And that's not all. I've always hated the silly fathead who shoves an important clue into his pocket and causes everybody trouble because he (or usually it's a she) won't speak; and then, when you find it, it's not worth the hunt. All right, here I am. And here's your clue."

From his waistcoat-pocket he took a Yale key with a chromium tag bearing the number 707, and tossed it across to Hadley.

"You mean," said Dan, "that you and Jenny have been _____"

"Have been what? Six kisses," said Wraybrun gloomily. "I counted 'em. She said the last one was for luck."

Hadley was curt.

"I think we'd better hear about this from the beginning," he said, only less satisfied than exasperated. "You didn't say anything about it when Mr. Rodney Kent was murdered."

"No, of course I didn't. Why should I? I didn't kill him."

"And yet, if you intended to marry her, his being dead must have simplified matters, didn't it?"

"This isn't going to be as easy as I had hoped," said Wrayburn, fixing his eyes grimly on the door-knob after a quick look at Hadley. "Try to understand this. I didn't think about it simplifying matters at all. I thought about it as an infernal shame and a piece of senseless brutality done by that fellow Bellowes when he was drunk. That's all I thought. It—woke me up."

"How long has this been going on? I mean the affair with Mrs. Kent."

"Well—it only really started on shipboard. Oh, Lord, these ships. The weather was cutting up rough, and only Jenny and I, and sometimes Dan, had our sea-legs. You know how these things happen."

"Mrs. Kent wasn't sea-sick?"

"Not a bit."

"We heard just a minute ago that she couldn't stand ships in any kind of weather."

Wrayburn glanced over his shoulder. As a rule, Kent knew, he was fond of the limelight; but he seemed to regret that he had perched on the table.

"Then all I can say," he retorted querulously, "is that somebody is mistaken. You ought to have seen her. That old tub was jumping about like a ball in a roulette-wheel, and Jenny would stand as cool as though she had just walked into a drawing-room. It was the—the humanest I ever saw her. How that woman liked to see things smashed up! Once the wicker furniture, and the gramophone, and all the rest of the stuff got loose in the palm-room when the ship was pitching badly. It sailed round from one side to the other, and simply busted the whole show to blazes. It was one of the few times I ever saw Jenny really laugh."

There was a stony kind of silence, while some members of the group shifted in their chairs. Dr. Fell was the first to speak.

"You ought to know, Mr. Wrayburn," he said, "that you're making rather a bad impression. That look on Hadley's face—I know it. In other words, you don't show any signs of being a broken-hearted lover."

"I'm not," said Wrayburn, moving off the table. "Now we're getting down to it."

He looked round the circle.

"You must be Dr. Fell. Will *you* explain what happened, even if I can't? I don't know exactly how it came about on that ship. The trouble with sirens, like Jenny, is that they win half their victories by their very reputations. They're attractive; you know they're attractive; but you have no intention of being attracted by them. Then they let you know—inadventently—how much interested they are in you; and you're so flattered that, like a chump, you wonder if you're not falling. Then you do fall. Finish. You're anaesthetised; for the time being."

"You needn't look so crushed about it," rumbled Dr. Fell cheerfully. "It happens, you know. When did you begin to wake up?"

His manner was so casual that Wrayburn stopped pacing.

" 'Begin.' 'Begin.' Yes, that's the word," he admitted. He dug his hands into the usual pockets; and once his animation had gone, he looked undistinguished again. "Let's see. It was—maybe just after the ship docked. Maybe it was when she told me she wasn't going down to Sussex because she couldn't trust herself to be with me. All of a sudden that struck a wrong note. Bing! I looked at her and knew she was lying. Finally, maybe it was when Rod died."

Dan had been waving a hand for silence.

"Will somebody explain this business about Jenny's 'reputation'?" he insisted. "What reputation? All I can say is that it's complete news to me."

"Of course," said Melitta.

"You mean to say you knew it?"

Melitta's thin voice kept to its monotone. "Of course, my dear, you will *not* listen to anyone; and you say everything is gossip, as it often is, and you're so terribly concerned with your own ideas—you and Chris, too—that naturally nobody ever tells you anything." Melitta was full of impatience. "All the same, I stick to my opinion, and I don't alter it. Jenny was a Sweet Girl. Of course, I know there has been a certain amount of gossip, and my grandfather always used to say that most gossip is probably true because it is what the people would like to do even if they are not doing it. But in Jenny's case there was *absolutely* nothing against her, and I was quite sure she could be trusted not to do anything foolish. And it was really most interesting to see what happened."

"Murder happened," said Hadley.

A wrathful superintendent had been trying to break through this screen of talk.

"It won't be necessary to explain your state of mind, Mr. Wrayburn. Just tell me what you did. Were you in Mrs. Kent's room last night?"

"Yes."

"Very well; let's get that clear. What time did you go in?"

"About twenty-five minutes to twelve. Just after the maid left, anyhow."

"At what time did you leave the room?"

"Midnight—I was also in there at seven, and again at eight o'clock this morning."

"And you tell us you did not commit this murder?"

"I did not."

During a strained pause of about ten seconds he met Hadley's eye. Then Hadley turned briskly and nodded to Dr. Fell and Kent.

"Good. Then just come across the hall with me to 707, and explain how you managed it. No! The rest of you, with the exception of these two, will remain here."

He very quickly shut off the protests. Opening the door for the other three, he ushered them out ahead of him and closed the door with a snap. Wrayburn, breathing hard, went out with a stiff gait which suggested that he might have been walking through a more evil doorway than this. In the corridor Hadley beckoned to Sergeant Preston, who was just coming out of the Reapers' suite. From room 707 the body had now been removed, leaving only a few stains on the floor.

"We've nearly finished searching, sir," Preston reported. "And so far, there's not a sign of that unif———"

"Shorthand," said Hadley. "Mr. Wrayburn, your statement will be taken down, and you will be asked to initial it afterwards. Now let's hear just what happened in here."

After looking round quickly, Wrayburn leaned against the foot of the nearest twin-bed and seemed to brace himself. His moustache was not now brushed up, either literally or metaphorically; he looked heavy and a little shabby.

"Well, it was like this. It's no good saying I was entirely out from under the ether. That's partly camouflage for the benefit of—" he jerked his head towards the other side of the hall. "But I was beginning to wonder whether I might have made a fool of myself aboard ship. Besides, we had had a roaring good time at Gay's."

"Wait. Had there been any talk of marriage between you and Mrs. Kent?"

"No, not then. She wouldn't bring it up, and I didn't. You understand, there was always Rod." He looked at Kent. "I swear, Chris, I never meant any harm to him."

"Go on."

"So, you see, I saw Jenny again for the first time last night. Considering what had happened—naturally, I didn't expect her to fly to my shoulder or anything of the sort. I was beginning to wonder whether I wanted her to; I didn't trust her. But I couldn't get an opportunity to speak to her alone. She seemed odd. At the theatre she arranged matters so that we were sitting at opposite ends of the row of seats, and between the acts she monopolised Gay. I had never seen her look—brighter.

"As you can understand, the only time I could get to see

her alone was after the others had gone to bed. I waited for fifteen or twenty minutes after we had all closed our doors. Then I nipped across the hall to there," he indicated the side door, "and knocked."

"Yes?" Hadley prompted, as he hesitated.

"I can tell you this. She was frightened about something. After I knocked there was no answer for a second or two. Then I heard her voice very close to the door, asking who it was. I had to repeat my name twice before she opened the door."

"Had she seemed frightened earlier in the evening?"

"No. At least, not noticeably. There was a stealthy kind of air about this; I don't know how else to describe it. And the door was bolted—I remember the noise of the bolt when she drew it back.

"She had changed her shoes for slippers, and was just beginning to unpack her trunk. The trunk, everything, looked just about as it does now. I don't want you to think I'm any more an ass than necessary. But when I saw her again, I didn't know what to say. I simply stood and looked at her; and my chest hurt. That's a devil of a confession to have to make, but it did. She sat down in a chair and waited for me to speak first. She was sitting in that one, over by the writing-desk."

He nodded towards it. The room was now grey with early-afternoon shadows, and the maplewood gleamed faintly.

"So I started in to talk—chiefly about Rod, and how bad it was. Not a word about ourselves. I knew she was waiting for me to do it. And she was listening with a kind of composed expression, as though she were waiting to have her photograph taken. You know: cool, and the corners of the mouth turning down a bit. She was wearing that bracelet with the black stone and the inscription. It was the first time I had ever seen it. As I told you, *I* didn't give it to *her*; she gave it to me, presently.

"There's something else I must tell you, because it fits into the story. I kept on talking, inanely, and wondered why I talked at all. During this time she got up once or twice; in particular, she went over to the dressing-table there, picked up her handbag, and got a handkerchief out of it. I noticed, when she ran through the things in the handbag, that the key to the room—the key with the chromium tag—was inside.

"By the time I was wondering if I ought to make jokes, she came to a decision. You could see it; all at once. Her face softened up a bit. She asked me straight out, in that trustful way of hers, whether I was in love with her. That broke the barriers. I said I was. I said a whole lot. Whereupon she said she was going to give me a keepsake, a pledge, all that kind of thing. She unhooked that bracelet and handed it to me, and I can remember exactly what she said. She said: 'You keep that for always. Then nobody will try to wake the dead.' Don't ask me what it means. I thought it was a high-flown kind of thing to say. Because, mind, one part of my intelligence was still awake. In these romantic moments—arrh!—I didn't seem any closer to her than to a clock ticking beside you. Also, she brightened up immediately afterwards. She said it was late, and what would anybody think if I were found there at that hour?

"I was still fuddled; I wanted to keep on with a good thing. So I had a romantic idea. I said, why shouldn't we get up early in the morning, and have breakfast together and go out and see the town on our own before any of the rest could join us? It would have to be early, because Dan Reaper is always up and roaring round the place just at the time I like to take the best part of sleep. I recklessly said seven o'clock. You understand. I didn't really *want* to go out at seven o'clock. God love you, I wouldn't want to get up at seven o'clock in the morning to walk through the Earthly Paradise with an unveiled Houri. But I stood there and said fool things. She welcomed the idea, with an out-you-go expression. Finally, she asked me whether I wasn't going to kiss her good night. I said of course. Instead of grabbing the wench, as I would have grabbed any other woman, I gave her a couple of chaste and tender salutes.

. . . Stop looking so damned embarrassed, coppers; you wanted the truth—and drew away. Then she put out her swan-like neck and said, 'And one for luck.' Then was when I saw her eyes sort of slide past my shoulder. There wasn't much in them; it was an expression like that of a woman in a foyer waiting for the lift to go up; they were blank and blue as marbles. And in that one second the cable was cut. My cable. In short, I saw————"

There was a click, and the wall-lights over the beds came on; Sergeant Preston was no longer sure with his shorthand notes. Nobody except Wrayburn, Kent thought, would have had the nerve to pour all this out to a notebook. He was now regarding them with sour poise and flippancy, his hands dug deep into his coat-pockets. The wall-lamps, behind their frosted-glass shades, made a sleek, theatrical light in the sleek, theatrical room.

"That's it," Wrayburn said complacently, nodding towards them. "Crafty little devil! I knew then; I felt it; though I couldn't imagine what the game was. I might have pursued the subject then, because all of a sudden it was beginning to hurt. But I couldn't—because that was when we heard the knock at the door."

Hadley jerked up his head.

"Knock at the door? Which door?"

"At what I suppose you'd call the main door: the one that had the sign hung on it later."

"What time was this? Do you know?"

"Yes. It was just a few seconds short of midnight. I know, because I looked at my watch when Jenny said good night."

"You were actually *in* the room when you heard this knock?"

"Certainly I was in the room—" Wrayburn was beginning with some asperity, when he stopped, and for the first time his eyes shifted. He added in a lower tone: "Oi! Here! You don't mean it was— Nobody told me————"

"Go on; what happened when you heard the knock?"

"Jenny whispered to me to get out in case I should be

found there. So I ducked out of the side door, with the 'keepsake' in my pocket. I think Jenny bolted the door after me. I walked straight across to my own side door and went in."

"The time being————?"

"Oh, midnight. It couldn't have taken more than ten seconds. I admit I was feeling a bit mixed-up, and not too good-humoured; but I was going to see the thing through. In case I should forget it, I rang up the porter on the telephone (or at least I put through a call downstairs) and told him I was to be waked up at a quarter to seven next morning. I also wondered, with a few less romantic fumes in my head, where we should get breakfast at that time; and what in the name of sense we were going to *see* at that hour. Most people get over calf-love by the early twenties. I waited for a brief, bad bout of it until the early thirties. I suppose I saw us riding on a bus in the snow. Anyhow, I asked the porter a lot of questions, and I must have talked for three or four minutes on the phone."

Kent found himself fitting together the pieces of evidence. Wrayburn's story coincided exactly with the ascertained and ascertainable facts as regarded the man himself. He had been speaking on the telephone (according to Hardwick's schedule) from midnight until three minutes past. If any wonder might have been felt as to what could have been the reason for such a fairly long call at so late an hour, there was now a strong and plausible motive behind it. Wrayburn also spoke with an air of weary earnestness which was difficult to disbelieve. The question was now how far this evidence coincided with Dan's. Dan had seen in the hall this goblin, the figure carrying bath-towels, at exactly two minutes past midnight—standing outside Jenny's door. If Dan's statement were accepted (and nobody had questioned it), Wrayburn could not possibly be the elusive figure in uniform.

But there was one extra question. Someone, undoubtedly the figure in uniform, had knocked on the main door at a few seconds before midnight. Would it have remained there for two full minutes after the first knock, without going into or being admitted into the room? Why not? At least, so it appeared to Kent, who was watching Hadley and Dr. Fell.

Hadley drew a design in his note-book.

"Did you see anything of the person who knocked at the door?"

"No," said Wrayburn shortly. "No gratuitous information. I'll answer what you like; but I'm not bubbling over any longer. Thanks."

"Are you sure your watch was right about the times?"

"Yes. She's a good timekeeper, and I set her early in the evening, by the big clock on the wall outside this room."

(The same clock Dan had seen. Well?)

"Just continue your story," Hadley said. "You left this room at midnight, with Mrs. Kent's bracelet————?"

"*And* I didn't sleep. I couldn't. There was no need to ring me; I was awake long before seven. I got dressed, feeling seedy. At seven o'clock I went over and knocked at Jenny's door. There was no answer, even when I knocked harder. That made me mad, rather. It occurred to me that, since she would be sleeping in one of the twin beds, she would be closer to the main door, and would hear me better if I knocked there. I went round to the main door. The shoes were outside it, and the 'quiet' sign was hung from the knob. Now begins the story of my derelictions. I looked at the sign, and saw 'Dead Woman' scrawled on it. I picked up the sign to look at it closer; then I could see, behind it, the key still stuck in the lock outside the main door."

Dr. Fell puffed out his cheeks. So far he had been shutting out the view of one window, but now he lumbered forward.

"The key," he said, "was in the lock outside the door. Kindly take note of that, Hadley. The night before it had been in her handbag. Well?"

"I opened the door with it," said Wrayburn obediently,

"and took the key out of the lock. Automatically, I suppose. I stuck my head inside the room, and saw her."

"That door wasn't bolted on the inside, then?"

"Naturally not, or I couldn't have got in. There was a heavy stuffy smell inside the room, and I thought, 'Doesn't the little so-and-so put her windows up at night?' Then I saw her; she was lying on the floor with her head inside that trunk. I went over and touched her. She was cold. I didn't investigate further; I didn't want to. But now comes the hardest part of the story to tell. I walked back out of the room by the way I had come, with the key in my hand, and stood in the hall. My first impulse, naturally, was to set up an alarm; to go and wake Dan, or wake somebody. But I'll admit it: I got the wind up. My trouble is that I always want to know what's going on, and I won't act until I do. Without saying a word I went back to my room and tried to think. This was about five minutes past seven o'clock.

"At a quarter-past seven I heard the maid coming on duty; I heard her jingle. And I was still racking my brains. Somebody had killed Jenny. I knew something queer had been going on last night, but *I* wasn't going to find that body. I had been the last person alone with her, and—you know. What bothered me most, and kept on bothering me, was *how* she had been killed. I wondered why on earth I had not stopped to make sure. There had been something done to her face; that's all I could tell, because it was early morning and very nearly dark. I felt I had to know, but I couldn't screw up quite enough nerve to go back to that room.

"It was going on towards eight o'clock when I remembered something that was nearly the last devilment. *I* had Jenny's bracelet. It's a distinctive-looking thing; it undoubtedly cost a lot of money; it would be certain to be missed; and if they found it in my possession————

"Well, no frills. I felt like that, anyhow. On top of this, I heard two men coming along the corridor saying something about 707. I got my door open a crack, and saw them go round, and heard them talking about a master-key in front of the main door of 707. How the devil was I to know one of 'em was you?" he demanded, turning to Kent. "I heard the door to 707 being opened, and closed, and then dead silence. The other man—the porter—was still out in the hall talking to the maid. On top of all this, the side door of 707 opened, and the first man (you) slid out with his head tucked into his overcoat collar. He didn't give an alarm; he hurried down the hall and got away."

Dr. Fell interposed again, this time turning to Kent.

"Hold on! When you got out the side door, Mr. Kent, do you remember whether or not it was bolted on the inside?"

"It was bolted," said Kent. "I remember that quite well —drawing the bolt back."

"H'mf, yes. Go on, Mr. Wrayburn."

"I'll tell you exactly what it was like for me," said the other, who had been reflecting, and could not stop his own garrulousness. "It was like standing in the street before oncoming traffic, and wanting to get to the other side. You think you've got good clear margin to get across before the traffic bumps you; but, all the same, you hesitate. Then, when it's almost too late, you suddenly make up your mind and dash for it. And the traffic nearly bumps you to glory after all. That's what I did. I had Jenny's bracelet in one hand, and the key in the other. Just after that fellow—you—had gone, I made up my mind to do what I should have done before. If the key opened the main door of Jenny's room, I was sure it would open the side door as well: my own key did. I went across the corridor and got in there while the porter was still outside. Mind, I kept *some* sense. I touched things only with a handkerchief. All I wanted to do was dispose of that bracelet, so I simply dropped it in the bureau drawer. That took only a few seconds; and there was Jenny on the floor. I had to see her and find out what was wrong, now I'd got my courage to the sticking-point. It was broad daylight, though the blinds were drawn. I wanted to see her face, but I couldn't because her head was still inside that trunk. I dragged her out. I took one look—and then bolted. I was back in my own room again, closing the door, by the time the porter barged into 707. And, of course, I walked off with the blasted key after all. There it is.

"That's what I did, and that's all I did. Call it what you like; I claim it was only natural and human. The trouble is that I'm a ruddy rotten criminal. I once picked up a pound-note off the floor in the foyer of a theatre and kept it; and afterwards I was convinced everybody in the place had seen me, and was ready to denounce me. That's how I felt to-day. I couldn't keep it down. So I decided, in the words of your favourite film-star, to come clean. I've now come so clean that I feel I've been through a wringer. Thus spake Zarathustra."

He ended with a deep breath, and sat down on the bed with enough violence to make it creak. He had sketched out a perfect characterisation of himself, Kent thought.

Dr. Fell and Hadley looked at each other.

"It it too early to inquire," said Wrayburn, "whether you believe me? Or is it handcuffs and bread-and-water. Arrh!"

Hadley looked hard at him. "It certainly fits all the facts," he acknowledged. "And coming clean, I don't mind telling you, was very wise. Well, Mr. Wrayburn, if your story about the telephone-call at midnight is confirmed, I don't think you've got much to worry about. One other thing. While you were in this room on any of those occasions, did you come across a silver linked bracelet set with diamonds, and belonging to a Mrs. Jopley-Dunne?"

"Eh? No. I never heard of it or her."

"For the moment, then, that's all. You might wait across the hall."

When Wrayburn had gone, Hadley whistled softly between his teeth. "So that's the story of the reappearing bracelet. Yes, I don't think we can doubt that the murderer was looking for it, and made a thorough search to find it. Only, it wasn't here. And therefore, presumably ————?"

"The murderer pinched Mrs. Jopley-D.'s property, wondering if it might be an old friend in disguise," said Dr. Fell. "Why not? The background of both, so to speak, is similar. Both are linked bracelets, and silver looks much like white gold. H'mf, yes. The murderer was looking for the bracelet with the black stone, all right. But that's not, I think, the really important point of the story. And, oh, Bacchus, Hadley, the real point is important! I mean the key left behind in the door."

"You think it clarifies anything?"

"I know it does. Look here!—Eh? Yes? What is it?"

A knock at the door was followed by the entrance of Sergeant Betts.

"Just finished, sir," he reported to Hadley. "And it's no go. I've been over every room, cupboard, cranny, and rathole in this wing; and there's no uniform hidden anywhere."

Chapter 11

The Solution According to Fiction

A WINTER evening, when there is good food behind plate glass, money in the pocket, and a warmth of light to be seen on snow from inside, may be considered the best of all times for argument. Christopher Kent, entering the Restaurant des Epicures in Lisle Street at seven o'clock that evening, was ready for all of them. It had been a long day—which, for him, only began when Hadley and Dr. Fell finished their questioning at the Royal Scarlet Hotel.

The most important business had been the establishing of his own alibi for the night before, and the cashing of a cheque to bring him to the surface again. The first was not difficult; the second enabled him to pour largesse on the clubmen at the coffee-stall who swore to it, and to redeem his suit-case from the landlady in Commercial Road, East. Once his alibi was beyond question, Superintendent Hadley became genial and almost talkative. Kent was accumulating facts, facts, facts. He felt somewhat surprised at this: facts had never before been a great concern of his. But, relaxing under the ministrations of the barber, and spending a fine hour steaming in the Turkish baths at the

Imperial, he began to tabulate the discoveries for reference.

1. The writing-printing in red ink on the "quiet" sign, which might have been so promising a clue, ended in nothing. It was so much printing and so little writing that it had to be classified as the former; and could never be identified.

2. The two sets of finger-prints found in the room were his own and Jenny's. Since the room had been cleaned and dusted by the maid just before Jenny moved into it, there were few old prints beyond smudges. Wrayburn, evidently by accident the first time and design the second, had left no prints at all.

3. Wrayburn was proved to have been speaking on the phone between midnight and three minutes past. Hadley, nothing if not thorough, set half a dozen persons to speak anonymously over the wire to Billings, the night-porter, and Billings had again identified Wrayburn's voice at once.

4. There was nothing wrong with the clocks, and no possibility of tampering with them. They were all electric clocks, with glass fronts which did not come off; all were operated on Greenwich time from a central switch. If Dan had seen the figure in uniform outside Jenny's door at two minutes past twelve, the time was exactly two minutes past twelve and no other.

5. Nothing, so far as could be ascertained, was missing from Jenny's possessions. Melitta Reaper went through them and said she was certain of this. There were several good pieces of costume jewellery in Jenny's trunk, in addition to £30 in notes in her handbag and travellers' cheques for £400 on the Capital Counties bank. But there was no silver or loose change whatever in her handbag.

6 The batch of small folded cards, bearing the room-numbers of each guest, had in fact been handed to Dan. He did not definitely remember seeing the card for 707 among them, since he had not looked at them. But he

confirmed Melitta's statement that he had put them down on the bureau in their bedroom.

7. A detailed deposition from each of the persons concerned, regarding where they were at about two minutes past midnight, produced the following statements: Sir Gyles Gay had been reading in bed. Melitta Reaper had been taking a bath in the private bathroom of their suite. Francine Forbes had been "doing her hair" in her own room. Wrayburn and Dan were accounted for. Kenneth Hardwick, the hotel-manager who had been questioned along with the others, provided another alibi: from midnight until ten minutes past, in his own rooms, he had been going over the next day's menus with the headwaiter of the Royal Scarlet dining-room.

Thus the facts stood; and Christopher Kent had been tinkering with them as though for a story. To be near the party, he had reserved the only vacant room in Wing A, and he wondered about a number of things. He had invited Francine, Dr. Fell, and Hadley to dinner that night. Hadley (as usual) would be detained at the Yard, but Dr. Fell accepted with heartiness and Francine after some consideration.

When he entered the Restaurant des Epicures at seven o'clock, he found Francine waiting for him. She looked rather lonely in that crowd, and he suddenly felt protective. They sat down by a shrouded window, with a yellow-shaded lamp between them, and he ordered cocktails; but, instead of taking advantage of this mood, he said, "Well?" —which was definitely the wrong thing.

"Well, what?" she said instantly, and put down her glass.

He had meant nothing by it, merely a sort of clumsy opening to start a conversation: which causes much difficulty. He admitted this.

"Look here, what's wrong between us?" he inquired in some desperation. "I'm not your worst enemy: I swear it. I'm not trying to put one over on you or do you in the eye. But———"

After a time she spoke in a reflective tone. "Oh, Chris, if you weren't so beastly intolerant!"

His own glass slid on the table as he put it down.

"Intolerant? *Me*?"

"If you could only hear yourself say that," said Francine, and was amused. "Oh, come on, let's face it. You think being intolerant merely means persecuting somebody for moral or religious reasons, or not liking lowbrows and fish-and-chips, or all the rest of it. But it doesn't. It doesn't!" she said fiercely. "It means that you simply go your own sweet way, and pay absolutely no attention to anything that isn't in your ken. You're tolerant on moral grounds because you sympathise with most of the offences, you're tolerant on religious grounds because you haven't got any religion, you're tolerant of lowbrows because you *like* Wild West stories and band music and merry-go-rounds. But if there's something that doesn't come into your ken, like doing some real good in the world—all right: I won't say that: I'll take something in your own province—like the work of certain great authors whose beliefs you don't agree with, then you simply don't discuss them as being beneath contempt. Grr! Your idea of being generous is merely to be ridiculously generous with money, that's all."

"Sorry," he said. "Is that really it? All right. Honestly, if it will make you any happier, I will even admit that Blank Blank or Dash Dash is a great writer; but privately ———"

"There. You see?"

"And if, in the latter part of the indictment, you were referring to certain gifts which you practically threw back in my face———"

"Trust a man," said Francine icily, "to take the conversation straight to the personal. You always do, and then accuse us of doing it." She paused. "Oh, I don't mind, really!" she cried in a different tone. "But you will *not* notice things, Chris; you sail through the world in your own sweet way, and you never do! For instance—Jenny."

The evil subject was back again; they could not keep it out. Francine spoke in an off-hand tone:

"I don't suppose you even noticed she was making a play for you, did you?"

"Nonsense."

"She jolly well was!" cried Francine, firing up.

He sat back and stared at her. Into his mind, doubtfully, had come a gleam of light; and with it a feeling of uproarious happiness sang through him. They looked at each other, each knowing the other knew.

"I wish I could persuade *you*," he said, "that I am the fair-haired prize-package you seem to believe other women think. Jenny? That's impossible! I never————"

"Thought of it? Neither did poor old Harvey Wrayburn, as decent a sort as there is, until she got after him during a long sea-voyage. She really was a terror, Chris. She did it as much to amuse herself as anything else. What annoys me is that I can't see how she did it, or how she had the knack. But she was most definitely going out to make a play for you."

"But I hope you don't think I—? To begin with, she was Rod's wife————"

"Your cousin's wife. Yes. And you wouldn't think of making love to the wife of a friend of yours, would you? In fact, the idea rather shocks you, doesn't it?"

"Frankly, yes," he admitted with what he hoped was dignity. "Your friends' wives are—well, damn it, I mean————"

"Not-to-be-thought-of-like-that," said Francine. "Oh, Chris, you are an old mossback!"

"Very interesting," he said coldly. "I suppose that in Russia————"

"Don't you say anything about Russia!"

"I was merely about to point out————"

"Don't you see, Chris," she urged with great sincerity, "that the moral issue involved is precisely the same whether the woman is your friend's wife or the wife of someone you don't know? You wouldn't make love to

Rod's wife; but you'd have no compunction—not you!—about making love to the wife of some poor devil who's making maybe two pounds a week, and has to stay at a factory all day, and hasn't your leisure to————"

"One moment," he said, rather dazed. "So far as I remember, I never said one word about roaring round the country after other men's wives. As a menace to the home I am practically nil. But will you explain to me how it is that we can never touch on any subject without your somehow coming round to the political and economic aspect of it? I'll swear you and the world and Davy Jones seem to have gone politics-mad————"

"Indeed," observed Francine with sweet savagery. "It must be so nice, it must be so stimulating, for you to sit on your Olympian height and watch all the little imbeciles crawl about in the valley. I was attempting to explain, in as elementary a way as I could, that it is your kind of outworn, stupid codes and shibboleths which have made such a mess of the country————"

"Well, would it please you any better if I made love *both* to my friend's wife and the factory-worker's wife? Do you think we should be happier then?"

"My God, Chris Kent, there are times when I could kill you. You go and make love to whom you like! You————"

"That's what I am trying to do, my dear. Only————"

"*Ahem*," said Dr. Fell.

They stopped. The vast presence of Dr. Fell towered over the table, beaming down with doubtful but benevolent interest, and following the thrusts with his head as you follow strokes in a tennis match. Now he cleared his throat. Francine, radiant with cold anger, put a handkerchief to her lips; but she burst out laughing instead.

"Ah, that is better," beamed Dr. Fell. "Heh-heh-heh. I dislike to interrupt; but the waiter has been hanging about the table for the past five minutes with the *hors-d'œuvre* wagon, and hesitating to say, 'Sardine?' for fear it should seem to have a personal application."

"He's a pig-headed—" said Francine.

"I have no doubt of it, my dear," said Dr. Fell, cheerfully. "In fact, it is a very good sign. The woman who does not think her husband is pig-headed is already beginning to dominate him, and that would be bad. I beg your pardon: I do not wish to begin an argument about equality or inequality in marriage. As the Frenchman said about love-making, 'Never before the fish!' But, if I might make a suggestion here, I should suggest that you get married; then you could stop being on the defensive and begin to enjoy yourselves."

"Jenny got married," said Francine.

"Not now," interposed Dr. Fell, with sudden strong authority. "Not that—just now."

That meal was like a loosening or unbuckling of armour, while the doctor's face grew redder and redder, and his chuckles more explosive behind the wine-bottles. However unbelievable his anecdotes became, however his rapid paradoxes gave his listeners the impression that they had just been whirled round a particularly fast switchback after having drunk two Seidletz powders, it was all directed towards one thing: putting these two at their ease. What a master of ceremonies he made Kent never fully realised until afterwards. But it was not until they were padded round against night and the things of night, over the brandy, that the subject was introduced again.

"Harvey should have heard that story—" began Francine.

Dr. Fell trimmed the ash off his cigar, and blinked sideways at her.

"Yes. Now is the time," he said. "What do you think of the whole affair, Miss Forbes?"

"I can answer that. It's the idea of—someone close to you—doing all that," she told him quietly. "Someone you've known a long time, but who's got a hinge loose. I don't think I'm afraid, though. I think it's all over."

"Why?"

"Because the poker was left behind this time." She took

a deep inhalation of her cigarette, and spoke in the same even tone. "It wouldn't have been left stuck in those towels if somebody had had a further use for it. Unless, of course—well, unless someone has grown too fond of blood. But I can't credit that. I was trying to tell Chris what I thought, a while ago."

She considered.

"Some people might have been able to take Jenny, and Jenny's ways, lightly. I could, for instance. Probably most people could. But the tenth person mightn't be able to see her in so light-hearted a way. I've often wondered what Rod thought of her. Oh, she managed him, and her noted devotion to him, beautifully. Do you know, it was all so skilful that it was rumoured—and many people believed, at the time—*Rod* was marrying *Jenny* for her money?"

The glasses almost dropped off Dr. Fell's nose; he gave one wheeze through that nose. Then he said:

"Repeat that, please."

"It's true! It went all round our crowd in South Africa; and it's the first thing Sir Gyles Gay joked Rod about (subtly, of course) when we came over here; so the version was pretty broad and pretty garbled. It hurt Rod a good deal, though he simply said nothing about it and never even bothered to deny it. But I think some people even in our crowd believed it."

"Was she wealthy?"

"Well-off, anyway. I think."

"From what source?"

"From her parents, we thought, though a stony veldt farm isn't usually—and then her dressmaking business must have been very profitable. She had wonderful taste in clothes, there's no getting away from that."

"But why are you so interested in that piece of gossip?" demanded Kent.

"Because it's merely the motive for your cousin Rodney's murder," groaned Dr. Fell. "Oh, Lord, what a duffer I've been! What a thundering idiot! And yet there was no hint—!" He knocked his fists against his temples. "You see, the first murder was the one which wouldn't fit into any rational scheme of things. It wasn't rational sense; it wasn't even rational insanity. But Rodney marrying the woman for her money: that provides a very deadly and sane explanation."

"How? If you know anything," urged Francine, her too-fair skin flushed with wine, and looking less poised and more beautiful than Kent had ever seen her; "if you know anything, or guess anything, *won't* you tell us? It isn't just curiosity. It's to keep the devils out."

"That's fair enough," said Kent.

It was a little time before Dr. Fell answered.

"No!" he roared. "No, by the temple of Eleusis! And there's one main reason why I don't. I think (mind you, I say I think) I know just half this affair; with luck I may be able to get the other half. But there's a strong possibility, on which I am balanced at the moment, that the explanation may be exactly opposite to what I think it is: for that reason I haven't even dared to explain fully to Hadley. And he has some new information. I don't want to raise your hopes, and put you off-guard in case————"

"Eleusis," repeated Kent, as Dr. Fell stopped in mid-sentence. "If Wrayburn were here, with his mine of good-for-nothing lore, we might get that explained. Didn't the Eleusinian mysteries celebrate the descent of Persephone into the underworld, and her return to the light of day? System of rewards and punishments?" He added, " 'To wake the dead.' "

Dr. Fell chuckled. " '*Pale beyond porch and portal, Crowned with calm leaves she stands—*' It's a curious thing about Swinburne, but the more intolerably doleful the poem, the more the rich gusto with which you can recite it. '*Who gathers all things mortal, With cold immortal hands———*' "

"Who does?" inquired Francine, who had a practical mind. "What on earth are you talking about?"

"Yes, we had better stop it. But the character of Mrs. Kent fascinates me as it unfolds. If we had only seen her, if we had only known after Rodney Kent's death what we know now, we might have been able to prevent Mrs. Kent's death." Dr. Fell brooded. "Or could we? I don't know. I doubt it."

"You think there's still—danger?"

"There's no danger," said Dr. Fell, "if you keep your door locked at night. I'm sorry if I seem to act as a Job's comforter; but we have got to take care of all possibilities. Can either of you help me? You must have some ideas. Where would you look?"

Kent thought of his sheaf of notes.

"My trouble is," he replied despondently, "that even now I can't look at the thing with an eye of human reason. All I can think of is how I should make it work out if I were writing the story. That's the phobia of all fiction-writers. I tell you, according to the laws of fiction there's only one possible solution and only one possible murderer! But it's not only guessing at an artistic solution; it's a very strong case. And yet————"

Dr. Fell looked at him with interest. "I know," he said guiltily. "I thought of that, too."

"You thought of what?"

From the breast pocket of his coat Dr. Fell began to take out an enormous collection of old papers and envelopes (there were enough of them to stuff a waste-paper basket) until he found the stub of a pencil. On one comparatively clean surface of paper he wrote a few words. Then he turned the paper over and pushed it across to Kent.

"Write down," he suggested, "the name of the person who springs to your mind as the murderer. That's it: thank you. Now, Miss Forbes, take this piece of paper and look at both sides."

Francine stared at it.

"But you've both written down the same name!"

"Of course," agreed Dr. Fell gloomily. "Kenneth Hardwick, the manager of the Royal Scarlet Hotel."

Chapter 12

Above Suspicion?

FRANCINE, it appeared, could not understand whether they were joking or whether Dr. Fell's glum face was as serious as it looked.

"But you don't honestly mean that? Or is this another of Chris's ridiculous—That nice quiet man?"

"You really will throw suspicion on him if you talk like that," Dr. Fell grunted. "Let's hear the case against him."

"To begin with, it's a question of keys," said Kent. "Somebody got into that linen-closet and took out fifteen bath-towels and one face-towel. Therefore somebody had to open the door of the linen-closet: unless the maid failed to lock it last night. There's no sign of burglarious entry, so apparently the door must have been opened with a key. But, according to this new system of locks—here I'm quoting Hardwick himself—it's impossible for any unauthorized person to open even so much as a linen-closet. Now I remember it, he used the word 'linen-closet.' On the other hand, again quoting him, he alone can open any door in the whole building. That's a short and simple point to start with."

"Good," said Dr. Fell. "Go on."

"Next, the question of disguise. There couldn't be any more admirable disguise for him than the uniform of one of his own attendants. It's like the story he told about the porter who dressed up in pyjamas and pretended to be a guest. If Hardwick were seen by one of the real guests, he wouldn't be recognised even if someone got a glimpse of his face: the uniform would do the trick. He would know, furthermore, that he ran very little danger of being spotted by one of his own employees: the only employee who could come upstairs after eleven-thirty would be one of the under-porters, and on such large floors he wouldn't have much difficulty in hiding himself if he saw the under-porter coming. As two additional points, I might mention that his private rooms are on the seventh floor; and that he would have easy access to any kind of uniform he chose to wear. You notice that the mysterious costume hasn't been found. But, if it were a real uniform belonging to the hotel, why should it be found?"

"Chris, that's awfully good," said Francine. "Do you think it's true?"

He reflected.

"I don't know; I'm only saying it's the way a story should work. For the crux of it is this: the production of an alibi."

"The clocks!" said Dr. Fell with a wheeze of great pleasure.

"Yes. You think of the dozens of wall-clocks in that hotel, all worked from a central switch, and you've got it first shot. I remember we had the same sort of system at school. One day, in the Schoolroom, roars of delight were caused when the clock on the wall went crazy: its hands began to whirl round the dial and point to all hours like something in a pantomime. What had happened—a master informed us acidly—was that all the clocks in the building had stopped, and were being re-set from a controlling-station in the headmaster's study.

"Now, you can see the beauty of that device. Suppose a murderer wants fifteen minutes out for an alibi, and this person has access to the master-clock. Well, he gets hold of the dupe who is later to swear to his presence; he talks to the dupe between (let's say) 11:55 and 12:10; then he dismisses the witness. Whereupon he goes to the master-clock and sets it back to 11:55: *thereby altering every clock in the building.* Out he goes to commit his murder. He may even let himself be seen. Afterwards he returns to his office, and puts every clock right again. He has created a hiatus in time of ten to fifteen minutes; and his dupe will later swear to his alibi during the time the murder was committed. The excellence of it is that he runs no risk of being caught out, or having anybody notice a discrepancy in time; no matter who looks at no matter what clock, they will all have precisely the same time. And, at the Royal Scarlet, in whose charge would the master-clock be? I'll lay you a fiver it's the manager. Hardwick, you observe, has an alibi for just those minutes."

He stopped in some doubt, and finished his brandy with a feeling of defiance.

"It really is good," admitted Francine. "It's so horribly ingenious that I can't believe a word of it."

"I am afraid that will be the general impression," beamed Dr. Fell. "Though I like the idea very much myself. It might, you see, cause some curiosity if a chance guest glanced at one of the clocks and saw its hands suddenly jump fifteen minutes in one way or another."

"At midnight? How many people were abroad in the halls then? I'll acknowledge," said Kent, hunching his shoulders, "that it still leaves much to be explained." The grizzled, amiable figure of Hardwick rose in his mind. "Where's the motive? Unless he's somebody out of Jenny's dark past; you appear to think she has one. What's the reason for all that hocus-pocus with shoes and 'Dead Woman' signs? Why, after getting into the room, does the murderer take Jenny's own key and shove it into the lock outside the door————"

"H'mf, yes. I told you that was an intriguing point."

"—and, lastly, which in sequence was firstly, why was

the same uniform worn at Gay's place in Sussex? Every explanation of the case, as you said this morning, takes a violent header over the first apparance of the uniform in a country house at two o'clock in the morning. Unless ———"

"Keep at it!" urged Dr. Fell. "You're going great guns. That's the point on which I vary badly need help. Why?"

"Symbolic meaning in a uniform?"

"Harrumph—well. Maybe."

"I believe I've got it," said Francine, putting down her cigarette and looking at the lamp in a startled fashion. "Did Hardwick know Dan had booked rooms for all of us at the Royal Scarlet?"

"Yes, naturally. Dan arranged it a long time ago, before any of us left South Africa."

"The murderer," she told them, "was seen at Northfield in a uniform because he *wanted* to be seen. That was the reason for it! He wanted to draw attention to the uniform. If he hadn't been observed by the drunk on the sofa, he'd have said Boo to someone else. Think of him walking straight down the hall, like—like someone behind footlights, do you see? It was easy. He shook the drunk by the shoulder, and then let himself be seen much too obviously. But that must mean—no, don't say anything, Chris!—that must mean he was preparing everybody's mind for his appearance later, when he came to kill Jenny —preparing our minds to see—but where is there any indication in just a coat and a pair of trousers?" She paused. "I'm afraid that's the best I can do."

Dr. Fell studied her with an odd frown. "I should not be surprised," he commented, "if that remark came closer to the truth than anything we have heard."

"Meaning?" asked Kent.

"Meaning that Hadley and I are trying to work out a plan of campaign. To-morrow we are going down to Northfield; and we're—h'mf—well, we're going to ask all your party to go down there as well. In the first place, Sir Gyles Gay's house interests me. In the second place, I want to go to the jail and see Mr. Ritchie Bellowes; specifically, I want to find out what he was really supposed to see."

"Supposed to see?"

"Yes. Isn't it fairly obvious?" inquired Dr. Fell, opening his eyes. "I think you're quite right in one respect, Miss Forbes. There had to be a witness to see our figure in uniform walking down the hall. What do you think of the theory that Ritchie Bellowes was deliberately chosen?"

"Hold on," protested Kent; "I don't follow that. How do you mean, deliberately chosen? The murderer couldn't have known that the village toper would have come wandering in conveniently on the very night of the murder."

"Oh, yes, he could," said Dr. Fell, "if the village toper had been summoned."

For a time he remained wheezing, his eyes half-shut, and then he went on in an abstracted tone:

"Very well, I'll give you a hint; and you can see what you make of it. Not enough attention, I think, has been paid to the first murder. First tell me this: did any of your party ever meet Bellowes before he was found in the house that night?"

"No, we didn't exactly meet him," said Francine. "Our amiable host brought him in one night during the first week we were there, as a sort of hired entertainer, to show us his mental tricks. You'd riffle through a pack of cards in front of him and he'd afterwards tell you each of the cards in the order he saw them. You mix up several dozen articles on a table, and he identifies them all after one second's look; that sort of thing. Tall, hollow-eyed chap, very pleasant-spoken. He talked to us casually. Then our host took him out to the kitchen and sent him home full of whisky. I thought it was rather rotten of Sir Gyles, because that used to be Bellowes's home, you know. That was why, when Rod was killed, we thought at first———"

Dr. Fell shook his head, fiery with argumentativeness.

"Now consider the following indications! I pointed out to Hadley this morning Bellowes's importance in the case.

You see, his presence there on the very night of a particularly brutal murder was a little too fortuitous. The man himself was unquestionably dead drunk and incapable of mischief. His presence there might be a coincidence, a somewhat painful tearing of coincidence; but there were certain indications against it.

"First (you recall), when he was found on the sofa at two o'clock in the morning he had a key to the house in his pocket. That meant either that someone had given him a key, or it was an old one of his own; but, in either case, it meant he had left his lodgings early that evening intending to go to his old home—and intended it before he had taken a drop to drink! What, then, becomes of the homing pigeon reeling back by instinct?

"Second, he concluded his evening at the pub, contrary to custom, by drinking whisky and going away with a pint of it. Now, I don't know whether you know anything about the habits of village pubs. I, to my joy, do. The drink there is beer, because spirits are too expensive. Whisky is a luxury reserved for rare and mystic occasions. Bellowes, we know, was almost penniless; his usual tap was beer; but on this occasion, *with* a key to the house in his pocket, he orders whisky. It looked as though someone had been supplying him with extra cash. Why?

"Third, you recall that Bellowes's finger-prints were actually found in the room where Rodney Kent was murdered—which made it look very bad for him—although Bellowes absolutely denied ever having been in that room. He had at least looked in there, since the prints were round the light-switch. But he didn't remember it.

"Suppose Bellowes had been summoned or invited to the house at a certain hour. But why? It assuredly was not to be a scapegoat for the real murderer. If this had been so, he would have been made a far more thorough-going scapegoat. The poker, instead of vanishing mysteriously from the house, would have been found in his hand. There would have been blood on him; and finger-prints in more damning places than merely round the light-switch.

Furthermore, the real murderer would have known—stop; or would he wonder?—that Bellowes's nearly paralysed left arm would make it impossible for him to have strangled Rodney Kent in the crushing two-handed grip that was used.

"Yet, the more I turned it over, the more it seemed to me certain that Bellowes had been invited there. In short, he was to be a witness: as he was. A far from sober witness: as he was. An incurious witness: as he was. A witness with a photographic memory: as he was. And a complete witness to some skilful and evil design for strangling, planned to throw suspicion on the wrong person: as, alas, he was *not*. He got too drunk. What might he have seen when he looked into the room where Rodney Kent was killed? In other words, what lies just under the surface of this first crime, which is rather more devilish than the second? Bellowes saw part of what he was meant to see. But was there anything else? Archons of Athens! I wish I knew! And we are going down to Sussex to find out."

Ending on a note of some savagery, Dr. Fell drew out a large red bandana handkerchief, mopped his forehead with it, and blinked at the other two from under its folds. He added:

"I trust you take my meaning?"

"But if someone invited or got Bellowes to the house," muttered Kent, "it must have been the murderer. Consequently, Bellowes must know who the murderer is?"

Dr. Fell put away the bandana. "I wish it were as simple as that. But I'm afraid it's not. Bellowes, you see, could hardly have been paid to keep silent when he himself was in danger. I don't think he suspects at all; if he did, perhaps it's just as well that he's safely in jail. What I am going to do, you perceive, is find out what he was supposed to see on the night of January 14th. I am going to dig into the subconscious; and digging into the subconscious, we are assured by the tenets of the newest science, inevitably produces a nightmare. Shall we have a final brandy?"

Their cab prowled up Piccadilly, the chains on its wheels clanking faintly. Dr. Fell had gone home, more silent than was usual with him; and Kent had told the driver to take a turn anywhere he liked. It was warm enough to be pleasant inside the cab. Pale lamps looked in on them; the street was churned to slush, but by the time they turned into the high dimness of the Park, there were lawns of snow outside the windows and the bare trees wore bonnets. Francine, a bundle of furs topped by yellow hair that fluffed out over them, leaned against his shoulder and stared straight ahead. He had just put his hand on a cold hand when she spoke.

"Chris, do you know who he suspects?"

"Who—?" For a moment Kent was puzzled; it seemed incongruous at such a time. Though she pressed his hand, she did not turn round. "I don't know," he confessed. "Harvey Wrayburn seems out of the running, and my elaborate case against Hardwick was, I admit, sheer fireworks. I don't like to think of anyone else."

"He suspects Melitta Reaper."

It was so abrupt and so startling that he dropped her hand. Of her face he could so far see only the tip of her nose; now she moved, turning towards him squarely.

"Meli—rubbish!"

"It's not, Chris. I know. I can feel these things." She spoke with fierce intensity. "You think a minute and you'll realise it. Do you remember? I was maundering along, trying to find a reason for someone wearing the uniform. I hardly knew what I was saying—but I saw his eyes. I said, 'But where is there any indication in just a coat and a pair of trousers?' A pair of trousers, Chris; it was as though I had made some kind of slip of the tongue. And he didn't thunder out. He just said it was closer to the truth than anything else. It was enough to give me goose-flesh, because I saw. Why would a murderer be so horribly anxious every time to print a picture in our heads of a man, a man in an especially mannish kind of uniform? You see? Because it's a woman."

He looked at the white face over the furs, with the large, long brown eyes shifting slightly. The run and crossing of car-lamps among the trees shifted like her eyes; and the wheels seemed to hammer loudly.

"But that's crazier than any of my guesses! You don't believe it, do you?"

"No; I suppose I don't, really, but————"

"But what?"

"Chris, I've been a beast. I suppose, from now on, I'll tell you every thought that's in my head; because I'd like to; but I'm always having them." She seemed rather incoherent from the strain of the past weeks, but she spoke in a quiet voice, looking up now and again. "Suppose it's Dan himself who's been tied up with Jenny? It's quite possible, you know: living in the same house, and Jenny being what she was. To say nothing of the fact that Dan's close to being a millionaire. You saw how queer Dan was to-day when we talked about Jenny's real nature, didn't you? And didn't it strike you that Melitta was just a little too quick to defend Jenny, and say bah-bah-my-dears-there's-nothing-in-it, and act in a way that's not exactly like her? If Dan is the man in the case, the one from whom Jenny has been getting all the cheques————"

He felt cold, though he would have nothing to do with the idea.

"Well, old girl, in my opinion it's still raving lunacy. Melitta: definitely not. Why should she?"

"You say I'm mad on economics. But you know how Melitta is about plain money."

"But how does Rod fit in?"

"Jenny lived off Dan; Rod was supposed to live off Jenny————"

"Come here," he ordered. "And forget that gibberish. If we go on like this, there'll be nobody at all we can dare trust. We can't go on feeling that everybody round us is a hobgoblin. Why not Dan himself? Why not me? Why not you?"

"Why not?" she said, and plucked at a button of his overcoat. The bundle of furs stirred; the cab jolted slightly, and moved on into the darkest curve of the park. "I wonder," she added in a small voice, "just what that chap Bellowes will say?"

Chapter 13

A Welcome at Four Doors

ALL I can say," replied Ritchie Bellowes, "is what I have said. I'm sorry I went there, but I don't see that I did any great harm."

He sat back on the bunk of the cell and regarded his visitors with an air of polite cynicism which was not even marred by the stubble on his face. He was that rare product, a gentleman; and it was all the more odd to meet him in a jail in Sussex. Tall, with dark hair in a wide parting, he looked even more hollow-eyed from his fortnight's enforced sobriety. He wore a grey shirt open at the neck, and a pair of brown braces with one button missing made him hitch his shoulder frequently.

They had gone down to Sussex early on the morning of February 1st, Christopher Kent accompanying Dr. Fell and Hadley, and the others arranging to follow on a faster train. The nine-fifteen from Charing Cross idled through the succession of tunnels which make the Kentish hills seem to shut away London as though with a wall. The flat lands beyond were stiff with snow. Dr. Fell was occupied with a vast series of notes, spreading over from one small piece of paper to the other, so Hadley gave up any attempt to talk to him and settled down glumly with a crossword puzzle. They changed at Tonbridge; and, the nearest station to Northfield being Eglamore, a police car was waiting for them there.

Northfield, an attractive enough village in summer, now carried out its reputation sufficiently to look like something off a Christmas-card. Great pillars of yew-hedge before the church, and arching over the lychgate, were powdered with snow. The village green, hard earth, sloped down to the public-house of the Stag and Glove, as though tilting its inhabitants there; it was fronted by low houses of white weather-boarding and others of that faded half-timbering which looks brittle to the touch. The visitors, after having been inside several of the houses, thought that they had never seen so many oak beams; oak beams seemed to sprout and crowd, to the manifest pleasure of the owners; but living inside too many oak beams, Kent decided, must be like living inside the stomach of a zebra.

They did not go to Four Doors, Sir Gyles's house, since Gay himself had not arrived. After (at Dr. Fell's insistence) testing the local brew at the Stag and Glove, and finding it good, they went on to the district police-station on the road to Porting. The station consisted of two converted semi-detached houses, and was presided over like a householder by Inspector Tanner. Dr. Fell—one or two of whose great sheaf of notes had suffered from having fallen into the beer—was determined to conduct the examination of Bellowes. After a great unlocking of underground doors, they found Bellowes reasonably courteous, but apathetic and cynical.

"Look here, I'll be frank," said Dr. Fell, getting down to business with a directness which pained Hadley. "We're here because we're not satisfied you told the whole truth about the night of January 14th."

"Sorry," said Bellowes. "But I've already said it a hundred times. I—did—not———"

"Now, steady!" urged Dr. Fell, with a redder tinge in his face. "The question is not what you did; the question is why you did it. Quick! Did someone tell you to go to Four Doors on that night?"

Bellowes had been reading a well-thumbed Wild West magazine. Now he put it down on the floor beside the bunk; and, stirred out his apathy, regarded the doctor with what Kent could have sworn was genuine surprise.

"No," he said.

"You're sure of that, now?"

"I'm certain of it. What's all this? Why should—well, why should anybody want me there? Why should anybody want me anywhere?" he added, with a rush of bitterness which was dangerously near self-pity.

"You still maintain you wandered there of your own accord, while you were drunk, and had no intention of doing it beforehand?"

"I don't know why I went there. Yes, I suppose I do know; but you understand what I mean. But I hadn't any intention of doing that early in the evening. I honestly don't go about breaking into people's houses as a rule, and I can't understand how it happened."

"How do you explain the fact that there was a key to the house in your pocket?"

"Key? But I always carry that key; I've carried it for years," replied Bellowes, bringing his heel down with some violence on the floor. "Ask my landlady. Ask anybody. I don't suppose I'm entitled to it; but Sir Gyles knows I have it————"

"Forgive my mentioning this: but you were rather in funds on the night of the fourteenth?"

The other's face grew pinched.

"I was."

"Well?"

"You may have heard," said Bellowes gravely, "that I gave a little tame conjuring entertainment for the guests at Four Doors. As I was leaving Sir Gyles pushed an envelope in my pocket. There was more in that envelope than I deserved; and, just between ourselves, than I had—hoped for. We used to learn a lot of tosh about people being too proud to accept charity. I was not."

"Damn and blast!" said Dr. Fell. He opened and shut his hands; he would have surged up with oratorical thunder had the size of the place permitted it. After a curt remonstrance from Hadley, he subsided to mutterings, and pursued the subject with almost ghoulish hopefulness.

"Would you maintain in court that nobody prompted you to go to that house?"

"I would."

"Humph. Ha. If you don't mind, I'd like to take you over that statement of yours. But, first, as a general thing: you know Sir Gyles Gay fairly well?"

"I'm acquainted with him. That is, I've been to the house two or three times in the past year."

"When you went there to entertain the guests, I suppose you met all of them?"

Bellowes frowned. "Yes, I was introduced to all of them—I think. I didn't talk much to them, barring when they asked questions: except to Mr. Reaper. I liked him," said Bellowes, staring at the past. "He's my style, somehow. He asked me if I'd like to get a new start in South Africa, and I think he meant it."

"Did you meet Rodney Kent, who was later————"

"It's a queer thing about that. I suppose he must have been there, because he was one of the party: as I have good reason to remember, God knows. But I can't remember seeing him at all."

"Did you ever see any of the others on any subsequent occasion?"

"Yes, but not to speak to. Mr. Reaper dropped in at the pub one evening later, but he was in the private bar and I was in the public. I didn't have—have the nerve to walk in and say good evening. Then another of them was in the pub early on the night—the night it all happened; but that was very early in the evening."

"Which one was it?"

"I think the one named Wrayburn. But he was only there to order half a dozen of sherry, and didn't stay more than a minute or two."

Dr. Fell made another note. Hadley was growing restive; and Bellowes, whose long sobriety had done him no good, was beginning to twitch.

"Now, about the night of the 14th in question," rumbled the doctor. "Let's begin with the time you were in the bar of the Stag and Glove. What made you change to whisky and go away with a bottle of it?"

"Oh, I don't know. Why do you ever do anything like that? I thought of it, and so I did."

"Yes. I know," admitted Dr. Fell. "With the idea of going out to this clearing called Grinning Copse and drinking the bottle?"

"That's right. If I take a bottle home, Mrs. Witherson always starts to preach. She waits up for me. I hope you find this helpful," said Bellowes between his teeth.

"How drunk were you?" asked Dr. Fell blandly.

"I was—padded. Muzzy."

"Have you got a strong head?"

"No."

"You started for Grinning Copse, I understand, at closing-time: ten o'clock? H'mf, yes. You sat down on an iron bench or chair in the copse and began on the whisky. Never mind; I know you've made a statement; but just tell me everything that comes back to you in connection with it."

"There's nothing more I can tell," answered Bellowes, with a duller colour in his face. "Things began to run together and mix up then, but that was what I wanted them to do. I've got a hazy idea that at one point someone was talking to me; but don't take this too seriously—I was probably speaking aloud myself. Reciting or something. I'm sorry; that's everything. The next thing I knew I was sitting on some different kind of surface, which turned out to be leather; and in some different kind of place, which turned out to be the upstairs hall at Four Doors. You know what I did. I thought it was as good a place as any, so I just lay down on the sofa."

"Can you put a time to any of this; even an approximate time?"

"No."

"You say in your statement to the police—where are we?—'At this time I do not think I went to sleep immediately. While I was lying there,' and so on to describe the appearance of the figure in uniform. Are you certain you did not go to sleep?"

"No, I'm not sure."

"What I am endeavouring to establish is this," persisted Dr. Fell, with such unwonted sticking to the point that Hadley was disturbed. Every wheeze seemed to emphasise a word. "Were you conscious of an interval, any time between your lying down on the sofa and the time you saw the figure?"

"I don't know," groaned Bellowes, massaging the veins in the back of his hand. "Don't you think I've been over all that a hundred times? I think there was an interval, yes. Something to do with the light—the moonlight. But I'm not sure what." He broke off. "Are you a lawyer, by the way?"

Dr. Fell certainly sounded like one, though it was a suggestion which at any other time he would have repudiated with some heat.

"You'd call it a kind of semi-conscious state, then?"

"Yes, that's a polite way of putting it."

"While you were lying there, do you remember any sounds, anyone moving, anything like that?"

"No."

"But what roused you? I'm digging in here, you see. Something must have made you look up, or stirred you in some way?"

"I suppose it did," the other admitted doubtfully. "I have a vague impression that it may have been someone talking, or maybe whispering. But that's the closest I can get."

"Now listen. I'm going to read over a part of your statement again.

I should describe him as a medium-sized man wearing a uniform such as you see in the big hotels like the Royal Scarlet or the Royal Purple. It was a dark-blue uniform with a long coat, and silver or brass buttons; I could not be sure about colours in the moonlight. I think there was a stripe round the cuffs, a dark red stripe. He was carrying a kind of tray, and at first he stood in the corner and did not move.

Question: What about his face?

I could not make out his face, because there seemed to be a lot of shadow, or a hole or something, where his eyes ought to be.

Dr. Fell put down the sheet. In the light and warmth of a town, in a soft-carpeted hotel, such a figure had seemed merely fantastic. Here in the sealed countryside it was beginning to assume hues of something else altogether. Kent, who had not before dwelt too closely on that description of the face, felt a sensation very similar to that with which he had first seen Jenny's body.

"Have you anything to add to that, Mr. Bellowes?"

"No. I'm sorry."

"Would you recognise the face if you saw it again?"

"No, I don't think so. It was a fattish kind of face, I think; or the shadows or something gave it that effect. Man," cried Bellowes, and, to everyone's acute discomfort, the tears of raw nerves or self-pity overflowed his eyes, "what do you think I am? I wasn't in any condition to see it. If I hadn't been what they call a camera-eye observer, I shouldn't have seen anything at all, probably, and maybe I'm all out of focus as it is."

"Now, steady!" urged Dr. Fell, disturbed. He wheezed violently. "You make a reference here to the 'Blue Room.' Was that where Mr. Kent was killed?"

"So they tell me."

"And you didn't go in there?"

Bellowes grew more quiet. "I know all about those finger-prints, or alleged finger-prints. But, in spite of them, I don't honestly think I did go in there, even when I was drunk. From the time I was a kid I never liked that room. It was my grandfather's, you see, that's the reason for all the old-fashioned furniture, which went when I disposed of the house: and to keep me quiet, when I was a kid, my father turned the old man into something like an ogre."

"One last point, Mr. Bellowes. Do you remember this tray or salver?"

"I remember seeing it."

Dr. Fell leaned forward. "Was there anything on it?"

"On it?"

"Carried on it. Think! A number of small articles are put out in front of you, and you remember them all. It's your gift. You must use it. Was there anything on that tray?"

Ritchie Bellowes put up a hand and rubbed his forehead; he stared down at the Wild West magazine; he shuffled his feet; and nothing happened.

"I'm sorry," he apologised for the dozenth time. "No. There may have been. I don't remember."

"Thank you very much," Dr. Fell said in a dispirited voice. "That's all."

But even so he had not finished. When they were on their way out he went back to ask the prisoner still one more question; whatever it was, Bellowes seemed to return a decided negative, and this appeared to cheer the doctor somewhat. During this interview Hadley, who had been corking himself down, had with some effort managed to keep silent. But when they were driving back to Northfield he let himself go.

"All right," said the superintendent grimly. "Let's hear it. I asked you much the same sort of question once before. What was being carried on that salver? Somebody's head?"

"Yes," replied Dr. Fell with every evidence of seriousness. "Mine. A sheep's head, and a whacking great one, too. You know, I never realised until last night the purpose or meaning of that salver. It presented a real problem; and yet it's quite simple. I must be running on senile decay."

"Good," said Hadley. "I mean, I'm glad you find it so easy. I confess that so far it escapes me. But that's not the main point. You're not going to divert me from the solid information I got from South Africa. You were bombarding me with a hell of a lot of 'suggestive' points yesterday evening, among them your new idea that somebody invited Bellowes to the house early in the evening on the night of the murder. What becomes of that now?"

Dr. Fell made a handsome concession. "I withdraw it in the form in which it was presented. I also call your attention————"

"More suggestive points?"

"Didn't you see any?"

"As soon as I begin to hear the call of mumbo-jumbo," Hadley snapped, "I begin to have an idea (yes, I'll admit it) that you're probably on the right track. But I still don't like it. One of these days, my lad, you're going to come a cropper; and it will be the world's most outstanding cropper. Why do you want our party buried down here again? If you want a look at the house, couldn't you do it without bringing them back here? When they're in London, at least I've got an idea I could keep my eye on them. But I've got no such comfortable feeling about Northfield."

For a moment Dr. Fell did not reply. Their car circled the green at Northfield, and eased its way down a gravel road beside the church: a road dusted with snow as lightly as you might dust finger-print powder. At the end of a gradual descent the hedges curved and opened on the small grounds of Four Doors. The house was of that style of Queen Anne architecture which seems at once massive and yet squeezed together, as though the designer had tried to crowd too many arched windows into deep walls. The bricks were of a grimy colour; the front door, painted white like the window-facings, was as square as the house's heavy length; and dead wistaria clung to its face. An abrupt little garden, with a herbaceous border and a sundial in a brick path up the centre, also clung to the front of it. The party from London had evidently arrived from the station: a big black sedan, cut ropes hanging from its luggage-grid, was slewed round in the drive. Behind the house you could see the slope of the hill, and one great elm against the sky. A wind blowing down from the east brought, very distinctly, the sound of the church clock striking noon.

They looked at it for a time; while that wind rattled in the bushes and a little dust-devil of snow danced round the sundial.

"You see what I mean?" inquired Hadley.

"I do not see what you mean," said Dr. Fell. "Will you accept my assurance that there is absolutely no danger?"

The door was opened for them by Sir Gyles Gay, before their car had even come to a stop. Gay stood on the threshold with that slightly shivering air, as of one on the edge of a pool, with which many hosts either welcome or bid good-bye. He seemed still interested, even smiling, his hands behind his back as though in meditation. But his very correct tie was rumpled, and he greeted them with a certain gravity.

"Come in, gentlemen. I was wondering how long you would be. We have been here only an hour, but even in that time there have been certain happenings. Country air seems to have a curious effect."

Hadley stopped dead on the doorstep.

"No, no," their host assured them, with wrinkled amusement. "Not what you may be thinking; nothing serious. I mean that country air seems to bring about a sense of humour. But it is an unusual and perverted sense of humour, and,"—he looked back over his shoulder into a warm, comfortable hall—"I can't say I like it."

"What's happened?"

Again Gay looked over his shoulder; but he made no move to go inside.

"You remember my telling you yesterday that we played all sorts of parlour games down here, including that of pinning a paper tail on a paper donkey?"

"Yes; well?" said Dr. Fell.

"I did not know, when you asked whether we would all come down here, whether you wanted us for the day only, or for several days. Anyhow, I set aside rooms for you gentlemen, in case you should care to honour me with a visit." He looked at Dr. Fell. "It concerns the room which is at your disposal, doctor. Within the last half-hour, someone has had the highly humorous notion of taking a paper donkey's tail and pinning it to the door of your bedroom."

They looked at each other. But nobody was amused.

"That, however, is not all," Gay went on, sticking out his neck and looking round each corner of the door. "The humorist has gone even further. Put in a highly ingenious place—where somebody was certain to find it soon—I discovered this."

He took his hands from behind his back and held out a piece of stiff paper. It was a group photograph some eight by ten inches, taken by one of those professionals who lie in wait at amusement resorts and persuade you to buy the photograph afterwards. Kent recognised it easily as being the inside of the "fun-fair" at the Luna Park outside Durban. He remembered the slope of a rafter, a lemonade-stand by a window. The picture was taken from the top of the broad platform of one of those big slides or chutes by which you sail down into darkness. All the members of Dan's crowd were standing at the top of the chute, most of them turning laughing faces towards the camera—though Melitta was looking dignified and Francine annoyed. Someone, who could not be seen because Dan's body blocked the view, appeared to be sitting on the edge of the slide and making a sudden protesting gesture against the descent.

"Now look at the other side," said Gay, turning the photograph over.

It was scrawled in exactly the same printing-handwriting they had seen before. It was in red ink, and had a sloppy look. It said:

THERE IS ONE MORE TO GO.

Chapter 14

Red Ink

VERY funny, isn't it?" asked Gay. "I was inclined to split my sides when I saw it. But you had better come inside."

Four Doors, centrally heated, was as warm as the hotel had been. Gay took them across a comfortable hall and into a lounge where an additional fire had been lighted. Though the house was of massive build, with fan-lights over the pillared doors and white woodwork round high ceilings, Gay had overlaid it with furniture of genuine comfort. There was no sight or sound of anyone else about. But Gay closed the double-doors.

"Where did you find this?" Hadley asked quietly.

"Ah, there's another piece of subtle humour," said their host. "I went into the bothroom to have a wash. Then I reached out after a towel off the rail, and this fell out from among the towels."

"When did you find it?"

"Not ten minutes ago. By the way, I have established one thing. When we arrived here at eleven o'clock, there was no such delightful piece of mummery hidden in the towels. You see, I keep a cook and two maids. When we got here Letty had just finished tidying up the bathroom and putting out fresh towels. Consequently————"

"Who knows about this, besides yourself?"

"Only the humorist who put it there. I hope you do not think I was indiscreet enough to tell Letty anything. I also pulled that donkey's tail down off the door before (I hope) anyone spotted it. I don't know when it was put up. I noticed it when I was coming out of the bathroom, on the principle that jokes never come singly."

"Yes. And what do you think this means?"

"My good friend," replied Gay, drawing himself up and looking Hadley in the eye, "you must know very well what I think it means. I am fond of good crimes in the abstract; but I do not like funerals. This has got to stop." He hesitated, after which his face altered, and he addressed Kent with great gravity. "Sir," he added, "I beg *your* pardon."

"Granted readily," said Kent, who liked him. "But why?"

"Because I was more than half inclined to suspect you. Er—you have been with Dr. Fell and the superintendent? Between eleven and twelve o'clock, I mean?"

"Yes. We were at the police-station then. But why suspect me, in particular?"

"Why, frankly," responded Gay, with an air of candour, "because your turning up at the hotel yesterday seemed almost too good to be true. Also, because there has been a persistent rumour that you were more than a little interested in Mrs. Josephine Kent————"

"That can wait," snapped Hadley. He turned to Dr. Fell and held out the photograph. "So you'll give me your assurance that there's no danger? How does this fit in with it?"

The doctor put his shovel-hat under his arm and propped his stick against his side. Settling his eyeglasses with a vaguely troubled air, he studied the photograph.

"I don't mind the donkey's tail," he said. "In fact, I think it rather moderate. There are times when I feel I deserve the fate of Bottom the Weaver. But this, honestly, is not one of them. On the other hand, it's a complication I definitely do not like. Someone is growing frightened." He looked at Gay. "To whom does this photograph belong? Did you ever see it before?"

"Yes, it's mine. That is to say, I don't know whether you're aware of Reaper's passion for having photographs taken. He sent me on a batch of them, showing his friends on aqua-planes, and his friends holding up glasses of beer, and so on."

"H'mf, so. Where did you see it last?"

"I think it was in the desk in my study, with the others."

"What is more, this isn't ordinary writing-ink," pursued Dr. Fell, scratching the nail of his little finger across the thick and flaky surface of the inscription on the back of the photograph. "It's too viscid. It looks like————"

"Drawing-ink. That is what it is," supplied Gay. "Just come with me."

He seemed much stiffer than yesterday; he retained that hard glaze like the polish on a tombstone, even to his smile. As though coming to a decision, he led them to another pair of double-doors at the end of the room, and into a room fitted up as a study at the back of the house. Its windows looked out on a back-garden raked by the wind: on a gate in the brick wall, and the elms in the churchyard. But the study also was cheerful with firelight. It was conventional enough, with its bookshelves and busts above, except for an inner staircase ascending along the end wall: a room antiquated rather than ancient. Their host glanced towards this inner staircase before he indicated an open roll-top desk.

"There are, as you can see, four or five bottles of drawing-ink. Various colours," he pointed out. "I seldom or never use them; but the winters pass slowly for me, and, one winter, my hobby was architecture. By the look of that printing, I should think the pen used was this."

He lifted the stopper out of a bottle of black ink. To the stopper, inside, was attached a broad pen-nib—a feature common to bottles of drawing-ink—for testing it before use. He waggled it at them. Kent did not like the expression of his face now.

"I suppose you can guess where that staircase leads?

The door at the top of it is beside the bathroom door upstairs. This humorist, this *slim* fellow, can simply walk down here, scrawl on that photograph like a child on a wall, and walk up with it."

For the first time Hadley was indecisive. Apparently he did not like it either, and there had been a strain ever since they entered the house, but he was studying Gay in a very curious way.

"Do you keep the desk locked?"

"No; why should I? There's nothing of value in it. Half the time the top is not even closed, as it is now."

"But where are the photographs?" asked Dr. Fell. "I've come a long way to see those photographs, you know."

Gay turned round quickly. "I beg your pardon? You've what?"

"Come a long way to see the photographs. Where are they?"

Their host reached towards his trouser-pocket; then he shrugged his shoulders and pulled open a drawer in a tier at the right-hand side of the desk. "I am afraid you will not be well rewarded," he said sardonically. "There is very little to—good God!"

He had jerked back his hand quickly. What oozed out from between his fingers, what he moved back to avoid in case it should splatter on his clothes, was not blood. It looked like blood. But it was red ink. Gathering round him, they saw that the inside of the drawer was what Dr. Fell literally described as an incarnadined mess. In the drawer there had been photographs: some loose ones of all sizes, and others which had obviously been taken of or by Gay himself, for they had been pasted into an album. All were ripped and torn into many shreds, a kind of pudding, over which had been poured some half a bottle of red drawing-ink.

Dr. Fell groaned. Sir Gyles Gay did not. Standing with his hand stiffly outstretched while he swabbed at the fingers with a handkerchief, he began to curse. He cursed with such careful, cold-voiced, measured authority that it showed a new side to the man, a new use for marble teeth. He cursed in English, *Afrikaans* and Kaffir, the sort of thing which would have skinned the hide either from an offending houseboy or a Government department: yet Kent could not help feeling he had heard exactly the same tone of voice on a golf-course when someone has just foozled about the sixth easy stroke. Kent saw the veins in his neck.

"I hope," Gay continued, without changing his even tone, "I can be called a good host. I like my guests. I have enjoyed their presence immensely. But this—by God! this is going too far. That ink is still running in the drawer. It hasn't been put in for much more than half an hour. And where are my guests now? Why, I'll tell you. Without a doubt each is sitting or standing in his own room. Without a doubt nobody has ventured out, as on other occasions. It is all beautifully quiet; by the so-and-so it is."

Dr. Fell scratched his chin. "Do you mind my saying," he observed, "that you're rather a rum sort of bloke?"

"Thanks very much."

"No, I mean it. When a murder is committed—even one in your own house—you are helpful, philosophical, and all good things. It is an intellectual problem. It stimulates you. But you go off the deep end, with one majestic volplaning sweep, when someone plays a senseless practical joke that makes you mess up your hands. You don't mind a throat being cut; but you can't stand a leg being pulled."

"I can understand murder," said Gay, opening his eyes. "I cannot understand this."

"You don't see any meaning in it?"

"Ah, there I am not qualified to judge. But I want to know what has been going on. Up to this time 'somebody' has confined his or her inane scribblings to nighttime. Now this humorist walks about in the light of day and writes—Chequebook!" said Gay, breaking off.

Now not minding the confusion in the drawer, he began to grub in it. With some relief he produced a leather-bound cheque-book on the Capital Counties Bank; it was by some chance not stained at all, and he put it gingerly on the desk. Then he drew out a small leather purse, of the sort used by countrymen for carrying loose change, and snicked it open.

"Something wrong here," he added in an altered tone —a natural tone. "There's some money missing."

"Money?" said Hadley. "I thought you said you kept nothing valuable in that desk."

"Quite true, superintendent; I don't. All this purse ever contains is a little silver in case I have to pay for a parcel, or hand out a tip, or the like. There's never more than a pound here at any time."

"How much is missing?"

"Twelve shillings, I make it," said Gay with competence. "Is this some more highly subtle humour, do you think?"

Hadley took a deep breath and studied the room with a vindictiveness that equalled Gay's own. With his hand in a handkerchief, he picked up the bottle of red drawing-ink from the desk. It had undoubtedly been used to deluge the drawer; it was nearly empty.

"Yes," he growled, "yes, I'm taking precautions about finger-prints in going after a practical joker. I remember a time, Fell, in the Mad Hatter case, when the answer to a piece of tomfoolery was the answer to a murder. You know—" Hadley stopped and cooled off. "We'll settle this up right now. Will someone—will you," he looked at Kent, "go and round up all the others? No, never mind sending a servant, Sir Gyles; I want all the servants here now, if you'll send for them. We'll begin with them. If you've got two maids, I don't see how it's impossible for someone to have raised the devil like that without *anything* being seen." He added to Kent, grimly: "Yes. Tell 'em what you like. It won't do any harm."

Kent went up the inner staircase to the hall of the floor above. He went quickly, because he did not want time to think. Four Doors, according to the plan of its (would-be) period, was severely oblong, with a central hall running broad-wise through the building. And he had no difficulty in finding three out of four of his quarry. Francine, Dan, and Melitta were sitting together in a sort of upstairs den whose big oriel window looked out over the main door. They sat round a gas-fire in an atmosphere of grousing.

Dan greeted him peevishly.

"I must say you're a fine sort of friend. You walked out last night with the wench here—well, that's understandable enough. But this morning you up and walked out with the police————"

It was the home atmosphere again.

"I walked out with the police," Kent said, "because Dr. Fell countenanced it, and because I wanted to see whether I could find anything to help us out of this mess. And there's a lot more to say now." He looked round; Wrayburn's absence was a noticeable gap. "Where's Harvey?"

Dan's intuition was disconcertingly keen: keener, perhaps, than Melitta's. He had been sitting with his elbows thrust out and his hands on his knees; now he got up as though he were levering up a boulder. On one side of him sat Melitta in stout discontent and a Chanel dress. On the other, Francine smoked a cigarette and looked properly attentive. He always remembered them at that moment, because of the home atmosphere which seemed to connect this with bright-hued villas in Parktown. What had happened this morning was like a home-bickering become distorted: a clash of wills or a bad joke, like breaking into somebody's liquor-cabinet or setting a booby-trap. The worst of it was that it was real. It could happen, and did happen—on a scale that ended in murder. And Dan guessed. He was standing so close to the gas-fire that you could smell the fire scorching a tweed suit.

Dan said: "Harvey? He went up to the pub after cigarettes. What's up?"

"Somebody's been acting the fool." Kent stopped. It was not actually that, in spite of every ludicrous attempt at a jeer in the actions that had been done this morning. "How long have you three been in here together?"

"Mel and I just came in. Francine has been here all the time. What's *up*?"

Kent told them.

The way in which they received it might or might not have been considered curious. They were very quiet. It was like Melitta's what-a-holiday mood, as though they had taken seaside lodgings where it rained steadily for two weeks. Only at the end did something appear to rouse Dan.

"I never heard of such tomfoolery in all my born days!" he said, looking for the perpetrator in corners of the room. "Let me see if I have this straight: somebody takes that photograph, writes on the back of it, and puts it in among the towels. Somebody tears all the other photographs to pieces and douses them with red ink. Then someone steals twelve shil—oh, here! Why steal the money?"

"You've got it," said Kent, realising. He knew at last what was wrong with the picture. "I've had a feeling that something didn't ring true, and you've got it. It's the money. The rest of it might have been perverted humour, or there might be an explanation for most of it; I think I can see one. But stealing the money doesn't fit in."

"May not have anything to do with it," Dan pointed out. "Suppose one of the maids took the money, or something like that?"

"Jenny had none, you know," interposed Melitta.

"Jenny had none of what?"

"No silver, coppers, small change of any kind," she answered obediently. "In her handbag at the hotel. I know, because they asked me to go through her things."

It was true; Kent remembered having written it down in his notes. Melitta, whose handsome nose was pink this morning, warmed up.

"Now do not tell me I don't know what I'm talking about. I thought it was awfully queer at the time, and I told Mr. Hadley so; because whoever travels, you know, *always* carries some change, and I am quite sure Jenny always did. When I saw it was not there I felt somebody must have taken it, though of course I knew it was no good saying anything."

"But she had thirty pounds in notes, and that wasn't touched."

"So she had, my dear; but how did you know that?"

"Because I took charge of it," Dan returned grimly. He had evidently noticed no implication. "Somebody's got to take the responsibility here. I'm the fellow who cleans up afterwards. That's all right; I'm the executor; but I want this nonsense stopped. Do you mean that there's someone who goes around consistently stealing loose silver and coppers, and letting big banknotes alone?"

"I'm sure I don't know, my dear," said Melitta with her infuriating placidness, and smoothed her skirt. "As my grandfather used to say————"

Dan lowered his head for a moment.

"Mel," he observed, "there's something *I* want to say. And don't misunderstand me in saying it. I'm your husband. I'm fonder of you than of anyone in the world, if you'd only Snap Out Of It. What I want to say is this, man to man. Damn your grandfather, and your Uncle Lionel, and your Aunt Hester, and your Aunt Harriet, and your cousin Who-is-it, and all their garnered wisdom. There never was a man so afflicted with relatives as I am; and every single one of 'em is dead."

"Easy!" Kent urged, as Dan stalked gloomily across to the window. "This thing has got all our nerves to such a pitch————"

"I suppose so," admitted Dan. "Sorry, Mel. Only I'd give anything I've got just to hear you laugh again. Well, what do we do now?"

"If you could show, to Hadley's satisfaction, where you were between the time you arrived here at eleven o'clock and, say, a quarter to twelve————"

"Library," said Dan promptly. "I was fooling about

with the books, and wondering where everybody else was and why we were here at all."

"You don't mean Gay's study?"

"No, no; the library at the other side of the house."

"And you say Harvey went to the pub after cigarettes? When did he leave?"

"Almost as soon as we got here. He walked back with the chauffeur who drove us. So he's out of it—again."

They both looked at Francine, who had been unwontedly silent. "I hope, Chris," she said, and smiled while she contemplated the fire, "you haven't got round to suspecting me. I told them all about your grand case against Hardwick, so I imagine nobody's safe."

"I didn't mean that." What he meant was that he could not straighten out last night, when each had so very nearly spoken, and then there had come between them the dead wall of her mood. But he was not speaking of what he meant. "The police are going to ask you in about one minute————"

"Oh. Yes. I was up here, between my old room and this room. I didn't go downstairs at all."

"Melitta?"

"I was having a bath."

There was a silence. "You were having a bath?" repeated Dan. "You always seem to be having baths when these things happen. When? I mean, where?"

This time she did laugh, an honest and homely sound. "Well, really, my dear, there is only one place I do, usually. Though I remember, when we were first married, you used to have them in the water-butt, and nearly drowned the parrot each time. I was in the bathroom, of course. You got us up so terribly early to come down here, and I didn't have time at the hotel. I rang for the maid—Letty or Alice; Letty, I think it was—and she drew it for me. That was just after we got here. I know, because she was just finishing tidying up the bathroom, and putting new towels there when I asked her to start the bath running."

"Then—" said Kent. "How long were you in the bathroom?"

"I'm afraid it was well over three-quarters of an hour, really." She wrinkled her forehead. "I renewed the hot water twice. And then there was that nice church clock, and I think it is so nice that you can hear it from here. It struck the half-hour after eleven, and then the quarter-hour, before I was out of the tub————"

"Did you use the towels?"

"Fiddle-dee-dee! Of course I used the towels. Two of them. And that photograph was not there."

He spoke slowly. "We got here at just noon by that clock; we heard it strike. Gay met us at the door with the photograph. He said he had found it in the bathroom ————"

"You certainly got here at noon," interrupted Francine. "I was sitting up here at this window watching you; and I saw him standing down there with the photographs behind his back. But *I* wasn't going down to inquire. I didn't wish to be told to mind my own business."

"Wait!" he said, feeling as though he were half mesmerised. "Gay said he had found it in the bathroom ten minutes ago; or, in the exact words, 'not ten minutes ago.'"

Melitta smoothed her skirt again. "Well, I'm sure I don't wish to say anything against anyone's character; but you remember, Chris, and you too, Dan, I *warned* you. Of course he may have found it there, but I don't really see how he could have. Because I wasn't out of the tub until after I heard the quarter-hour strike: that was what made me get out, now I come to think of it: and then I dried myself, and tidied up the bathroom, and opened the upper part of the window to let the steam out, and actually, you see, I've only just got dressed."

Dan's face changed colour.

"You think the old devil wrote it himself?"

"I think," Kent said decisively, "we'd better go downstairs and Melitta had better tell this, before they get the idea that we're up here inventing a story to stick to. There's something damned funny about every move that's been made this morning. Gay's behaviour was odd. But so was Hadley's. He's got something on his mind. He made no objection to my coming up here and telling you everything. In fact, he practically directed me to, though I should think he'd want to spring it on you and see what happened. I tell you, there's something going on under the surface, and I wish I knew what it was."

In just two minutes he found out.

Chapter 15

Duello

IT WAS Hadley's voice which made him stop with his hand on the knob of the door. The voice was not raised; it had the unimpassioned tone of one discussing a business-deal; but Kent had not heard just that different tone in it before.

The door, at the head of the private stair leading down into the study, was open some two or three inches. He could look down on them with a tilted, theatre-like view, which was yet close enough to follow every movement of a wrinkle or turn of an eye. He saw the brown carpet spread out below, its ancient pattern of roses faded. Past the chandelier he saw Superintendent Hadley's head. Hadley was sitting by the fire-place, facing outwards, his back to the watcher above. Opposite him sat Sir Gyles Gay—his hands lifted, the fingers lightly interlocked as though he were inspecting them—a business man listening to a business proposition. The firelight shone fully on Gay's face, on his alert little look. There was no sign of Dr. Fell. Round the house the wind deepened in a winter afternoon; from the back of it drifted the smell of hot food being prepared for lunch.

What Hadley had said was:

"—and, since we're alone, I feel inclined to tell you a little of what I know."

It did not need Kent's fierce gesture to stop and silence the three persons following him. They all waited, and they all listened.

Gay assented to the proposition with a slight nod.

"You have just heard the testimony of the maid, Alice Weymiss?"

Again Gay nodded.

"You heard her say that that drawer in the desk, where the photographs were kept, is always kept locked by you?"

"I heard it."

"Was it true?"

"You see, superintendent, Alice has no business to know whether drawers are kept locked or not. If she does know, it puts her trustworthiness in doubt. You can see for yourself that the drawer is unlocked now."

Hadley leaned forward.

"Have you a key to that drawer, Sir Gyles?"

"I believe so, somewhere."

"Are you carrying that key in your right-hand trouser-pocket now?"

Gay answered neither yes nor no; he waited, and shook his head slightly as though the question were of no consequence.

"You also heard what the other maid, Letty King, said? She said that she prepared a bath for Mrs. Reaper at shortly after eleven o'clock: that Mrs. Reaper remained in the bathroom until five minutes to twelve: that she knows this because she kept an eye out in case the bathroom should have to be tidied up afterwards."

Their host looked puzzled. "Naturally. I don't deny any of that. When I told you I found the photograph there within the last 'ten minutes,' perhaps I should have consulted my watch. Perhaps I should have said five. But I did not consult my watch. I went downstairs and questioned Letty about whether the photograph had been there when she laid out the towels earlier."

"Therefore your position is that Mrs. Reaper put the photograph there?"

"Come, come, man!" said Gay, as though mildly disappointed. "My position is nothing of the kind. I don't know who put it there; I wish I did. To put the photograph there would have taken perhaps ten seconds—after Mrs. Reaper left, if you like. Or whenever you like."

After a pause there was a certain sort of amusement in Hadley's tone; it was not pleasant to listen to.

"Sir Gyles, I wonder if you think everyone who opposes you is blind. I wonder if you think we've been blind from the beginning of this case. Now, I've had instructions not to trouble you more than was necessary. You know, you're being favoured. So I've hesitated to come out with it until I had enough to trouble you a whole lot. But, after what you've said this morning, I've got no choice. The plain fact is that you've been telling me a pack of lies."

"Since when?" inquired the other, interested.

"Since yesterday. But we'll begin with to-day. Your story about this 'donkey's tail' on Fell's door was rubbish. Don't try to play with flourishes like that. Had you told any of your other guests that you expected to entertain either Fell or myself here overnight? Think before you answer. They will remember, you know."

"No, I suppose I didn't."

"Of course you didn't—sir. Then how could any of the others be expected to know even that he would be here at all; let alone what room you had 'set aside' for him?"

It is a sober fact that a reddish patch showed across Gay's forehead, though he kept the atmosphere of a business discussion.

"I think it was well known," he answered without hesitation, "that you both were coming down here. This house, as you know, boasts eight bedrooms. The others would have their old rooms; and I assuredly would not put anyone in the room where Mr. Kent was murdered. That leaves only two. There is not much margin for error. It is possible, you know, that the donkey's tail was meant for *you*."

"Just between ourselves, do you still stick to that flap-doodle?"

"There is nothing 'between ourselves.' You will see to that. Incidentally, I stick to the truth."

The fire was built of somewhat slaty coal; it crackled and popped, distorting the light on Gay's calm, interested face. Hadley leaned down beside his chair, picking up the photograph.

"Let's take this printing on the back. Even without calling in a handwriting man, I think we can decide that this was written by the same hand that wrote 'Dead Woman' on another card. Do you agree? Yes, so do I. Was this message written this morning between eleven and twelve?"

"Obviously."

"It was not. That's definite, Sir Gyles," Hadley returned. "Fell noticed it—maybe you saw him scrape his little finger across the ink. This thick stuff takes a very long time to dry. And this particular printing was not only dry; it was so flaky that it shredded off when he touched it. You saw that. That message has been written on the card for well over a week, if not more."

Again Gay would not be drawn. A dawning anger showed in his eyes, as (Kent remembered) he had shown before in that odd impression of a man foozling an easy golf-stroke, and knowing it. But he regarded his clasped hands from several angles.

"I gave an opinion, my friend."

"I give a fact—sir. Unless that writing was really done this morning, there seems no point at all to torn photographs and splattered ink. And it was not made this morning. So far, I understand, Fell and I disagree about this case. But we both agree about this, I think. . . . We'll go on to something else. Your maid swears that you always keep that particular drawer locked. You maintain that it is always open. Fair enough. But, when you were asked to open it and get the photographs out, you automatically reached for the key—in your right-hand pocket—before you remembered the drawer was supposed to be unlocked. You then jabbed your hand, much too ostentatiously, into the drawer, in order to get red ink on it and show how surprising the thing was. Anybody would have looked before doing that. You didn't. I know two burglars and a screw-man who made the same mistake."

After some deliberation, Gay crossed one leg over the other, shifted in his chair, and seemed to grow comfortable.

"You have talked for a while," he murmured. "Now let me talk. Do I understand that you accuse me of faking the whole thing? That I put the photograph in the towels; that I tore up the other photographs in my own drawer, and poured ink over them?"

"Yes, that ink was fresh."

"Quite so. Then am I accused of insanity? For there are two sides to your attack, and they won't fit. First you inform me that I did all this within an hour or so ago. Then you turn round and say that the printing on that photograph was made well over a week ago. Which is which and what is what? I'll try to meet your charges, Mr. Hadley, if I can understand them."

"Very well. To begin with————"

"Wait. Am I, by the way, accused of stealing twelve shillings of my own money?"

"No. You were really surprised when you discovered that: it was different from the other acting."

"Ah, then you acknowledge that someone else besides myself could have got into that drawer? So far, you've been building a good deal on the fact that I'm the only person who has a key to it. Excuse this insistence on small points," begged Gay, beginning to show his teeth; "but, since all your charges are built on nothing else, I want you at least to be consistent."

Hadley's tone changed again; Kent would not have liked to look him in the eye then.

"I'll give you a big one, Sir Gyles. You were acquainted with Mrs. Josephine Kent, then Miss Josephine Parkes, when she was in England four years ago."

Again the fire crackled and popped in a gush of light; a grain of burning slate exploded out towards Gay, but he did not notice it. His eyes were wide open.

"That, I concede, *is* something; if you think it is true. But what makes you believe even that she had ever been in England? You heard all her friends, her relatives, everyone say that she had never been out of South Africa in her life."

"Yes," said the superintendent grimly, "I heard it. I also heard them swear she never did any travelling at all, that she hated travelling, and could not stand even a short journey in South Africa. Then, yesterday, I saw her trunk —Fell called my attention to it. Have you seen that trunk?"

"No."

"I think you have. It is an old, battered, worn one; it has seen years of good service in trains and ships, as it shows by its handling. That trunk was certainly Mrs. Kent's own: she did not, for instance, inherit it from someone else who had done the travelling. Her maiden name, Josephine Parkes, was painted in it in chipped, faded lettering that was as old as the trunk; it had certainly got its knocking-about at the same time as the trunk itself. You see what I mean. The trunk had been used by her."

At the top of the stairs Kent turned round and glanced at Dan, who was looking guilty in the gloom of the hall. He heard Dan breathe. Nobody hesitated in the ancient practice of eavesdropping; they were listening with all their ears. And Kent remembered only too well the worn lettering on the worn trunk.

"We heard also how badly she was affected by train and sea-sickness; though she was one of the few who stood up to bad weather on the voyage out. Never mind that. But we learned that she 'turned up' unexpectedly in Johannesburg three years ago: she had come, she *said*, from her old home in Rhodesia. It surprised everyone that she had a great deal of money, which she had 'inherited' from her dead parents."

"But still————"

"Just a moment, Sir Gyles. It was worth looking up. I looked it up. I had her passport: or, rather, a joint husband-and-wife passport made out to Mr. and Mrs. Rodney Kent. Last night I cabled Pretoria about it, and got an answer. In order to obtain that joint one, she had to turn in a previous passport on the Union of South Africa, Number 45695, made out in the name of Miss Josephine Parkes." Hadley again opened his brief-case, without haste, and consulted notes. "Here I've got the immigration stamps on it.

"She landed at Southampton on September 18th, 1932. She then, at various times, paid any number of visits to France: here are the dates: but she was domiciled in England. She left England on December 20th, 1933, and landed again at Capetown on January 6th, 1934. Are you satisfied?"

Gay shook his head a little, as though fascinated.

"I won't deny your facts, of course. But still what has it to do with me?"

"She came to England to see you."

"Er—can you prove that?"

"I have proved it. Here are the papers. You were then, if you recall, Under-Secretary for the Union, and you should recognise this. Mrs. Kent said that she intended to take some kind of employment. She was given a form to fill up. She rather grandly wrote on it just this—here's the form—'To see my friend Sir Gyles Gay, who will arrange it for me.' Would you like to see it? I got it from South Africa House last night."

"I wonder, my friend, if you have any idea of just how many people passed through my office, in the course of a season, while I was on executive duty?"

"She was not a friend of yours?"

"No, she was not. I never saw the woman in my life."

"Then just take a look at this. They tell me it's a very unusual thing, nearly unheard-of, and shows direct personal intervention. Across here is written, 'Personal interview, satisfactory,' written and signed by you. Will you acknowledge this as your handwriting?"

Gay did not take the paper which Hadley was holding out. Instead he got up from his chair with an abrupt movement, and began to walk up and down the room under the dead marble busts on the bookshelves. The fire was simmering now, its light not so bright. Stopping by a humidor on a side-table, Gay tapped his fingers on the lid, opened it, and took out a cigar. He did not seem so much alarmed as very thoughtful. He spoke without turning round.

"Let me see. You think I knew, before Reaper's party got here, that a certain Mrs. Josephine Kent was really a certain Miss Josephine Parkes?"

"You might or might not. She had a different surname."

"Yet I must have known who she was? I had the photographs there, which Reaper sent on recently."

Hadley allowed a pause before he answered.

"Yes, you had the photographs, Sir Gyles. That was why they all had to be torn up and made unrecognisable with red ink."

"I confess I don't follow that."

"I mean," said Hadley, raising his voice a little, "that the photographs Mr. Reaper sent weren't the only ones you had in that drawer. There were a lot of old ones belonging to you, in your album. I'm suggesting that some of them showed you and Mrs. Kent together. That's why they had to go."

Gay closed the humidor with a snap and turned round.

"Damn your ingenuity. All very clever, all very beautiful, and—basically—all wrong. Whatever I am, I'm not as much of a lunatic as all that. It won't hold water, my friend. If what you say is true, I had week upon week's time to destroy everything long beforehand. Yet you say I waited until this very morning to do it; and then I went out of my way deliberately to call attention to it. How do you explain that?"

"I'm waiting for *you* to explain it."

"You mean that you cannot? Then there is that photograph with the obvious threat written on the back of it. According to you, the ink has been dry for over a week. Yet I am supposed to make use of it this morning, for some purpose which escapes me. Have you anything else?"

Evidently he was recovering his mental wind, after a bad attack of cramp, and had begun to fight back. But, in clipping the end off the cigar, he almost got his own finger. Hadley was not impressed.

"I have. We were rather busy last night. Sergeant Betts, following this lead, went down to Dorset to see Mrs. Kent's two aunts. We can rule them out so far as suspicion goes. They really never had seen her before. She hadn't thought it necessary to visit them when she was in England before: it seems she had other business. But they were very convenient. When she wanted to avoid meeting you, and keep up her pretence that she had never been in England, she decided to stay with them————"

"Curse it all," said Gay, in such a melodramatic way that he seemed to be shaken clear through, "why should she want to pretend she had never been in England before? Answer that, if you can. Had she committed a crime? Also, I think you forget that I did meet her, on the evening before last."

"The night she was murdered," agreed Hadley, as though merely confirming the fact. "Yes. I told you we had something else. While she was with her aunts, Mrs. Kent received two letters written from here. One was from her husband—the aunts had seen that handwriting before. One was in a handwriting they did not know."

"You have the letters, of course?"

"We have the letter from Rodney Kent. The other she destroyed. Why? But she answered both of them." Hadley leaned forward. "I'm suggesting to you, Sir Gyles, that you recognised Mrs. Kent from the pictures Mr. Reaper sent on. (No wonder she objected to making the trip to England.) You then wrote to her to assure her that you would be prepared to meet her as a stranger. And, the night before last, you did."

Gay lit his cigar. He said:

"You started on me with a charge of playing senseless pranks. Somewhere along the line the gears were shifted. It's beginning to dawn on me that you're running me straight into a charge of murder." He spread out his hands, crisping the fingers, and spoke past the cigar in his mouth. "My God, man, do you really think I"—the fingers opened and shut—"I took these and killed two inoffensive—" His voice ended in a kind of deep yelp. "It's p-p-preposterous!"

"I asked you for an explanation of certain things, Sir Gyles. You haven't so far answered one straight question. If you don't give me an explanation, I shall have to ask you to come back with me to London for further questioning. And you know what that is apt to mean."

Across the room Kent saw the white-painted door leading to the lounge at the front of the house. From outside this door there abruptly began a fusillade of knocks. Kent knew why it startled him: it was the first sign of life, of bouncing movement, that had echoed up in this house. The knocks were not really loud; but they seemed to have a heavy and insistent din in the quiet afternoon. From outside the door rose up Harvey Wrayburn's hearty voice. He did not stop for replies: he asked the questions and sang out the answers himself.

"Knock, knock," said Wrayburn.

"Who's there?"

"Jack.

"Jack who?

"Jack Ketch," said Wrayburn, suddenly opening the door and grinning at them. "Sorry; I know it's a rotten one, and doesn't even keep to the rules; but I'm just back from the pub, and I thought it was applicable."

Gay's face had gone muddy pale. You could see the Adam's apple move in his neck.

The others did not wait to hear what Wrayburn, apparently in careless fettle, would say when he saw Hadley. Behind Kent's shoulder Dan whispered: "Lets' get out of here," nor did any of them care for the smell of boiled lamb for lunch, coming up the back stairs across the upper hall. Melitta and Francine were the first to turn back. They all went on tiptoe like thieves: which, in fact, was what Kent felt like.

And the first thing they encountered behind them, towering up in the hall as though it would block the way, was the vast presence of Dr. Fell.

Chapter 16

The Woman on the Slide

I HAVE just been looking at the famous Blue Room," said Dr. Fell amiably. "And I think you're wise; you're not really wanted downstairs now, any more than I am. Why not sit down for a minute?"

He indicated the open door of the den looking out towards the front, and shepherded them in with his stick like a master of ceremonies. Kent, with a vague and warm feeling that he was being made a fool of, followed in some perplexity. For a few seconds nobody commented. Then Melitta Reaper, who had gone by instinct towards the gas-fire, turned round and summed it up (if inadequately) in one explosive word:

"Well!"

"You never heard Hadley run out his masked batteries before, eh?" inquired Dr. Fell, settling his chins in his collar. "Yes, it's an improving process. And anyone who can break down Sir Gyles Gay's guard has my sincere admiration. I wonder if he's done it? I wonder if he will do it?"

Dan regarded the doctor with a wary eye. "You heard all that, did you?"

"Yes, indeed. I was as interested as you were. Of course

I knew what was up his sleeve—in fact, I helped to stuff the sleeve myself—but I wasn't sure when or how he would produce it. Harrumph."

He beamed on them.

"Then Gay is guilty after all?" demanded Dan, who seemed on the edge of an explosion that never quite came off. "I never thought it. By God, I never did: down inside. And Jenny seems to have made roaring fools out of all of us with her past history. But even if he did it, why should he?"

Dr. Fell grew quiet. He lowered himself on the edge of the window-seat.

"Would it make you feel any happier if you knew he was guilty? Eh?"

"It would clear the air," said Dan, with a quick glance. "Every time I go round a corner or open a door, I've been feeling I ought to look a leedle oudt. The trouble is that it's nothing you can hit back at."

"But is he guilty?" asked Francine quietly. "You don't think so, do you?"

The doctor considered this.

"I merely wish to know more about it, you see. Being afflicted with a real scatter-brain, I am full of a hideous curiosity about very small details, and tend to let the main picture go hang. Hah!" He folded his hands over the head of his stick. "And I'll tell you the impression I got from that little episode," he added impressively. "Supposing always that things are what they seem, on every major issue Gay was floored. On every minor issue he floored Hadley. You might be able to make out a case against him as a murderer. But you cannot make out a case against him as a practical joker. You see, I am one of those people who honestly think it is funny to paint a statue red; and I can see the force of it."

"What's that got to do with it?"

"Well, look here! If that drawer full of photographs had really contained a picture of him with Mrs. Kent, or anything of a betraying nature, why should he have waited until this morning to destroy it? Why wasn't it destroyed quietly instead of being joyously besprinkled with red ink to call attention to it? Burning would have done it in one minute, with nobody the wiser. Gay made those points himself. And they were so pertinent that Hadley had to dodge them.

"Then there is the question of the fun-fair photograph. Hadley was quite right: the ink on the back of that picture is at least a week old, and probably a good deal more. Now, psychologically, that rather unpleasant-sounding threat, 'There is one more to go,' was inspired by precisely the same motive as a joke. But the whole point of such a trick is its immediate execution and its full, fine flavour while you are in the mood. I will give you an example. Let us suppose that I am a member of the House of Lords. One day, musing dreamily on the back benches, it occurs to me what an excellent thing it would be if I were to inscribe a piece of paper reading, 'Just call me Snookums,' or 'Ready-made, £1 3s. 6d.'; to pin this paper to the back of the unsuspecting fellow-peer in front of me; and to study the interesting effect as he stalked out afterwards.

"Now, either I decide not to do this, or (if I am made of nobler stuff) to do it. There is only one thing I assuredly do *not* do. I do not write out the sign and put it carefully away in my pocket, saying to myself: 'I will hang this paper on old Plushbottom's back exactly a week from next Thursday, the proper time for it, and meanwhile I will keep it always ready at hand, guarded against all ravages.' Why on earth should I? It takes only a second to scribble: I may have a different mood or a brighter thought: it is an utterly useless sort of thing to carry about, and may cause surprise if it falls out at the dinner-table.

"Don't think I am not serious because I use such an example. Exactly the same principle applies here. But it applies much more strongly. If I am caught, all I risk from old Plushbottom is a dirty look or a punch in the nose. The person who wrote this, and kept it about him, risked the hangman. So why should Gay do any such nonsensical thing as write it weeks ago and keep it at hand for a possible opportunity?"

There was a silence.

"I've wondered," Francine said demurely, "just where in this affair you would live up to your reputation and really begin to lecture. But, I say, I don't see that it applies only to Sir Gyles. It applies to anybody else as well, doesn't it?"

"Exactly. And therefore I have wondered why Hadley has neglected to ask the only really important, the only really significant question about the photograph."

"What question?"

"Why, the question of who is *in* the photograph, of course!" thundered Dr. Fell, and brought his hand down on the head of the stick. "Or, more properly, who isn't in it. It's not very complicated, is it? If this means a menace at all, it means a menace to someone in the group. And if it follows the distortedly jesting symbolism which is the only symbolism it can have, the victim indicated is the person who is being pushed down the slide in the picture: the one who seems to be making a protesting gesture about it. But that is the only person in the group whom you can't see. Mr. Reaper's back is in the way, and hides the view." He paused, wheezing, and added mildly: "Well, that's what I'm here to find out. Do you remember that picture being taken? And, if so, who was being pushed down the slide?"

He looked at Dan, who nodded.

"That's smart," said Dan thoughtfully. "Yes, naturally I remember it. It was Jenny. She didn't want to go down the chute; afraid she'd show her thighs or something; but I gave her a push."

"But that means—!" cried Francine, with a sort of inspiration.

Dr. Fell nodded. "It was Mrs. Kent. I thought so. And that's the whole sad, ugly story. Do you begin to see why the message, 'There is one more to go,' was written a fortnight ago? Eh? When Rodney Kent was killed, the murderer scrawled this message on the back of the photograph and intended to leave it on the scene of the crime: just as later he sardonically scrawled, 'Dead Woman' when the threat was fulfilled. 'There is one more to go' *applied to Mrs. Kent*. But the murderer changed his mind about leaving it: this murderer you see, can never seem to make up his mind about anything—that's what has betrayed him. But he was wise in not leaving it. That would have been incautious. And the photograph-cum-message has been calmly reposing in this house, probably in Gay's desk, ever since: until it was hauled out for some very curious monkey-tricks this morning. Well, do these heavy cogitations lead you on to deduce anything else?"

He watched them with grim affability. Getting out his pipe, he unscrewed it and blew through the stem as though he were blowing a particularly seductive whistle. He was still whistling for something, certainly.

"In Gay's desk," muttered Christopher Kent. "The heavy cogitations show that Gay can't possibly be the murderer."

"Why not?"

"It's pretty plain. If the picture was intended to represent a threat to Jenny, the murderer knew that the person being pushed down the slide *was* Jenny. But you can't tell that just by looking at the picture. She's hidden. You can't even tell it's a woman. So the murderer must be somebody who is either in the picture or was there when it was taken; and that rules out Gay."

"Won't do," objected Dan, shaking his head with decisiveness. "I remember telling Gay who it was, or writing about it, or—here! Seems to me I've seen that picture more recently, somewhere—seen it—seen it————"

"Yes," chimed in Francine abruptly. "And so have I. We saw it————"

Their voices stopped: that mutual jump at thought seemed to defeat itself as they came into conflict, like two people trying to open a door from opposite sides. Dr.

Fell's whistle piped enticingly, and piped again. Nothing happened.

"It's no good," said Dan. "I've forgotten."

"H'mf, ha! Well, never mind. But still is there anything else that strikes you?" prompted the doctor.

"But still, about Gay's innocence," persisted Kent. "I'd like to—er—yes, I'd like to think he's guilty. All the same, it comes back to what we were arguing about a while ago: the blazing fathead who would keep the thing in his possession for a couple of weeks. You say you think it was probably in Gay's desk. But, if he were the murderer, wouldn't he have destroyed it?"

"Warm," said Dr. Fell. "Unquestionably warm. Therefore?"

"The only thing I can think of was that it was planted on him." Kent started; it was as though his sight went into another focus, and he could see the other face in the moon. "I believe I've got it! Listen. Someone planted it in the desk two weeks ago. But Gay hadn't found it because he hadn't looked in that drawer in the meantime. When he came back home to-day, he did look in the drawer, and discovered it among the other photographs. Now, listen!————"

"Chris," said Francine coldly.

"He was properly scared out of his Sunday trousers, because he wondered whether it would be found or whether somebody mightn't have seen it among his things already. It was all the worse because he really had been tied up with Jenny in the old days; and, for some reason, has persistently denied it. So he pretended to 'find' the photograph-and-message somewhere else. To cover up its sudden appearance, and pretend that the murderer had been up to funny business again, he tore up the rest of the pictures and sloshed them with red ink. He invented a story about donkeys' tails and pinched some silver out of his own drawer. That's it! It would explain both his guilty and innocent actions; his behaviour to-day and the rotten badness of his acting when————"

"Warmer and warmer yet, I think," beamed Dr. Fell. "But not, I am afraid, quite on the mark. It is significant that the only picture left completely intact did not contain a likeness of Mrs. Kent. True enough, I managed to dig one out of the mess, one that had not been effaced by tearing or ink; but————"

He stopped. There were heavy footsteps outside. Hadley, with a depressed-looking Wrayburn who was not now inclined to bounce, glanced in at the door. He gave the others a perfunctory good morning.

"May I see you alone for a minute, Fell?" he said.

When Dr. Fell had lumbered out, Hadley was careful to close the door. There was an uneasy silence, while they all looked at each other. Wrayburn, jamming his hands again into the pockets of his coat, attempted a light note in speech. His face was glossy.

"It may interest you to know," he remarked, "that I've just dropped one of the world's heavier bricks. The trouble being that I haven't got the remotest idea what it is. I made quite a study of psychology once; but I still don't know. I came back from the pub enlivened with a couple of pints, and charged back to the study, and said something asinine: still, I don't see how it could have been as asinine as all that. Hadley rather prefers the measles to me. Our host, after a conference with Hadley, is sitting downstairs with his head in his hands, looking like death. Poor old cuss: I felt sorry for him. I knew a fellow once, fellow named————"

"Shut up," said Dan briefly.

"Oh, all right. But fair's fair, and somebody ought to talk to me. If I'm still in disgrace for making a fool of myself over Jen————"

"Shut *up*," said Dan.

There was another silence.

"Yes, but all the same," argued Wrayburn, "isn't that what's making everybody so frosty? I had to get a couple of pints inside me to ask it; but what have I done that others haven't done? You know, I've been wondering about something I never thought of before. Just why did we call her *Jenny*? Is it natural? The ordinary diminutive for 'Josephine' is 'Jo' or even, save the mark, 'Josie.' But she always referred to herself as Jenny, you know. Would it be Jenny Wren? No, I've got a better idea————"

"What the devil are you burbling about?" asked Dan, out of the thick wool of reflection.

Both of them broke off when the door opened, and even as Kent remembered Dr. Fell's remark that his first interest in the case had been in names. It was Dr. Fell who opened the door. He was alone.

"I am afraid," he said gravely, "that some of us will not be staying to lunch. But—hum—before we go, will you do me one favour? Believe me, it is necessary. Will you all come up to the Blue Room with me for just a short time?"

There was a noticeable shuffling of feet when they went out. The long hall which bisected the house, of rough plastering and beamed ceiling, had a large but small-paned window at each end. The windows were of slightly crooked glass, and held a reflection of snow. Kent knew which door would be the door to the Blue Room, since the famous leather sofa stood near it. They were all awkward about getting through the doorway.

The room in which Rodney Kent had died was at the back of the house, its windows looking out over the garden wall and the elms of the churchyard. Like the other rooms it was large but narrow, papered in velvety dark-blue stuff which now merely succeeded in looking dismal. The furniture, old-fashioned without being ancient, was of the fashion of some seventy years ago: a great double bed in oak, its headboard and footboard pointed at the top but sloping down shallowly to a curve by the little posts, showed much scroll-work and aggressively dominated the room. A bureau, and a dressing-table with a very tall mirror, both had marble tops like the round table in the centre. There were two chairs trying to break their backs with straightness, and a wash-hand-stand (marble-topped) bearing blue-and-white china. Face towels hung neatly from a rack beside it. On the dark-flowered carpet near the table there was a broad greyish mark of scrubbing. Tasselled draperies on the windows were not drawn close enough to shut out a view of a headstone or two, or of the church tower, whose clock now made the glass vibrate by striking one. Dr. Fell stopped by the table.

"Is this room," said Dr. Fell, "except for one exhibit, now just as it was when Mr. Kent was murdered?"

It was Dan who answered yes.

"There were no signs of a struggle?"

"None."

"I have seen it in the police photographs," rumbled Dr. Fell, "but they did not show what I wanted. Will you get down on the floor as nearly as you can in the position the body was lying? . . . H'mf, thank you; that's fairly clear. Right side; head almost touching the left-hand caster of the bed; feet near the table. The bruise on the back of the head was rather high up, I take it?"

"Yes."

"Where was the towel?"

"Draped over the shoulder."

"As in Mrs. Kent's case?"

"Yes."

There was a heavy finality in question and answer which was like the striking of the clock.

"All right, there's that," growled Dan. "But what does it show, now you've seen it?"

"I'm inclined to think it shows a great deal," said Dr. Fell. "You see, up until this morning I wondered if I might be wrong. Now I know I must be right. At least we know one thing that was in the dark before. We know how Rodney Kent really died."

There was not as much light as there should have been, either in the room or in their minds. They stared at him.

"This is really a lot of most unnecessary nonsense," interposed Melitta, who had been sniffing as though she were going to cry. "You are perfectly well aware we *know* how poor Rodney died."

"The murderer was talking to him amicably enough," said Dr. Fell. "Then the murderer distracted his attention to something, so that he turned his head away. The murderer struck him on the back of the head with a weapon smaller than a poker. When he was unconscious, the murderer first strangled him to death and then beat his face with the poker. Yes. But what I said before is still true: we did not know, before, how he was really killed. It is not a riddle. You see, the murderer was someone who hated Rodney Kent very much. And therefore the murder of Josephine Kent————"

"Jenny," said Wrayburn.

"*Will* you be quiet?" requested Dan, turning in exasperation.

"No, I mean it," said Wrayburn. "We all know how attractive a—a woman Jenny was. Excuse me: I was going to say 'piece of goods,' but that doesn't fit. With all the inane crookedness in the little piece of goods's heart and soul, it still doesn't fit. There are women like that. They sort of—hold on."

"You're drunk," said Dan.

"Not on two pints. No. I'm myself. I was telling them, doctor (or trying to tell them) that it occurred to me a while ago how she came to be called Jenny. Of course she liked it. But she didn't coin the name for herself. No. It was some man who did that. God knows who he is or where he is—and if I had an idea, I wouldn't tell you. But he's middle-aged, the sort Jenny liked. She was the ideal Old Man's woman; or has someone said that? And he's probably not far off now, wondering why he killed her and what life will be like now that he hasn't got anything to hate."

"Oh, brace up," growled Dan. "We're all getting soft-headed. Why don't you begin on verse?"

"I will," said Wrayburn. He nodded gravely, his hands jammed into his pockets and his eyes on the window.

"Jenny kissed me when we met,
    Jumping from the chair she sat in,

Time, you thief, who love to get
    Sweets into your list, put that in!
Say I'm weary, say I'm sad,
    Say that health and wealth have miss'd me,
Say I'm growing old, but add————"

Chapter 17

The Questions of Dr. Fell

MURDER—" began Dr. Fell affably.

"Hold on," said Hadley, putting down his tankard and giving the doctor a suspicious look. "There is something in your expression,"—it was, in fact, one of fiendish and expansive pleasure—"which tells me you're about to begin a lecture. No! We don't want to listen to any lectures now. We've got too much work to do. Furthermore, when Gay gets here————"

Dr. Fell looked pained. "I beg your pardon," he rumbled with dignity. "So far from demeaning myself to lecture to you, I was about to submit myself voluntarily to the intolerable process of listening to you lecture. I gather that for once in your life you are inclined to agree partly with me about a case. At least, you are willing to give a sporting chance to a belief. Very well. I have some questions for you."

"What questions?"

It was nearly ten o'clock, and a rush of last-minute customers at the bar penetrated through from the other side of the door. Dr. Fell, Hadley, and Kent sat alone in the comfortable, raftered bar-parlour of the Stag and Glove.

There was ample living-accommodation at the pub, and they had taken rooms there for the night. This Kent knew; but it was all he knew. That day had consisted of cross-currents and mysterious conferences about whose import he had been given (and had asked for) no hint. Dr. Fell had disappeared for a long time during the afternoon. When the doctor returned, Hadley disappeared. There was also a conference with the long and saturnine Inspector Tanner. What was to be done about Sir Gyles Gay, or whether anything was to be done, Kent had not heard. He had not seen Sir Gyles after that episode of eaves-dropping. To get away from the atmosphere of tension at Four Doors, he and Francine had gone for a long walk in the snow; but the tension was still there, and the silver of a winter sunset looked merely angry. The only memory he carried away from it was of Francine, in a Russian-esque kind of astrakhan cap, sitting on a stile in her fur coat, with the low grey hills beyond.

That same tension had not even disappeared in the bar-parlour of the Stag and Glove. They were waiting for something. Yet Dr. Fell showed it much less than Hadley. It was a bitter night, though without wind. A big fire had been built in the bar-parlour, so big that its reflections were almost wild: they flickered on Dr. Fell as he sat enthroned in the window-seat, with the leaded panes behind him and a pint tankard in front of him, beaming with pleasure.

He took a deep pull at the tankard, and assumed an argumentative air.

"Murder, I was about to say," Dr. Fell pursued, "is a subject on which my views have been somewhat misunderstood: largely, I confess, because I have muddled them in the telling or in the enthusiasm of controversy. I feel inclined to rectify this, for a very good reason.

"I have admitted to a weakness for the bizarre and the slightly fantastic. I have, in fact, worn it as a badge of pride. That affair of the Hollow Man, and Driscoll's murder at the Tower of London, and that wild business aboard the *Queen Victoria*, will always remain my favourite cases. But this does not mean that I, or any rational person, would take pleasure in a mad world. It is precisely the opposite, in fact, of what I do mean: and this is the only reason why I mention it at all.

"Now, to the quietest human being, seated in the quietest house, there will sometimes come a wish for the possibilities or impossibilities of things. He will wonder whether the tea-pot may not suddenly begin to pour out honey or sea-water; the clock point to all hours of the day at once; the candle begin to burn green or crimson; the door to open upon a lake or a potato-field instead of a London street. Humph, ha. So far, so good. For a reverie or a pantomine it is all very well. But, regarded as a scheme of everyday life, it is enough to make a man shiver.

"I have enough difficulty in finding my eyeglasses as it is, even when they remain where I last put them down. If they suddenly went sailing up the chimney as I reached for them, my language would be difficult to control. The precise book I am looking for on a shelf has no need of magic to elude me. A malevolent spirit already dwells in my hat. When a person goes from Charing Cross to Bernard Street by underground, he can think himself jolly lucky if he gets to Bernard Street. But if he makes the same journey—say for an urgent appointment at the British Museum—and gets out at Bernard Street, and suddenly finds himself not in Bernard Street, but in Broadway or the rue de la Paix, he would be justified in thinking that matters had become really intolerable.

"Now, this principle particularly applies to criminal cases. It would be a very dull business to have a calm, sane criminal in a mad world. The criminal would not be interesting at all. You would do much better to go and watch the nearest lamp-post dance the rumba. Outside things must not act on the criminal: he must act on them. That is why the eternal fascination is to watch a slightly unbalanced criminal—usually a murderer—in a quite sane world.

"This is not, of course, to say that all murderers are

mad. But they are in a fantastic state of mind, or they would not be murderers. And they do fantastic things. It would be, I think, an easy thesis to prove.

"We all know, in any murder case, the questions *who*, *how*, and *why*. Of those three, the most revealing, but usually by far the most puzzling, is *why*. I don't mean merely the actual motive for the crime itself. I mean the why of certain other actions, eccentricities of behaviour, which centre round the performance of the crime. They torment us at the time: a hat placed on a statue, a poker removed from the scene of the crime when by all reason it should not have been removed. More often the why torments us even when we know, or think we know, the truth. Why did Mrs. Thompson write those letters to Bywaters? Why did Mrs. Maybrick soak the fly-papers in water? Why did Thomas Barlett drink the chloroform? Why did Julia Wallace have an enemy in the world? Why did Herbert Bennett make a sexual attack on his own wife? Sometimes they are very small points—three rings left behind, a broken medicine-bottle, an utter absence of blood on clothes. But they are fantastic, as fantastic as mad clocks or the real crimes of Landru; and, if we knew the answers to the why of them, we should probably know the truth."

"What questions?" inquired Hadley.

Dr. Fell blinked. "Why, the questions I've just been indicating to you. Any of 'em."

"No," said Hadley. "I mean what questions were you going to ask me?"

"Eh?"

"I've been patiently waiting to hear. You said you were not going to lecture; you said it was an honour you passed on to me, and that you had some questions to ask me. Very well: let's hear 'em."

Dr. Fell leaned back with an evil dignity.

"I spoke," he retorted, "by way of preface to the document I am going to lay before you. I have noted down here, on various small sheets, a number of questions. They are mostly 'whys'; any of the 'what' variety are of the why nature. All of them must be answered and answered satisfactorily, before we can say we have a complete solution to this case. Look here, we'll put this up to an umpire." He turned to Kent, and went on doggedly:

"Between last night and this morning, Hadley became convinced that Gay was our man. I was not so sure. I doubted it then, and I am now certain he isn't; but I was compelled to regard it as a possibility. Gay has been given a few hours' grace to answer certain matters: he should be along any minute. We are then—um—going to test a theory of mine, which Hadley regards with at least an open mind. It is now ten o'clock. By midnight we may have the real murderer. Now, both of you, how are the following questions to be answered? How do they fit in with Gay's guilt, or anyone else's guilt? It is your last chance to have a shot at it before the gong."

He spread out his multitudinous note-sheets.

"1. Why, on both occasions, did the murderer wear the costume of a hotel-attendant? An old question, but still a stimulating one.

"2. What happened to that costume afterwards?

"3. Why, on both occasions, was a towel used in strangling the victim?

"4. Why was it necessary for the murderer to hide his face from Josephine Kent, but *not* from Rodney Kent?

"5. Why did Josephine Kent first begin to wear a curious bracelet, having a square black stone cut with a Latin inscription, only a few hours before she was murdered?

"6. Why did she pretend she had never been in England before?

"7. What is the explanation of her words to Miss Forbes, in reply to the latter's question about whether the inscription on the bracelet meant anything? Her reply, you recall, was, 'Only if you're able to read it; that's the whole secret.'

"8. How did the murderer get into a locked linen-closet at the Royal Scarlet Hotel?

"9. Similarly, how did the murderer—supposing it to be some person other than Gay—get into a locked drawer in the desk of the study at Four Doors: a drawer to which only Gay had a key? You observe that the murderer seems able to go anywhere without difficulty.

"10. Why was a small amount of loose change stolen from Mrs. Kent's handbag, and also from the desk in Gay's study?

"11. It must be presupposed, in Mrs. Kent's case, that the murderer placed a pair of odd shoes outside the door of 707, and also hung the 'quiet' sign on it. If he wished to make sure of not being disturbed, this is understandable. But he wrote 'Dead Woman' in red ink, as though to call attention to his presence while he was there. Why?

"12. Perhaps the most intriguing 'why' in the whole case. We believe (I think correctly) that the murderer, dressed as a hotel-attendant and carrying his pile of towels, was admitted to room 707 by Mrs. Kent herself. Very well. At this time, we know from another witness—Wrayburn—Mrs. Kent's key to that room was in her handbag. But the next morning this same key was found by Wrayburn in the lock *outside* the door. You follow the fascinating double-turn of that? The murderer goes in. For some reason he takes the key out of the handbag, having found it there in his search of the room, and puts it in the outside of the door. Why?"

Dr. Fell put the sheaf of notes together and made a mesmeric pass over them.

"Eh bien?" inquired the doctor. "Or which of them appears to you the most interesting?"

"As umpire," answered Kent, "I should say the second one. In other words, what has happened to that infernal costume? It applies to everyone else as well as to Gay. But the uniform seems to have disappeared like smoke. The murderer couldn't have got rid of it in any way I can follow. He couldn't have tossed it out of the window, or burnt it, or hidden it: I suppose you took care of that. We seem to be reduced to the logical certainty that it must be in the hotel somewhere. Which would make it a genuine uniform, borrowed or pinched from somebody. It's unlikely that the murderer went roaming about looking for a uniform at random: it looks like collusion. And so we get back to the hotel again—like my case against the manager."

"And nothing else suggests itself to you?" inquired Dr. Fell, with a curious look at him. "Hasn't any member of your crowd ventured on a suggestion? Come! Surely there would be an ingenious theory somewhere. A theory from Wrayburn, for instance?"

"No, I've seen very little of him. There's been no suggestion except————"

He stopped, having made a slip.

"Except what?" asked Dr. Fell quickly.

"Nothing at all. It was only————"

"It was enough. At a conference of the powers, I think we had better hear it."

"Some far-fetched idea about the possibility of the murderer having been a woman. I suppose you hadn't thought of that?"

Dr. Fell and Hadley exchanged glances. The doctor chuckled.

"You wrong me," he said with offhand geniality. "It was one of the very first thoughts that did occur to me. You mean as regards the uniform, to make us postulate a man from the sight of it?"

"Yes. But you see the reason why it couldn't be so? I mean," said Kent, "the suède shoes. In the first place, it's unlikely that a woman would have taken two odd shoes; she'd have selected a pair. Second and more important, she'd never have put out suède shoes, which can't be polished. That means it was a man. I can realise—once I think about it—that you don't polish suède. But, if I had been the murderer and simply wanted to shove a pair of shoes outside the door, I question whether I should have thought of that at the time. I'd have picked up the first shoes that came handy, as the murderer evidently did."

"Unless," Dr. Fell pointed out with relish, "it was the double-twist of subtlety. The murderer is a woman. She wants us to believe it is a man; that, I think you will acknowledge, would be the whole point of the deception. Therefore she strengthens it by deliberately choosing a pair of shoes which no woman would choose."

Kent regarded his tankard moodily.

"I know," he admitted. "It's a very useful device in fiction, because you can prove very nearly anything by it. But, deep down inside me, I've never really believed in it. You remember the famous passage in which Dupin shows how it is possible to anticipate the way a person's mind will work, and uses as an example the schoolboy's game of evens or odds. You have a marble concealed in your left or your right hand, and the other fellow gets the marble if he picks the correct hand: so on as long as your marbles last. After estimating the intelligence or stupidity of your opponent, you put yourself mentally in his place, think what he would do, and win all the marbles. Well, it won't work. I've tried it. It won't work because, even if you have two minds exactly adjusted, the one thing they will differ over is what constitutes strategy. And, if you try any such games when the other fellow is probably only leaving it to chance, you'll build up such an elaborate edifice that you can't remember where you started. . . . Don't you honestly think that most murderers are the reverse of subtle? They haven't got time to be; and I should think they would be pretty nervous about being misunderstood."

Across the room, the private door leading to the stable-yard opened, and Sir Gyles Gay came in.

By the expression on his face, it was evident that he had heard the last few words and was turning them over in his mind. Cold air blew in with him, making the firelight dance. Ten had struck loudly from the church clock. They were turning the last customers out of the bar; you could hear a noise of firm-shutting doors and final good nights.

Gay wore a soft hat pulled down on his forehead, and a heavy herring-bone coat. He carried a stick under his arm.

"I am a little late, gentlemen," he said formally. "You must excuse me."

"Will you drink something?" asked Dr. Fell, reaching for the bell. "We're putting up here, you know, and we can order it."

"Yes. I know," said Gay, stripping off his gloves. He studied them. "You prefer to come here rather than accept my hospitality. Does this mean that you cannot dine with a man you mean to arrest?—In any case, I cannot accept yours."

"There's no question of arrest yet, Sir Gyles," Hadley informed him sharply. "You were asked to tell us certain things. For some reason you wanted a few hours to 'think it over.' At Fell's insistence, I was willing to agree. Have you anything to tell us now?"

Gay put his hat and stick on the table, smiling at the hat. Drawing out a chair, he sat down with some care; he seemed to be listening to the chimney growl under a cold sky.

"Yes, I am prepared to tell you the whole truth." He turned round. "I warn you that you will find it disappointing. After I have told you, you will, of course, take what steps you like. What I wanted was time for reflection. I wanted to remember whether I had ever met Mrs. Kent before in my life. Wait!" He held up his hand. "I am aware what your evidence shows, superintendent. I know that I must have met her in the sense that I must have encountered her. You would not believe me this afternoon, when I assured you that a woman could have come to England claiming acquaintance with me—in fact, many people do just that—and such a staggering number of persons go through an Under-Secretary's office in the course of a year that he would require a card-index mind to remember a quarter of them. The plain truth is still this: I do not remember that woman. I have gone over very carefully in my mind everything I can remember for the year in question. I was then living in Norfolk. With the aid of my diary I can almost reconstruct the whole year. Mrs. Kent does not fit into it anywhere. I never had any 'dealings' with her, of the sort you mean; and I shared with her no secret which would have obliged me to kill her. That is my last word."

There was a silence. Hadley rapped his fingers on the table with slow indecision. Such seemed the sincerity of the man's manner that Hadley was evidently impressed.

"And that's all you have to say?"

"No, not quite all. Now comes my confession. I did put that photograph among the towels in the bathroom; or, rather, I did not put it there, since I never went into the bathroom at all and only pretended to find it. I also ruined the inside of a drawer with red ink. But that is *all* I did."

For some obscure reason, Dr. Fell was rubbing his hands with pleasure. Hadley studied Gay, who returned his look with a sardonic smile.

"Oh, yes, it was quite asinine. Was that what you were going to say?"

"No," interposed Dr. Fell. "A more important matter. Did you tear up the other photographs?"

"I did not."

"Good. In that case," said Dr. Fell, "I think you had better tell us about it."

"It is to be conceded that my first and only venture into crime was not a success," observed Gay. This seemed to sting him more than anything else. He was prepared for an attack; he did not appear to be prepared for the casualness of his hearers. "I suffered from the delusion that, if I made the thing grotesque, it would therefore be believed. It is a weakness of mine, which————"

"We can omit that," said Hadley. "Why did you do it?"

"Because I was not going to be framed," retorted Gay, with the blood now in his shrunken face, and a certain violence about his dry fingers. He leaned forward. "If you can ever believe me again, listen to the sober truth. I had not your eye or flair for detecting that the ink on the back of that picture was so old; it occurred to me afterwards, and made me curse myself. I thought it had been put there this morning.

"We returned to Four Doors at eleven o'clock. Good. That at least you don't dispute. And there is something I fear you missed, for all your deductions. I don't keep a regular chauffeur. I hire the same man when he is needed. This man—Burns—drove us back from the station this morning. Consequently, I had to pay him. I was going to pay him out of the small-change-purse in the drawer of my desk. Shortly after we arrived, and the others had gone upstairs while Burns was taking the luggage off the grid, I went back to my study————"

"Wait. Is that drawer, as the maids say, usually kept locked?"

"It always is. I was not aware, however, that my in-quisitive staff knew it. I shall remember such possibilities when I commit my next crime. Very well. I went back to my study. As I passed through the lounge I heard some-body moving about in there. And, when I opened the door of the study, I was just in time to see somebody on his— or her—way out, slipping through the door at the head of the inner staircase."

"Who?"

"Ah, there we are. I honestly do not know. I want you to believe that. I was just in time to see the upper door closing."

"But noises, footsteps?"

"Yes, I believe there had been footsteps. But I can't describe them. I called out, and there was no answer. If I said I was not uneasy, I should be lying; I *was* uneasy, particularly as I had no idea what might be up. While I was thinking of this, I unlocked the drawer of the desk. I found all those photographs torn to pieces; and, on top of them, the picture announcing another—murder. Or so I interpreted it."

"How long had it been since you looked in that drawer last?"

"Probably three weeks."

"Go on," said Hadley quietly.

Gay's voice grew cold. "You are not a fool, my friend. You know what I thought and what I still think. It was a plain, barefaced attempt to saddle me with the blame for these crimes. You wish to know why I burst out against my guests this afternoon? That is the reason. Somebody had put that there. In a very short time somebody would have had it 'found.' That is how some genial friend repays hospitality." His fingers twitched, and he put them flat on his knees. "Wasn't it obvious? I am the only person with a key to that drawer. Yet someone else had got one. How, I don't know. Why, I know only too well. If you can think of any better evidence of a premeditated attempt to throw the blame elsewhere, I should be interested to hear it."

"And so————"

"Well, there is an ancient truism about beating someone to the punch. Possibly I acted like a fool. I don't know. I know that I was more furious in that moment than I can remember being since the days of my encounters with official stupidity in the Government. I compressed several years' rage into my feelings then, nor have I even yet recovered my usual child-like good temper."

He exhibited very little sign of child-like good temper. Yet it seemed evident that he sincerely believed in this quality as belonging to himself. Nobody commented; and, after a wheezy breath Gay went on:

"If I had known who put the picture in the drawer ————"

"A picture," interrupted Dr. Fell dreamily, "on which the message had been printed two weeks ago."

"And a fact," replied Gay, "which I did not know. There was certainly a prowler in my study just after eleven, and up to no good. I repeat: if I had known who did it, I should have been after him with great pleasure. I should have tried my hand at counter-framing. But I did not know, and I was unwilling to make a guess which might be wrong. You see, I am more charitable in several ways than the real murderer. But above all I was exceedingly curious to mark the effect if I should fight back with a return stroke against 'somebody.' Perhaps it would have been more sensible to have got rid of the picture and the torn fragments. But I was not willing to have the matter drop altogether. Being innocent, I wanted the police to find such clues. But, by God, gentlemen, I was unwilling for the police to find such clues in my desk!"

"It didn't occur to you to come to us and tell the truth?"

"It did not," said Gay quite simply. "That was the only course which did not occur to me."

"Go on."

Gay cocked his head on one side. Amusement crept into his wizened face, the sort of amusement which had been absent from it for some hours.

"I concede that I was a trifle too spectacular. The donkey's tail, too, was an error; and I am not sure that I gained much by ruining the inside of the drawer with red ink. But I wanted to draw attention to it. Believe me, gentlemen, there was absolutely no thought in my mind of making the snapshots in the drawer unrecognisable. I admired, even when I felt my hair rise on my scalp, the ingenuity with which you dove-tailed these bits of evidence to-day. Can you understand this?—that I was stunned into a kind of detached interest, a contemplation of myself, by the way in which you spun a case out of nothing? I was Pickwick listening to Sergeant Buzfuz, and hearing my chops and tomato sauce used against me."

He paused.

"I think that's all I have to say. You understand, I did not have to create a prowler. There really was someone in my study. You have got a valuable piece of evidence, even if you got it in a way for which I am heartily sorry. I have no dark and terrible secrets connected with the past of Mrs. Kent. There is my story; you may believe it or not; and (just between ourselves) be damned to you."

Hadley and Dr. Fell looked at each other. Hunching

his neck into the upturned collar of his overcoat, Gay blinked at the fire.

"You don't find the atmosphere so hostile now, do you?" asked Dr. Fell amiably.

"Well—no. To tell the truth, no."

"Just a question or two," suggested the doctor, as Hadley scowled at his note-book. "Can you think of any reason why this person should have torn up all the pictures in that drawer?"

"No. I cannot. *That* could not be for throwing suspicion on me. Or at least I don't see how."

"H'mf, no. Would it be easy to have got a duplicate key to the drawer?"

"I shouldn't have thought so. It's something of an elaborate and intricate lock, for a desk drawer. But it's quite possible, since it was done. I am not exactly aware how these things are done. From a wide acquaintance with sensational fiction, I know that it is customary to use wax or soap; but if somebody handed me a sheet of wax or a bar of soap and said, 'Get on with it,' I don't think I should know how."

"You say you heard footsteps when someone was in your study. Light or heavy footsteps?"

"The best I can do," answered Gay, after reflection, "is the old and unhelpful 'medium' of this whole affair."

"It could not have been one of the maids?"

"Why should it be? They would have told me."

"Has your staff of servants been with you for a long time?"

"Oh, yes. They came with me from Norfolk. I—er—well, yes, I trust them absolutely, in so far as I trust anybody in this world."

"I think you told us you were living in Norfolk at the time Mrs. Kent was in this country?"

"Yes, if I have the dates down right."

"H'mf. Well—just at a guess, Sir Gyles, have you any notion as to who is responsible for all this?"

Gay shook his head without taking his gaze from the

fire. An odd smile twisted his mouth. "That is your business. Mine, too, I acknowledge; but in a different way. Will you answer me, truly and freely, one question?"

Hadley was cautious, and interposed before Dr. Fell could speak. "All depends on what it is, Sir Gyles. What question?"

"Why," said Gay, still without taking his eyes from the fire, "why have you two got a police-officer watching Miss Forbes?"

Chapter 18

Hands Across a Grave-stone

KENT remembered the thump as he put his own tankard of beer down on the table. He glanced quickly round the little group; and he realised by the quiet that Hadley and Dr. Fell had taken the words with the utmost seriousness.

"What makes you think that?" Hadley asked.

"I see," said Gay, half humorously. "Don't you ever give anybody information on any subject whatever? When Miss Forbes and Mr. Kent here went for a walk this afternoon, you had a man following them. I am not certain who it was, but it was one of the sergeants I saw at the Royal Scarlet Hotel. When they came back to Four Doors, he followed Miss Forbes. I'm inclined to suspect that the reason why you—hum—lured me here to the pub to-night, instead of coming to my home, was for the purpose of getting a man inside. I don't object. But if my house is to be used for any purpose, I think I have a right to know what is going on. The place seems to be full of policemen. There was another in the bar to-night. You can't expect to disguise things like that in a village, you know; and I've been wondering what is going on."

"You'd better tell him, Hadley," said Dr. Fell. "I've

been urging it all along. He could give us a lot of help; and, if things went wrong in any way, he might wreck the plan."

"Why," interposed Kent, "have you been having Miss Forbes watched?"

Hadley smiled without enthusiasm. "Not for the reason you think. Just to see that she doesn't get into any trouble. As she might." He turned to Gay. "Very well. The whole story is that, with luck, we may get the murderer to-night."

Gay whistled two notes and sat up. "Interesting—also attractive! Where and how?"

"Your house is unusual," said Hadley. "It really lives up to its name. Unlike Seaview and Parkside, it really does have four doors, one on each side of the house. All those doors must be watched. If Fell is right, we hope to meet someone coming out of the house by one of those doors in the middle of the night."

"Leaving the house? Why?"

"That," said Hadley, "is as far as the story goes now."

Gay looked puzzled. "But I still don't follow this. If you merely caught somebody sneaking out of the house in the middle of the night, would that, *per se*, prove it was the murderer? I have always thought"—he frowned in a meditative manner—"that, when these traps were laid and someone is caught suspiciously prowling, the person caught is almost too ready to break down and admit his guilt. Suppose he were to fold his arms and say, 'This is a frame-up; I refer you to my solicitors?' Where would your evidence be?"

"We've got reason to hope," said Hadley, "that it would still exist." His tone changed. "What I'd like to ask of you, Sir Gyles, is this. If you should happen to see a police-officer in the house: in fact, no matter what you do see or however suspicious it appears: do nothing and say nothing to anybody. Let the household go to bed in the ordinary way, just as usual. At some time early in the morning you may be waked up; but by that time, if we have any luck, it may be all over. Will you promise that?"

"With pleasure. I—er—take it you accept my own story as being true?"

"If I didn't accept it, would I confide this to you?"

"I don't know," said Gay, with candour. "However, you can depend on me. If I scent the presence of dirty work, I also like the presence of dirty work. Good night, gentlemen. I hope I shall see you soon."

He pulled down his soft hat on his forehead, got up, and put the stick under his arm. By the door—the same door as that by which he had entered—he studied them for a moment before he made a brief salute and slipped out. The night, which remained cold and almost absolutely still, sent in hardly a chill after him.

Hadley looked at his watch.

"I'd better see the landlord," the superintendent commented. "We want none of *that* interference."

And he reached up and switched off the electric lights.

While the uncertain firelight rose up, and they heard Hadley blundering out into the bar, Kent looked at Dr. Fell. Dr. Fell drained his tankard without comment; he seemed to be listening for the sound of the church clock, which should be close on the half-hour.

"Am I allowed to know what's up?" demanded Kent, yet speaking in little above a whisper. "What's this about Francine? I've got a right to know————"

He could not see the doctor clearly, though he heard the wheezy breathing. "Miss Forbes," declared Dr. Fell, "is in no danger of being hurt. Set your mind easy about that."

"But if she's in any danger I want to————"

"H'mf, yes. That, I believe, is a part of the idea."

"I mean, I want to be on the spot to————"

"No," said Dr. Fell. "Never again. I allowed it in that case of the Eight of Swords; and I swore a mighty oath that it should never happen again. It merely meant tragedy. It's a professional's job, my lad; and a professional's doing it. But you can make yourself useful, if you will. We want two men on each of the four doors, and we're short-handed. If you like, you can share the watch. Without stretching the matter in the least, I can tell you that we may run foul of someone who is apt to turn infernally nasty if certain schemes go wrong."

The church clock struck the half-hour.

Hadley returned with the tankards filled. Very few words were passed. Sitting down close to the fire, so that he could keep his eyes on his wrist-watch, Hadley bent over it. Nor were there many sounds except the scrape of pewter on wood, the watch ticking, and the fire: which had turned to a red-glowing bank. The quarter-hour rang, and then the hour. Northfield was asleep.

At a few minutes past eleven Hadley, who had been going from one window to the other to pull back the curtains, moved across to the door opening on the stable-yard. He opened the door wide and stood peering out. A patch of cold crept over the floor like a carpet, widening against the walls, while the smoke of Hadley's breath blew back over his shoulder. There was a creak in the stable-yard, and a whisper.

"Tanner!"

"Superintendent?"

"Men in position?"

"All ready, sir."

"Hold on."

Hadley moved out on to a creaking board, and there was the mutter of a conference. When he returned he picked up his own overcoat from a chair. He faced Kent.

"Your beat," he said, "will be with the inspector at the back door of the house. He's got his instructions, so you just follow the leader. You're not to go into the back garden. Miss Forbes's room overlooks the back, and you might be seen if the moon should come out. Stay just outside the iron gates to the back garden, on the edge of the churchyard. You'll have a clear view of the back door from there. Haven't got the wind up, have you?"

"I don't think so."

"In any case—" Hadley bent down, picked up the poker from the hearth, and handed it to him. "In any case, just take this along. You're a private citizen, so you can be armed. All right."

Hadley went with him to the door. Inspector Tanner was waiting, his flat cap looking belligerent; but he muttered little beyond issuing directions. They moved out quietly through a gate opening on the green.

Or, at least, Kent supposed it must be the green. It was his first experience of that puzzling, disquieting phenomenon, the complete pitch-blackness and silence of an English village at night. We use terms loosely. Few urban streets, few parts of the remotest town in the deadest hour of the night, are ever without *any* light or *any* sign of movement. There is always someone awake. The African veldt is lighter and more aware than this core of a well-populated district, a village. Venture into one after nightfall, and you will never know you are there until you are in the middle of it: a house is as startling as a ghost. Your impression is that people must fall into a drugged sleep at nightfall. Even when a public-house remains open until ten o'clock, the blinds are so sealed or the lights so remote that it looks as dead as the rest; it might be a public-house in Pompeii.

Though he walked slowly beside the inspector, Kent heard his own footsteps sound with such distinctness on the frosty ground that he might have been making footprints for trackers to follow. It was a night of smoky cold, in which you could smell mist without seeing any of it. Later there might be a moon. Their own heavy footfalls went ahead of them round the green. There did not seem, Kent thought, to be any dogs in Northfield.

Instead of going down the dim road past the church Inspector Tanner softly opened the lych-gate of the church itself. Kent followed him through under the great pillars of yew. The poker had grown blistering cold in his hand; he was gripping it too tightly; so he thrust the end of it into his deep overcoat pocket and crooked his arm round it. They moved down a flagged path, still slippery with snow, and round the church. Beyond it was so dark that each of them kept a hand out in front. Then they went into the churchyard, which sloped down with some abruptness and in whose maze flat stones made obstructions.

"Which way?"

"Down here. Look sharp!"

Great elms were materialising out of the sky in front of them. Beyond ran a wall pierced by iron gates, and he could see a faint light. Evidently someone at Four Doors was still awake.

Kent, who had had it drilled into him as a boy that you must never step on a grave, had been doing some unusual walking to avoid them. He barked his chilled knuckles several times on the stones. Then, just as they stopped on the edge of the churchyard, the light at the house went out. But his eyesight was now growing accustomed to the dark; he had lost that naked feeling such as is experienced on groping into a dark theatre, and losing the usher with the flashlight half-way down the aisle. He could see a sort of shine on the iron gates. Beyond that, the white window-frames and white back door of the house loomed up with some clarity. He could even pick out the line of the chimneys. If it were not so infernally cold———

The church clock struck the quarter-hour.

He was leaning, incongruously, against the headstone of a grave, only a few feet from the gates. Objects were now assuming a night-time clarity; he made out the steps to the back door, the dust-bin, and all white paint seemed to shine. But he wished he had brought a pair of gloves. His hands felt raw, and a shiver went through him. "Walking over somebody's grave" was the thought that occurred to him: it was the same sort of feeling.

All the same———

What was going on in that house? Who or what did they expect to slip out of a door, when only the church clock was allowed to talk? He put the poker, which was beginning to irk him, down in the rimy grass by the headstone. Bending forward, he made certain that the rear gates had been left unlocked. They creaked softly, and he drew back. It seemed to be the consensus of opinion (good old sober phrase) that there was no danger. But there must be danger inside, or they would not have surrounded the place with a ring of guards. If they had let him go in to Francine, he would have felt better. The roles (he mused) were reversed. Those inside the house, those tucked into stolid steam-heated walls, were the persons who ran a risk; the people outside, in loneliness where there was no cover, were safe.

After touching the padlock on the gates, he crouched back to the headstone. He would get a crick in the back if he stood long like this. Sit down? That would be the easiest thing. The damp headstone, worn to a wafer by time, was scrolled along the top like the bed in the room where Rodney Kent had died. His fingers brushed it as he bent down to pick up the poker. And the poker was not there.

The poker was not there. His fingers groped in sharp patches of snow. He squatted down, moving his hand wide. He remembered just where the end of it had lain, and it was not there.

"What the devil—?" he whispered to his companion beside him.

"I have it," whispered the other voice.

Kent turned round in relief. His companion was standing just where he had stood when they took up their posts, still motionless and large. Kent's eyes, accustomed to the gloom, could not pick out details. He saw the blue coat, no overcoat being worn; he saw the silver buttons shining dimly; and he saw something else.

It was not an inspector of police who had been walking through the churchyard with him.

Then it moved. The noise of the poker in the air was a kind of *whup*; it sang in brittle air, and struck the headstone as it was intended to strike a head. Kent had not dodged: he had stumbled, or so he always remembered it afterwards. He heard his own knee strike the ground. He rolled, and bounced to his feet like an india-rubber cat, as the poker rose up and fell again. Then they were standing, breathing hard, with the headstone between them.

Now it seemed a very long time, minutes by the church

clock, before any other movement was made. The longest adjustment is an adjustment of thought. In front of him, at not much more than arm's length, was the person they had been looking for. How this person had come there was not the question. The question was what to do. It never once occurred to Kent to cry out and call for help. And this was not bravery, for he was frightened green and he could hear a thick beating in his ears. It is possible that he did not have time to think. He stood looking at the other through the mist of his own breath.

"Put that down," he whispered. "Who are you? Put it down."

The other did not reply. Instead he began to edge round the headstone.

"Put it dow———"

If it had been a longer weapon that his adversary carried, he might have risked a grab at it. But it was too suitable for murder at close quarters; that last blow, if it had landed, would have smashed his skull like an orange. As the indistinct figure shuffled round, Kent moved back. His adversary was moving the poker a little, like a boxer about to feint. Then he struck again—and overshot his mark.

Both were turning at the time. Kent felt no more than a faint burning sensation, as of pins-and-needles, in his thumb: which then seemed to be warm and soft and numb. It was the mound of the grave itself, wiry and slippery underfoot, which tripped the other in his forward drive. His body struck the headstone. His feet, off-balance, clawed for support. Thrown almost against Kent's chest, his neck was across the stone; and the poker rattled on stone as he tried to swing it. Kent, out of sheer fear, struck once the worst blow he knew. He struck with the closed fist, in the form of the rabbit-punch, across the back of the neck; and it caught the back of his adversary's neck on the gravestone as you might catch iron on an anvil.

Even as he heard the poker drop and roll in wiry grass, there was another and more rapid rustling. Three men came into the dimness under the bare elms; and two of them carried flashlights. He heard them breathe. And he recognised the heavy but not quite steady voice of Superintendent Hadley.

"No, don't call me anything," Hadley said. "I didn't turn him loose on you. I didn't know he was anywhere near here. The swine stole a march on us————"

He paused, drawing in his breath. Kent coughed, and kept on coughing for a moment.

"Whatever happened," he said, "*I've* probably committed the murder this time. There wasn't anything else to do. You'd better see if his neck's dislocated."

The figure had slipped down and rolled like the poker. Hadley bent over it as more heavy footsteps sounded, and Dr. Fell wheezed into the group.

"No, he's all right," said Hadley. "He'll be in proper shape to have it dislocated in another way. But he nearly got just about what he gave his victims. All right, boys. Roll him over. Make sure nothing has fallen out of his pockets."

Kent stared at his late adversary as the flashlight moved, and turned round again.

"Is that—?" he said.

Dr. Fell, who had been mopping his forehead with the bandana, got his breath. He ran the bandana through his fingers, blinked, and looked down in a disconsolate way.

"Yes," he said. "That's the real murderer, of course— Ritchie Bellowes."

Chapter 19

The Gentler Crime

AND he wore—?" asked Kent.

At the head of the lunch-table Dr. Fell leaned back expansively.

"He wore," said Dr. Fell, "for reasons which will be indicated, the spare uniform of an inspector of police; which is so exactly like that of the liftmen at the Royal Scarlet Hotel that I have sometimes been tempted to address them as 'officer.' You have not forgotten the description of the liftmen's uniform as given us by Hardwick? 'A short single-breasted blue coat high at the neck; silver buttons, shoulder epaulets.' You observe that they were the only uniformed men who wore *short* coats, like a police officer: the others had frock coats or tails. The only true and honest witness who had seen our phantom in blue (Mr. Reaper) said that he believed the phantom wore a short coat. Thus the field was tolerably narrow in drawing analogies. But all Ritchie Bellowes wanted anybody to notice (and calculated on anybody noticing) was the blue coat and silver buttons. You will see."

"But how did he get out of clink?" roared Dan. "And why———?"

To say that an atmosphere of tension had lifted from this group: to say that a hobgoblin had drifted away and a bad smell faded, would be to understate the case at Four Doors on that frosty morning of the second of February. Melitta Reaper was said to have cried all night, a proceeding which was generally thought to reflect great credit on her. A brittle sunlight showed at the windows of the dining-room, where Gay had provided a lunch that was something in the nature of a celebration. Kent's thumb, it is true, had given him a bad night after catching the weight of the poker in Ritchie Bellowes's hand; but he was too easy with wine and relief to be troubled about that. Dr. Fell presided at the head of the table like the Ghost of the Christmas Present. And Dr. Fell, wagging his cigar drowsily, said:

"Ahem. Yes, I am inclined to lecture, if only because I have so far had no opportunity satisfactorily to oil the wheels of my eloquence. But there is another and (if this can be credited) even more cogent reason. Academically, I like this case. It affords one of the better opportunities for gathering up pieces of evidence into one whole; and, to such of you as enjoy deductive orgies, it should prove of interest. The superintendent and I," he waved his cigar towards Hadley, "followed its tail together. If it is I who tell you about it, this is not because I have any great farsightedness; it is simply that I am the more enthusiastic and inexorable talker.

"The most satisfactory way to approach it will be to outline it to you from the first as we followed it. Now, when I went to the Royal Scarlet Hotel at first, I had only one firm idea in the welter: that Mrs. Josephine Kent was not what she seemed. Hadley, in his sharp brush with our host yesterday, outlined the reasons for investigating this; they began with the scuffed condition of the lettering on the battered trunk, and they did not end with some suggestive information we received from South Africa. They woke certain doubts to ally with others.

"At the inception, again, I had little doubt of Ritchie

Bellowes's story. The police were fairly sure he was not guilty; there were too many physical objections to it—notably his paralysed left arm, which would have made it impossible for him to have strangled Rodney Kent. Again, he certainly was very drunk at two o'clock when he was found. If he had committed a murder at midnight, he would not have gone to sleep on a sofa outside his victim's door and waited to be found at two o'clock. Again, the weapon was missing. Again, there was a complete lack of motive. Finally, I was inclined to credit his story of the 'man in the hotel-attendant's uniform' simply because it was too preposterous not to be true. This is not merely a congenital sympathy with the preposterous. I mean that it was not the *sort* of story which would do a deliberate liar any good. If Bellowes were the murderer, he would try to shield himself with a lie; but presumably not a lie so (apparently) meaningless and unrelated to the whole affair. At first glance the story of the hotel-attendant had no point unless it were true. If he were a liar, he might say he had seen a burglar in the hall: but not that he had seen an Arctic explorer, a ballet-dancer, or a postman.

"Thus, when we first came to the hotel, I was inclined to believe the murderer was actually in the hotel. More specifically, that it was one of the guests on the seventh floor. Then two points appeared to trouble me very badly about this.

"First, the utter disappearance of that uniform. Where in blazes had it got to? It was not hidden, burnt, or tossed out of a window; we should have found it, or traces of it. If a guest wore it, how was it conveyed into limbo afterwards? You see, it amounted to that. You might say that a guest was in collusion with an employee of the hotel, and had borrowed a real uniform for use in the masquerade, to return it later. Even if this were true, how was it spirited out of Wing A? The only entrance to that wing was watched all night, and up until the time the police arrived, by the three men working on the lift. Was it dropped out of a window by the guest, to be picked up in

Piccadilly or in the air-well by an employee in the conspiracy? This seemed unlikely; and yet the uniform was gone.

"Second, a circumstance which brought much light. Musing, it occurred to me that a door had been found strangely open. This was the spring-locked door of the linen-closet. Now, we had heard much of these varied new locks, which cannot be opened from the outside by any unauthorised person. The linen-closet was locked by the maid on the night before. It was found open in the morning. Therefore (and not unnaturally) ominous sideways glances were directed towards Mr. Hardwick, the manager.

"But my own mind is of a simpler nature. Nobody could have unlocked that door from outside. But anybody on earth can open a spring-lock from *inside*. You turn the little knob on the lock; and the thing is done. It therefore interested me to glance into the linen-closet. H'mf, ha. By the way, has anybody else here done that?"

Kent nodded.

"Yes. I looked in there when the superintendent sent me down to get Melitta," he answered, with a vivid recollection of the place. "What about it?"

"Good," said Dr. Fell. "Now, at the beginning of the whole case, we brought up the various ways by which an outsider could have got in and out of the hotel without being seen by the men working on the lifts. These were (1) climbing up and down the face of the building into Piccadilly; (2) climbing up and down the face of the building from inside the air-well; (3) by means of the fire-escape outside the window at the end of the corridor. All these were ruled out as 'so unlikely as to be very nearly impossible.' There were obvious objections to (*a*) and (*b*). As for (*c*), this would have been a broad highway of entrance and exit—an obvious lead, a dazzler of an easy way—but for one apparently overpowering fact. The locked window guarding the fire-escape was stuck and could not be opened; hence a sad eye passed over (*c*). But we looked into the linen-closet and got a shock. You," he turned to Kent, "looked in there on the morning after. What did you see?"

"A window," said Kent.

"Open or shut?"

"Open."

"H'mf, exactly. Since it would be a nuisance to take you back to the hotel in order to demonstrate this," pursued Dr. Fell, "we might just glance at the plan of Wing A. You see the window in the linen-closet. You also see that the commodious fire-escape outside comes within a foot—one foot—of that same window. A man would scarcely have to be a steeple-jack in order to stand on the fire-escape and climb in through the window.

"I stared. I saw. I was uneasy.

"For values had shifted backwards. Unless Hardwick or the maid had opened it, that linen-closet door could not have been unlocked from outside in the corridor: not by a guest, that is. And, if Hardwick or the maid opened it, they must first have got upstairs past the lift-workers: which they did not do. Therefore the linen-closet door was unlocked from inside the linen-closet itself, by the simple process of turning the knob. Therefore the murderer came into the linen-closet from outside. Therefore the murderer was (not to be too painfully repetitive about it), an outsider."

Dr. Fell put his large elbows on the table, seemed in danger of scratching his head with the lighted end of the cigar, and frowned at his coffee-cup.

"I hesitated, let me confess, on the brink of the deduction. I was not amused. Cases are not solved by one flying leap. The man who says, '*Only* this can be true; there can be no other explanation,' excites my admiration as much as he inspires my regret. But of the twelve major queries to be answered—the queries I propounded last night to Hadley and Christopher Kent—this theory would take care of two. These were (7), 'How did the murderer get into a locked linen-closet at the Royal Scarlet Hotel?', and (2) 'What happened to the costume afterwards?' The answers being, 'He came in from outside,' and 'He walked away in the uniform when he left the hotel.'

"But, if it might—might, you understand—be an outsider, what outsider? Our little coterie was all under this roof. Every person who had been at Four Doors on the night of the first tragedy, the night the uniformed figure had first been seen, was in the Royal Scarlet Hotel that night; and therefore segregated. Everybody— H'mf, well, not quite. Ritchie Bellowes was missing, for instance. And this for a good reason, since he was locked up at the police-station. In any case, he had never met Mrs. Josephine Kent—for she had not come to Northfield.

"This had been a fascinating query from the first: why did she rush away to riot in the home of her aunts? Why did she refuse to go to Northfield at any time, even after her husband had been murdered? We had then reason to suspect, and shortly afterwards reason to know, that she was not what she seemed. She had been in England for well over a year; she had returned to South Africa with a packet of money; but this visit she carefully concealed, and swore she had never been here before in her life. Why? Now note: she makes no real objection to travelling: she makes no objection to coming to London: she makes no objection to meeting people (such as Sir Gyles Gay, for example); but she will not *go to Northfield*. In a woman whose real character we were already beginning to see, that attack of 'utter nervous prostration' after her husband's death seemed to be overdoing it.

"This, then, was what one part of our simple minds registered. The other part of our minds registered still another question.

"As troublesome as the uniform was the murderer's consistent weakness for towels. Why, in the case of both murders, was a towel used to strangle the victim? As I pointed out to Hadley, it is assuredly a cumbersome and clumsy kind of attack, an unnatural kind of attack. Above all, it was unnecessary. The murderer assuredly did not use it for fear of leaving finger-prints: he would know what anybody knows, that you cannot leave finger-prints on human flesh, and that the marks of hands on a throat cannot be identified. We also know, from the universal lack of finger-prints on furniture or other surfaces, that the murderer must have worn gloves. We are therefore faced with the incredible spectacle of a murderer who uses *both* gloves and a towel to avoid leaving marks. And that will not do. We must look for another reason.

"Kindly note, to begin with, that Mrs. Kent was not strangled. No. She was put into the Iron Maiden trunk, and it was closed on her throat, with the towel wrapped round her throat so that the edges should not cut: so that it should leave bruises on the throat *like* strangulation. But why again, such a clumsy device? It would have been much simpler to have strangled her in the ordinary way, as (presumably) Rodney Kent had been strangled. This unnaturalness plus the unnaturalness of the towel began to make such a tower of inconsistencies that there must be method in them. What, off-hand, would that Iron Maiden device suggest to you?

"Why, it would suggest that the murderer was of too weak strength for ordinary strangulation—or a person who had the full use of only one arm.

"The full use of only one arm, the right arm.

"What else? The body is propped inside the trunk. The trunk is supported and propped against the left leg; the right hand pulls it powerfully together against that support of the murderer's left leg, and the thing is done.

"But this did not square with the murderous two-handed grip which was used on Rodney Kent. It seemed to put the matter out of court as a fantastic suggestion, until I reflected dimly on the subject of Rodney Kent's murder. Hadley had already described the furniture in the Blue Room here at Four Doors. The matter was not a certainty until I came here and saw for myself, but I could envision the scene. I have seen furniture of a much similar type. Just recall the foot-board of the bed. It is a heavy piece of work, pointed at the top and sloping down shallowly to a curve or round depression by the little posts. Thus."

He took up a pencil and drew rapidly on the back of an envelope.

"Like, you might say, the neck-piece or collar of a guillotine, in which the condemned man's neck lies. Rodney Kent was lying with his head almost touching the leg of the bed. Suppose the neck of an unconscious man has been put sideways into that homely guillotine. Suppose that neck were wrapped in a face-towel: not a bath-towel, which might be too thick and woolly to leave the proper sort of marks. Suppose the murderer stands over him; and, with one hand gripping one side of the neck, lets the other side be gripped by that broad curve of the wood, the victim's windpipe being pressed against the edge. When the murderer's work is finished—the marks being neatly blurred and made unrecognisable *as fingers* by the towel —you will have bruises in evidence of a crushing two-handed grip which went round both sides of his throat.

"Once might be coincidence. Twice could not be. It would explain the use of the towels. It would indicate that the murderer was a man who had the complete use of only one arm.

"Humph, hah! Well! I began to see the indications expanding like the house that Jack built, into (*a*) the murderer came from outside the Royal Scarlet Hotel; (*b*) he wore a uniform and went away in it; (*c*) he is, to all intents and purposes, one-armed. The only person who corresponded to this description was Ritchie Bellowes. The very thing which had so operated in his favour at first— namely, the partially paralysed left arm—was the thing which now rebounded against him. Everything began to rebound against him, once you considered. For, even if you still believed him to be ruled out as a suspect because he had been locked up at the police-station, the next connection was clear to any simple straightforward mind: I mean the connection between police-stations and blue uniforms.

"This point I indicated a while ago. 'A short single-breasted blue coat high at the neck, silver buttons, shoulder epaulettes.' Ladies and gentlemen, you have seen that costume on the streets every day; if the connection did not occur to you, it was because the prowling intruder was without any head-covering. If I wished (as I do not) to coin a bad riddle, I should cryptically inquire: When is a policeman not a policeman? And I should answer, amid universal groans, but quite sincerely: When he is without his helmet. This astonishing difference will have been noted by anyone who has ever gone to a trial and seen the police in court without their hats. Wearing their own hair, they are a different race. They look like attendants: as a matter of fact, in that capacity they *are* attendants.

"But to return. Ritchie Bellowes was locked up at the police-station. It was not reasonable to think that he said to his jailers: 'Hoy! Let me out of here and lend me a spare uniform, will you? I've got to go to London and commit a murder; but I'll be back later to-night.''

"Nevertheless, we begin to reflect on one feature of national life—the village police-station. Like the village bank, it sometimes surprises observers. It is not a great grim temple of stone, erected in some city for the especial purpose of housing a hundred drunks overnight. No; it is an ordinary converted house (like the one at Northfield) such as you and I might live in. It has been taken over for the purpose of turning it into a police-station. But somebody had to build it. And, whispering back through the halls of consciousness, we hear the information that Ritchie Bellowes's father, the grand old man and 'character,' was a builder—who, as Hadley had informed me, had put up half the modern houses in the whole district.

"We heard of old Bellowes's taste for doing the work with his own hands. We heard in particular of his very particular sense of humour, much of which has been twisted and burnt to more ugly purposes into the soul of his son. We heard of the old man's fondness for tricks and gadgets and ingenious deceptions: in particular the trick door or passage. We heard of the 'greatest joke in the world' he was going to bequeath to the village. Since I share the same liking, I can have a radiant vision of what *would* seem a private joke of this kind: a joke of the ripest vintage: a use to which such a device, so far as I know, has never before been put: I mean, ladies and gentlemen, a trick door in the cells of a police-station."

Dr. Fell sat back, musing.

"Of course we have one precedent several thousand years old. You recall Herodotus's story of the sardonic builder who did the same sort of thing in King Rhampsinitus's treasure-house? But, with regard to young Ritchie Bellowes, observe one suggestive fact. This story he told —of the hotel-attendant seen at Four Doors at the time of Rodney Kent's murder—when did he tell that story first? Did he tell it immediately after he was nabbed on the night of the murder? Not at all. He only told it late next day, when he found himself in the police-station. Eh? Not only in the police-station, but in a particular cell of that place. Suppose he knew quite well that he could get out of that cell whenever he liked? Suppose he had badly bungled and ruined the first crime, for reasons I will indicate in a moment? But, if another crime is committed, he is now safe from suspicion. And so, with a hysterical cleverness I cannot help rather admiring—for adolescent hysteria, as you may have observed when we talked to him, was the keynote of his character—he told a certain story. . . .

"A story which, as Hadley said, was either delirium tremens or prophecy or truth. And, by thunder, but it was prophecy! Calmly considered, it was too prophetic. It not only put the cart before the horse: it set the cart running uphill without any horse to push it. Not only did he describe a hotel-attendant, but he actually and barefacedly gave the name of the hotel at which the attendant was employed. You recall: 'I should describe him as a medium-sized man wearing a uniform such as you see in the big hotels like the Royal Scarlet or the Royal Purple.'

"Of course this was necessary to implant the image in

our minds. If it is definite to a nearly damning extent, it had to be; and he had, fortunately, his reputation as the camera-eye observer to sustain him. He had to turn a blue coat and silver (or brass) buttons—which might have meant anything, and to an innocent observer would probably have suggested something altogether different—into a concrete figure. Hence the salver. The meaning of the salver plunged me into a spiritual abyss until I had hit on Ritchie Bellowes's guilt. Naturally, it was merely an extra flourish to limn out and establish his picture; there never had been any such salver or any such figure. But I am afraid I am running ahead of the actual evidence. Incidentally Hadley, where did you find the trick entrance in the police-station?"

Hadley glanced round the table as though reluctant to speak of matters in mixed company. But he saw only interested faces: the refreshed alertness of Gay and Harvey Wrayburn, the heavy admiration of Dan Reaper, Melitta's surprising cheerfulness, and the blank absorption of Francine.

"Find it?" growled Hadley. "We've been finding nothing else all morning. There were three of 'em; and nobody ever knew. This is going to cause a number of smart remarks in the Press when it all comes out. Of course it wasn't quite as simple as it looked for Bellowes. The trick doors to the cells, you know, connected only with the cellar of the inspector's private house next door. He didn't have the run of the station. Consequently, though he could walk through the inspector's house and out of the place, he couldn't go————"

"Go where?" asked Gay.

"Where he really wanted to go," said Dr. Fell, "and needed to go. That is, up from the cells into the charge-room and waiting-rooms of the station itself. There were several barred doors, including that of his own cell, in between. Also, there were men on duty at inconvenient hours in that part of the station. It was a nasty knock because, to a man planning what he had planned, two things are vitally necessary. He needs clothes, and he needs money.

"Bellowes, as you know, was being charged with burglarious entry. Well, there are certain formalities attached to that. They had put away his money, they had put away his tobacco, they had put away his overcoat. All these things were safely locked up upstairs in the station, where he could not get at them, and he was naked without most of them. Do you begin to see? He could not return to his own lodgings in Northfield without exciting some curiosity on the part of the landlady. He could not wake up a friend in the middle of the night and ask to borrow a mackintosh or ten shillings for train-fare. He was either in jail or he wasn't: there could be no middle course: and he must *not* be seen. The only thing he could take for the night, without being detected, was a spare uniform from the inspector's place next door. He must take it, for, oh, Bacchus, he needed that uniform! You recall, when we talked to him in his cell, he was in his shirt-sleeves on not too warm a day. There was no sign of a coat or jacket or sweater in the cell, because he hadn't been wearing one when he was arrested. Now the cells were heated and warm enough for him to stay there without discomfort. But he couldn't walk about on a snowy January night without discomfort, to say nothing of the more vital necessity to attract no attention. Hence the inception of his rather brilliant triple-barrelled scheme of the uniform; first as covering, second as an excellent disguise, third as the phantom attendant at the Royal Scarlet. Between the night of January 14th, when Rodney Kent was murdered, and the night of the 31st, he had plenty of time to explore; and to prepare the ground. He knew what everyone else knew (as you shall see) that the whole party was going to the Royal Scarlet: that Mr. Reaper had specifically insisted on booking rooms in Wing A of the new seventh floor: that Josephine Kent was joining them there on a specified date————"

"But how could he have known it?" cried Francine.

"H'mf, wait. One moment. Finally, to kill small Josephine had become the deepest and strongest obsession of his life. You can guess the reason why."

"Well?"

"She was Ritchie Bellowes's lawfully wedded wife," said Dr. Fell. "But she could hardly be very garrulous about anything without admitting that she had committed bigamy."

Chapter 20

The End of the Stone

ONCE that tumbler falls into place," said Dr. Fell, "the safe-door opens by itself. You understand why she was so positive in pretending she had never been in England before. You understand why she was so anxious to keep away from Northfield, where she had previously lived. You understand why, though she knew quite well that Ritchie Bellowes had killed Rodney Kent, she had no intention of denouncing him or his motive. You understand why she was not unduly apprehensive about her own safety, since she thought Bellowes was in jail. And the hub of it is this: Josephine Parkes Bellowes was supposed by everyone except her husband to be dead. But I beg your pardon. I must give you the reasons which led us to think this."

Kent, at that moment, was remembering a face. He was remembering Ritchie Bellowes sitting on the edge of the bunk in the cell, fidgeting. Tall and thin and hollow-eyed, Bellowes seemed to look back at him now as he had looked back last night across a gravestone. But most of all Kent remembered an atmosphere and two gestures. The first gesture was that of Bellowes's fingers massaging the veined hand of his withered left arm. The second was Bellowes's suddenly stamping his foot on the floor, when there was addressed to him a question he did not like: stamping his foot on the floor of the cell like a child in a tantrum. It was an oddly revealing gesture like the whole atmosphere of this man who had never quite grown up.

"I have told you," said Dr. Fell, "reasons for believing in Bellowes's guilt and Josephine Kent's past connection, in some fashion, with Northfield. If we looked for a motive, it could only be in some relationship which had existed between this woman and Bellowes in the past. What, offhand, did we know about Bellowes himself? I knew from the beginning—Hadley told me—some pertinent things about his past history, and the sudden moral collapse of this well-to-do builder's son. He had been married, and his wife had 'died of typhoid at the seaside': a term which stirred my interest when I heard it. She did not die under the eyes of the Northfield villagers, then. In any case, from this time on began the abrupt disintegration of Bellowes into a thoughtful, polite, sober-pacing toper. Beware of such, my lads: especially when they go out to wintry copses to drink alone and 'recite' in the moonlight, as Bellowes admitted he did. But you will note that Bellowes's change was not merely one of stamina: it was a crashing financial collapse as well. One moment he was tolerably well off, and the next he was stony. It surprised people. In murder trials they are fond of quoting the Latin proverb. 'No one ever became suddenly the baset of men.' I will affirm that nobody ever became suddenly the brokest of men, unless there had been a snatching away of great proportions somewhere.

"And 'Miss Josephine Parkes' arrived back in Johannesburg from England with— Well, let us consider her and certain of her actions. On the evening she was murdered, the first evening she had ventured out from the shelter of her aunts, she was wearing a bracelet of an extraordinary sort. Nobody had ever seen it before. It seemed unlikely that she had got it in the country. To a simple mind it seemed much more likely that the bracelet was something out of her past life: something which, up to that time, she had carefully concealed. Why? Why bring it out now? She herself throws out hints which convince Miss Forbes that it had been given to her by someone she fears. She hints that she may be in danger, and that the bracelet is a safeguard against danger, because it contains a clue to the identity of the man she fears. To Miss Forbes she says 'If anything ever happens to me, which I don't anticipate, you shall have it.' Then she changes her mind, and in a fit of night-terrors she turns it over to Mr. Wrayburn with the words: *'You keep that for always. Then nobody will try to wake the dead.'*

"To wake the dead——

"That her fears were justified, and that the murderer also thought it was a danger to him, are indicated by his frantic ransacking of her hotel-room to find the bracelet: even to the extent of stealing another linked bracelet resembling it, in the ghost of a hope that it might be the right one in disguise. But I couldn't help thinking of Bellowes's 'dead' wife at the seaside. Was she dead? Or had she quietly kissed sad finger-tips and slipped away with Bellowes's money in her pocket: leaving him to explain as best he could how he had been made a laughing-stock? That also was worth investigating."

Wrayburn made a wig-wagging gesture as though he were trying to stop a bus.

"Wait!" he urged. "What's the point of that damned bracelet anyhow? What's the secret?"

"I will deal with the bracelet," said Dr. Fell, "shortly. Here I feel inclined to tell you in a few words the facts, as we have got them now, of the Bellowes-Parkes marriage. Hadley got them this morning, from Ritchie Bellowes himself. He does not deny his guilt. Considering the evidence against him, I don't see how he could.

"He met her and married her after two weeks in London in March 1933. It was, perhaps, inevitable. She had come to England looking for fresh woods and pastures new; and she had failed. Her bluff of knowing Sir Gyles Gay, and of being put on to something good in the way of employment, had succeeded only in getting her an interview with him————"

"Thank you," said Gay gravely.

"It must have been a sore setback, for I think she had great confidence in herself. A man like Ritchie Bellowes was her obvious move. He was quiet, he was obscure, he was emotionally immature, he was idealistic, he was content to worship; and he was moderately well off, which could be useful. In short, I think you will find his outward semblance much like that of Rodney Kent. She married him in her real name; but she did not tell him she came from South Africa. If she should wish to change her plans later, it would be a snag to let herself be traced. So they married, and they went to Northfield, and she made him an excellent wife (admired by all for her devotion) for eight or nine months. But she could not stifle here; and besides, being an abstemious woman, she disliked his fondness for drink. At her suggestion, and as a sound business principle in case anything should happen to the somewhat shrunken business he had inherited from his father, most of his money had been transferred into her name. She went for a seaside holiday. Just before doing so, she withdrew six thousand eight hundred pounds in cash; she left him a gentle, reproachful letter; and she disappeared. Well, you cannot do that without running a man into debts he can't pay, and nearly everything he has got must be sold to meet them. But banks, you know, don't tell.

"And there is one thing you must not do to a man of Ritchie Bellowes's type: you must not make a fool of him.

"These facts, night before last, I did not know. But, suspecting that Bellowes would do anything else in the world before letting this be known, suspecting that he had gone to some trouble and frenzy to create a mythical 'death' for the benefit of the neighbours, we had new questions ahead. How would Ritchie Bellowes learn that

'Josephine Kent'—the attractive wife of a South African who was coming to visit Sir Gyles Gay—was in reality his own nimble lady? The photographs, of course.

"You, Sir Gyles, were not living in Northfield at the time Josephine Bellowes-Kent was in England. You lived in Norfolk, as you told me, and moved here when Bellowes was compelled to sell this house. (You observe, though, how it brings our dates into line with the departure of the lady out of England?) But you were well acquainted with Bellowes. He had been several times to see you here. You were full of the subject of your visitors. You showed him all the photographs, didn't you?"

"I did," said Gay grimly. "*And* I talked. He seemed interested."

"On the other hand, it was not likely that many people from Northfield would see these photographs, and have their curiosity roused by the strange reappearance of Mrs. Bellowes. By your own confession, people are kept away from you by your manner; though Bellowes—drawn here by the fondness for his old home—you made hearty friends with as you are willing to be friends with anybody. The servants, usually local people, would not stumble on anything; you brought them from Norfolk. But Bellowes could not risk anything. Sooner or later, he had to see that those unfortunate pictures were destroyed—for when she died there must be no picture of her in a newspaper.

"Unfortunately it was you—the night before last—who threw a sizable spanner into *our* machinery. Just before I went out to dinner with those two"—he glanced sadly at Francine and Kent—"I had a conference with Hadley. He had got his cable from South Africa and his information from South Africa House. It threw light on Mrs. Kent; but, by all the top-hats of hell, it also threw suspicion on you. My stride was interrupted by you. It was possible that my idea was as wild as wind; that one Sir Gyles Gay was the man in the case and the murderer at the Royal Scarlet Hotel. Harrumph. Heh. Hah. Therefore, Miss Forbes, when you said to me, 'Won't you tell us who is guilty so that we can sleep soundly,' or words to that effect, I had to————"

Francine sat up.

"Yes," she said, "I've been waiting to ask you about that. Why did you deliberately sit there and make out (partly, anyway) a case to show that Bellowes was innocent, and had been brought as a witness to Rod's murder————?"

"I don't think you understand," said Dr. Fell humbly. "I deliberately sat there, as you put it, and tried to make out the strongest case I could in favour of Bellowes, in order to convince both myself and you that he *must* be guilty. Particularly to convince myself."

"*What?*" said Kent. "Hold on! The paradoxes are coming a bit too————"

"It's not very complicated, is it? I prayed that you would knock holes in my case. An intelligent sneer would have been manna to me. But you didn't, worse luck. You see, I was quoting all the points which in my mind told against Bellowes—(1) his having a key to this house in his pocket, with deliberate intent beforehand; (2) his whisky-drinking to screw up his courage for the murder of Rodney Kent, which drinking made him foozle the job after all; (3) the fact that his finger-prints were in the Blue Room—and I was trying to see whether innocent explanations of them could be found. If Bellowes were *not* guilty, those facts had innocent explanations. I raked my wits to find 'em. For these innocent explanations did not satisfy me. I hoped you would say, 'Bosh,' as I felt b-o-s-h. I hoped you would say, 'Gideon, *mon vieux*, all this is the merest eyewash. Your facts damn Bellowes; your explanations do not exculpate him. Witness? Do you expect us to believe that a murderer is so fond of witnesses to his crime that he pays one to come in and watch it? In all your fog of words, where is the sense?' I should then have said, radiantly, 'Good. Excellent. That is what must be so.' But you didn't. You appeared to accept it. Perhaps you noticed my strange behaviour, which caused me to mop my forehead resolutely; and I went home, a most unusual thing, before it was time for the party to break up.

"I was particularly despondent because you, Miss Forbes, had almost burnt your fingers a moment before on just what I believed to be the reason for the masquerade in the blue uniform. I can hear you yet, 'That must mean,' you were saying, 'he was preparing everybody's mind for his appearance later, when he came to kill Jenny —but where is there any indication in just a coat and a pair of trousers?' I came close to uttering a cheer; I stimulated you with my fiery glance; but the light went out.

"For this is what I thought, and know now, had really happened—beginning with the first murder:

"Bellowes coolly determined to kill Rodney, in a quiet and workmanlike manner. There was to be no flourish of hotel-attendants. Bellowes had met all of your party at his memory-entertainment; he knew Rodney; it would be easy to find out which room Rodney occupied. By the way, he made one more hideous slip when he told me an unnecessary lie at the police-station: Bellowes told me that he (the memory-expert) couldn't remember a single feature of Rodney's face. And his motive? You, Miss Forbes, told me about that at our celebrated dinner. It was believed by many people—and well known to Sir Gyles here, who liked to joke about it—that Rodney Kent had married Josephine for her money. Her money? Ritchie Bellowes's money. You must not tamper with men of Bellowes's kind. I can imagine him looking at the colourless figure of Rodney, the pleasant and colourless Rodney; and I can imagine the inside of his mind turning black with pure hate. Conjure up before you a picture of Bellowes's face, and you will see what I mean.

"But the murder was to be a workmanlike job. It was to be a murder by 'strangling,' since Bellowes's arm is paralised and he can strangle nobody. He had had a long time to think about it, you know. Did he know about the useful furniture in the Blue Room, which would enable him to do it? Of course he knew about it; that furniture was there in his father's time, and Sir Gyles Gay must have bought it with the house; Bellowes told us so himself.

"Bellowes left the pub at ten o'clock, with just the right amount inside to steady himself, and a bottle of whisky to keep him at it. He waited until the household at Four Doors had gone to bed at about midnight. He allowed a few minutes more, and then let himself into the house with his key. He went upstairs quietly. He was then wearing gloves; he was carrying a life-preserver in his pocket, and a poker under his overcoat, supported by his more-or-less useless left arm. He went into Rodney's room. Rodney, just retiring, would be surprised to see him; but not startled or alarmed. Any excuse for his presence would suffice. He distracts Rodney's attention, and knocks him unconscious with the life-preserver. Then he does what has to be done.

"Afterwards (at, say, about twenty minutes past twelve) he slips downstairs. His work in the house is not finished. He goes to—why, the study, of course, where his father's old-fashioned furniture remains in the house exactly as it remains in the Blue Room upstairs. He opens— the locked drawer of the desk, certainly, with the paternal keys he has kept as he has kept everything else he can. Who else could have opened that (admittedly, by Gay) elaborate lock? That is where he knows he will find the photographs.

"The whole scheme is arranged. Josephine is to go next. In fact, he has already written to her, announcing coolly that he will do this; for he knows it is one letter she will never dare show to anyone. (You recall, she received two letters postmarked Northfield, one from her husband and the writer of the other unknown?) She replied to this. She replied with equal coolness that he had better not try any tricks, for if anything happens to her she still has a bracelet which will hang him. Hence the reappearance of the bracelet. Meantime, Bellowes will give a turn of the screw to her feelings by killing her bigamous husband, Rodney; still knowing that she will not dare to speak.

"After the murder of Rodney, then, Bellowes crept down to the study. He closed the curtains and turned on one small lamp. It will interest you to know what we heard this morning, the place he had chosen to hide his murder-properties—the poker, the life-preserver, the gloves, the key to the desk, and so on—until he should need them again. Well, they were actually in the desk all the time. They were in a false compartment at the back of it, another of the devices of his father. It was the best of all hiding-places for them: if by any remote chance they were found, they would only serve to incriminate Sir Gyles or some member of the party.

"After stowing them away, he proceeded systematically to tear to pieces every photograph in the desk drawer, Sir Gyles's own as well. But a new idea occurred to him. I told you this man could never be satisfied with anything. I told you he could never let well-enough alone; and that is what betrayed him. The only photograph he did not destroy was the big group one, the slide at the fun-fair ——"

Gay interposed.

"There is another question here," he said. "I suppose he kept that picture because he could use it as a threat against Mrs. Kent without ever leaving behind a view of her face. But how did he know it *was* Mrs. Kent in the photograph? I imagine I must have shown him the picture, at one time or another; but I didn't learn who it was until you people had actually arrived here——"

"The memory-test!" said Francine.

"I beg your pardon?"

"That's it," agreed Dan, opening his eyes. "Damnation! I've been trying to remember just where I'd seen that picture recently. We were both trying to remember it yesterday. The memory-test, of course. When Bellowes gave his demonstration, I mean. One of the inevitable tests is to shove a photograph under somebody's nose, a group photograph with lots of details, and ask him to quote the smallest detail after one look. We used that picture! And somebody remarked that the unseen figure was Jenny. All right. Go on."

"The sight of the bottles of coloured inks," resumed Dr. Fell obediently, "put into his head the idea of writing, 'There is one more to go,' and of putting it beside his first victim. He did write it. But he rejected the idea as much too dangerous. He wanted the woman to know she was in danger. But he didn't want anybody else to know it. So he sat there by the desk in the middle of the night, puzzling the matter through his little brain—and at the same time (now his job was finished) gulping down steady pulls at a bottle of neat whisky.

Wrayburn stared. "You mean, with a dead body upstairs, he sat as cool as anything in somebody else's house———"

"You forget," said Dr. Fell, "that he wasn't in somebody else's house. That's the keynote to the whole affair. He was in his own house, the only place familiar to him. The others were interlopers, whom he hated. And, instead of hurrying out of the house, the fool proceeded to get drunk. As you might have guessed, the more he took the more indecisive he became, the more uncertain; for he could *not* let well-enough alone. Was everything all right upstairs? Was there anything he had omitted? It was Ritchie Bellowes's form of self-torture. And, when he was three parts gone, he had to see. He left the photograph in the desk. He went upstairs in the dark, with no glove on his hand and hardly a thought of precaution in his head. Scarcely in a condition to see, he opened the door of the Blue Room wide—as it was found—and proceeded to leave finger-prints by turning on the light. He had enough sense left to realise that he had been a fool; but it was too late. He had no sooner turned out the light and gone out (in the moonlight) when you, Mr. Reaper, opened your own door. He couldn't run; he could barely walk. So he did the instinctive thing. He tumbled down on a sofa and pretended to a stupor which was only half pretence.

"That, in the wrecking of the plan, was the story of the first crime and the reason for the second.

"I have told you how, out of necessity and his own cunning, he got the scheme for the second. He was going to kill Josephine at the Royal Scarlet, and he was going to be an 'attendant' in uniform; hence his story. He knew you were all going to the Royal Scarlet, he knew about the new top floor, he even knew the date: heaven knows you all talked enough about it. Then you altered the date, and went one day earlier; a piece of information which was kindly passed along to him by Inspector Tanner in Tanner's daily questionings.

"They lock up the cell-row for the night at nine-thirty. Before a quarter to ten he was out of jail, dressed, in one of those pitch-black village nights where nobody would have noticed him even if he had been seen. If he were going to London, as I told you, he would need money. But nothing could be simpler. He still had his key to Four Doors. There was nobody here except servants. In the drawer of the study desk, as he knew from his visit two weeks before, there was a purse containing at least enough money to pay his bus-and-train fare to town.

"And, of course, he had to come here to get his invaluable poker as well. . . .

"Hence the mysterious theft of loose change. With good connections by train and bus, the time from here to town is an hour and ten minutes. This would get him to Charing Cross at just gone eleven. A bus to the hotel, the poker wrapped in a newspaper; now (invaluable!) the status of his police uniform, which is not only a passport anywhere, but will allow him—unsuspected—to question car-starters or outside-porters about where fire-escapes lead; and within fifteen minutes he is on the fire-escape outside the corridor of Wing A in time to see your party return from the theatre.

"He had to wait until the departure of the maid before he could get into the linen-closet through the window. But even then, he waited until midnight before he attacked: why? Because he was patiently waiting for someone to *see* him. With his cap off, he was now disguised; he was transformed into an employee. He mustn't be seen by a real employee, of course, which will blow the gaff immediately. But he wants a guest to catch a glimpse of him —and they obstinately remain in their rooms. The linen closet will be his refuge if anyone should come too near It was lucky for him, however, that he did not attack Wrayburn was in the woman's room, though he couldn' tell that because Wrayburn had entered and left by the side door to 707; and, as it was, they narrowly missed each other.

"They would have missed each other by a still narrowe margin if Mrs. Kent had not prudently waited a couple o' minutes to make sure the coast was clear before she opened the door to the attendant, who murmured, 'Extra towels, madam.' She was not afraid then. Her attacks o' tremors had passed; Bellowes was safely under lock and key; and Wrayburn was within call. In this brief interval you, Mr. Reaper, glanced out to set your watch. If you had looked a second longer, you would have seen an attendant walk into 707 with the towels—and he wouldn' have minded if you had. In fact, it was what he was hoping for. He posed for you.

"Mrs. Kent, with a comforted heart, opens the door to a mound of towels. She says, 'Yes?' He gets just across the threshold and lowers the towels, and she has one good glimpse of his face before he does what has to be done He couldn't catch her on the back of the head as he had caught Rodney. She knew him.

"But, above all things, he must find that bracelet. It will require, as we decided before, an intensive search of the room. To keep himself secure against interruption, he hastily puts a pair of shoes (or what he thought to be one) outside, and hangs the 'quiet' notice on the door. He is wearing the same old gloves he used for Rodney's murder. But he can't find the bracelet! He comes across the key to the room, and he pockets all the loose change in her handbag; he is not (he will now point out to you, somewhat frenziedly) a thief, and he doesn't want any other money. But still he can't find any bracelet except

Mrs. Jopley-Dunne's. Do you know what he did with that bracelet later, by the way? He threw it down a drain out of sheer spite, proving that there are vagaries to the character of even the most altruistic murderer.

"Next observe how the technique of this crime is exactly like the first. Again, though with better reason this time, he cannot let well-enough alone. He is convinced that the right bracelet isn't anywhere in the room. Yet he is nearly wild with indecision. Once he actually does leave the room—and takes the key to 707 with him—because he knows he's going only as far as that linen-closet; and he will come back. He wavers exactly as he wavered here. Yet he can't delay too long, or he will miss the last train back. Back he goes to that room for one last look. The little devil has tricked him, even if she's dead. Where in the name of Satan is that bracelet? In the same kind of jeer at her as he had thought of once before, he takes the 'quiet' sign off the door, he scrawls 'Dead Woman' on it with a pen he has found in the trunk. Leaving the key in the door, he goes at last."

Dr. Fell drew a deep, wheezing breath, and put down his dead cigar.

"Well, you can guess our plan of campaign. If our views about Bellowes were correct, we already had enough evidence to convict him. But he would be damned beyond excuse if we could once more entice him to come out in that uniform. I had to handle him warily when I spoke to him at the police-station; I wouldn't let Hadley get in a question edgeways. It was all the worse because Bellowes was in a bad state of nerves: he hadn't had a drink in two weeks, and he really was in a state of enforced sobriety as great as though he had been locked up there beyond any getting out. You see, he couldn't get out except at night when the watch was withdrawn; and, by the time he could reach a pub where he wouldn't be recognised, our beautiful licensing hours had closed the pubs.

"I gave him firmly to understand I believed in his innocense. I outlined to him my bogus theory of himself as a 'witness.' He was so surprised at the novel idea that for a minute he was thrown off balance, and couldn't play up to it; believe me, I cursed in my sleeve at that. By the time he was tentatively agreeing to it, it was too late. What I had to do was bring the missing bracelet into the conversation somehow, without exciting suspicion. I finally got round it by the wild expedient of suggesting that the 'phantom attendant' had been carrying something on a salver at Four Doors. I couldn't go further without making the thing apparent. When we were leaving, you recall, I went back and spoke to him. I said that we had found a piece of evidence which the late Mrs. Kent had said would be important, a bracelet: I described it: I asked him if it might have been in the possession of the blue-coated phantom. He said no. I said, with a thoughtful shrug of my shoulders (which could, I fear, only be measured with a seismograph) that we were sending it for expert inspection, and showing it about to a few persons: I said Miss Forbes was keeping it for us.

"I believed, you see, that he would be fool enough and in a bad enough state of nerves to have one more go at that bracelet, and wouldn't hesitate if he thought he was dealing with a woman. He didn't hesitate. But the plan nearly miscarried. Everything was all right—we were going to let him get into Four Doors, let him pinch the bracelet, and catch him with it coming out—as we saw it. I assure you (cease this uproar) that Miss Forbes was in no danger: there were two men in her bedroom, although she didn't know it, and would have been at him if he had come within two yards of her. Things went well until Bellowes, who knew Hadley and I were staying at the pub, came close to reconnoitre on his way down. Hadley (quite naturally, in that dead blackness) mistook him for Tanner. And Bellowes couldn't run again. From what Hadley said, he knew the game was up. The only question was what he should do about it. I think he pondered it very carefully in his usual quiet style. After reflection he decided that, since he was going to be caught, he would simply take somebody with him; and he was not particular who. When the real Tanner turned up at the pub ten minutes later, your humble undersigned turned suddenly ill. That there was no casualty was not our fault. I salute your courage, sir; I congratulate your future wife; and I think that's all."

They looked at each other, and Wrayburn smote the table.

"No, by the gods, it's not all," said Wrayburn. "What about that bracelet? Where is the secret writing on the bracelet or the acrostic or whatever it is? I've made a fairly extensive study of puzzles; but I can't make head or tail of it."

"The secret," said Dr. Fell, "is that there is no secret writing."

"But there's got to be! You've quoted what Jenny said to me. What about the things she told Francine, particularly: 'Has the inscription any meaning?' 'Only if you're able to read it; that's the whole secret.' "

Dr. Fell chuckled.

"She was quite right, correctly and literally right. I am not here referring to one fact which does not concern us: namely, that originally there was an inscription 'J.P. from R.B.' engraved on the inside, which she had had removed some time ago. Bellowes, of course, thought it was still on there, covered over in some way. The real secret is something quite different. Josephine thought it was quite sufficient to damn Bellowes, if it were found, and she was right. There were only two of those black stones—originally belonging to Bellowes's father—and set in rings. Ritchie had one of them put into a bracelet for her, keeping the other himself. Many people had seen them; and the secret was so curious that it would be remembered. Do you know what the secret was? It lies in two words, a description not of the jewel itself, but of the device which that jewel represented."

"Well, what was it?"

"It was a sober-stone," said Dr. Fell.

After a pause Wrayburn struck the table more softly. "Of course," he said. "By Xenophon's ten thousand, of course! Why didn't I ever think of it? To wear a sober-stone ring was the mark of the well-bred Roman at banquets. Suetonius is very serious about it." He grew excited. "Hang it, it's such a good and practical device that it ought to be revived to-day. The sober-stone was a semi-precious jewel of any kind on the flat surface of which could be engraved a few lines of writing. Some good text: this one was especially applicable, and in clear but small print. The noble Roman began drinking at a banquet, and from time to time he consulted his ring. Whenever he could not clearly read the text written on it, he knew he had got over the line of being sober and that it was time to stop. *'Claudite jam rivos, pueri, sat prata biberunt.'* 'Stop singing; enjoyment has been taken.' And, 'Only if you can read it; that's the whole secret.' Oh, my *eye!*"

"Exactly," said Dr. Fell with benevolent placidness, "though the device, far from commending itself to me, is so conscientious that it makes my flesh creep. The interesting point is that Ritchie Bellowes gave it to her. They plighted their troth to each other with the stones. It was her good influence, you know, her sweetness and light, which turned Bellowes from a potentially sound and likeable man into a murderer with a fixed idea. I don't think I blame him, morally."

Dan Reaper drew a deep breath. "All I've got to say is," he declared, "that I wouldn't go through that again for—well, for a lot of money. I didn't know what to think. Half the time————"

"Whom did you suspect, my dear?" asked Melitta placidly.

They all started a little, and looked at each other. It was the letting out of a secret, a releasing of tension, which made them all sit back with a jerk. And then, gradually, a shamefaced grin appeared on several faces.

"Yes," said Wrayburn. "Let's have it. Who?"

"I suspected *you*, you cuss," Dan told him with some

violence. "Maybe I had been reading too many of Chris's tomfool ideas. But, since you had a cast-iron alibi and were ruled out of it practically from the start after having been once suspected—well, it looked funny. Sorry about my rotten manners————"

"Oh, that's all right. Here, what about another glass of wine? To tell you the truth, I should have voted for our good host————"

"The notion," agreed Gay, "seems to have occurred to several persons. For myself, since frankness seems not to be resented, I first favoured Mr. Kent there. But I very quickly shifted to Miss Forbes————"

"Me?"

"Especially since," insisted Gay, "it was you who were prowling about in the study yesterday, just before I found that long-lost photograph in the desk. I saw you closing the door at the top of the stairs————"

"But I was only looking in there to see what had happened to everybody! I never even thought of it afterwards."

"—and, when I saw the police had a man following you," pursued Gay, "I was sure of it. I should have been very sorry. You observe that I shielded you. Have you any views, Mrs. Reaper?"

Melitta, almost beaming, had already wound herself up. "Well, of course, I shouldn't like to venture any opinion, but I felt sure my husband must have something to do with it. I do not say, mind you, that he is any worse than other men; but then that is what other men do, and I have felt most horribly unhappy about it. As my grandfather used————"

"So now I'm guilty," said Dan. "Well, you're luckier, old girl. With Chris's case against the hotel-manager, that makes a pretty big round, and you're the only one who has escaped suspicion."

"No, she hasn't," Kent pointed out. "Melitta has been suspected by Francine here————"

Francine looked at him sadly. She said: "Chris, you

didn't really believe that?" and she stared at him in genuine perplexity.

"Believe it? Why, you told me yourself————"

"Chris, you are a blockhead! Of course I thought it was you. Why do you think I've been acting like such a harridan? I thought you were carrying on with her. I always thought so. That's why I was so terribly anxious to get that bracelet and find out if it concerned you. And at the restaurant, and afterwards much harder in the taxi, I was trying and trying to get you to tell me if you had killed her by saying it might be Melitta————"

Kent stared round.

"Let me understand this," he said. "Things have come to a fine pass. You don't know what people are thinking even when they tell you. What do you call that?"

From the head of the table Dr. Fell put down his glass and spoke.

"I call it," he said, "a detective story."